THE DEVEREAUX AFFAIR

Ladies of the Order - Book 1

ADELE CLEE

The Devereaux Affair
Copyright © 2021 Adele Clee
All rights reserved.
ISBN-13: 978-1-8383839-2-3

Cover by Dar Albert at Wicked Smart Designs

PROLOGUE

Witherdeen Hall, Hampshire, 1807
Seat of the Marquess Devereaux

"DON'T GO! Don't go to her!" Bennet's young eyes flashed with terror. His breath came in shallow pants. "Let's hide. I know where. Stay. Don't let her take you."

Bennet did not give Julianna time to respond. He seized her trembling hand and pulled her down the broad oak staircase, past the portrait of a stern man in a white wig and scarlet robe, past pictures of women with soulless eyes and gaunt faces. Sad women like her mother. Lonely creatures desperate for someone to fill the void. Past the mounted stag heads. The marquess liked collecting trophies.

The shouting upstairs shook the ceiling, had the hanging lantern swinging on its chain. Somewhere glass smashed. High-pitched yelling battled with the marquess' gruff growls and thunderous roars in a war no one would win.

"Whore!"

Julianna knew what it meant. Men had called her mother the name before, always when angry or consumed by a jealous rage. Giselle de Lacy reacted by stuffing her clothes and jewels into her valise, always captured Julianna's hand and dragged her away from the terrible place, to start a new life with a new lord who would take care of them until they were forced to flee again.

"They'll stop bickering soon," Bennet whispered, "and everything will be as it was before."

But Julianna had witnessed the performance so many times she knew the curtain was about to fall and she'd have to leave Bennet tonight.

Tears filled her eyes.

She didn't want to say goodbye to her only friend.

She didn't want to sleep in a new bedchamber with dolls for company, their lifeless faces filled with nothingness, their eyes as dead as the ladies in the paintings.

"It's no good, Bennet," she whimpered, tugging on the boy's hand.

"No. She'll not take you. I'll fight them both if I have to."

Bennet hadn't always been brave. He was nothing like the quiet, withdrawn boy she'd met on her first day at Witherdeen. For a month, they'd barely spoken. Everything changed the day he received a whipping from his father. The day she found him sobbing in the cupboard beneath the stairs where he'd been told to remain until morning. She'd brought him a slice of cake wrapped in a napkin and an apple she'd stolen from the pantry. They'd been inseparable ever since.

"Quick, we'll hide." Bennet dragged the marble table away from the wall, though the fancy gold legs scraped the chequered floor. He pressed the oak panel until it clicked open a fraction to reveal the small cubbyhole. "They won't expect us to hide in here."

She followed him into the dark space, used by the marquess as a torture chamber to punish his ten-year-old son, knowing someone would notice they had moved the table. In a matter of minutes, Julianna would be ripped from the arms of her beloved friend, torn from the only place that had ever felt like home.

They tried to calm their breathing, but there was little chance of anyone hearing them. The thuds above stairs were louder than the rumbles of thunder outside. A door slammed.

The boards on the landing groaned beneath stomping footsteps. The vile words and curses grew louder.

"You devil-crazed witch!" The marquess was in the hall now.

Julianna's heart thumped in her chest.

Bennet gripped her hands and squeezed tightly.

"Denver will tire of you within the week," the marquess bellowed. "He'll not tolerate your incessant whining. Does he know you have the French Disease?"

"If I have, I've caught it from you! Julianna! Come quickly!"

"You'll have to send the brat away. Denver won't want her."

"Don't listen." Bennet covered her ears with his hands.

But she shrugged from his grasp. She didn't want to be in that quiet place, alone with her thoughts. Hearing the blazing row was better than the endless silence.

"Julianna!" her mother cried.

"I need to go, Bennet."

"No." He cupped her cheeks, wiped away her tears. "I need you."

"It's no good." There was no point fighting. "It won't be forever."

"Stay." His throat was thick with fear.

Shouting erupted in the hall again.

"No man will tolerate your harlot ways. Go. Take your heathen spawn. My son deserves better than a whore's waif for a companion."

Her mother ignored him. "Julianna, we're leaving! Come down now!"

"They're in the cupboard, fool. The girl doesn't want to leave with you."

With seconds to spare, Julianna gripped the open neck of Bennet's nightshirt. "Promise you'll find me when you're old enough."

"I promise," he panted. "Promise you'll return if you can."

"I promise." She hugged him, tried to gather her courage when the cupboard door flew open and an enraged Giselle de Lacy grabbed Julianna by the sleeve of her white nightgown and yanked her out into the dimly lit hall.

Everything happened quickly then.

Bennet charged out of their hiding place, shouting as loud as his father.

Her mother dragged her across the cold floor while the marquess gripped Bennet by the scruff of his nightshirt and brought him to heel like a disobedient pup.

The couple shouted nasty things, cruel things, hurtful things.

"I'll miss you!" Julianna cried numerous times as her mother hauled her out into the rain, down the stone steps and into the waiting carriage that did not belong to the marquess.

"Come, Julianna, we're leaving this wicked place."

The carriage reeked of cologne—a new smell, just as sickly, just as choking. Some things never changed. And when they reached their new home, Giselle de Lacy would make Julianna sound like an asset when really she was a noose around her mother's neck.

Look at her pretty red hair.

She can play the pianoforte better than any girl her age.

The carriage jerked forward. Rain lashed the windows. Tears lashed Julianna's cheeks. Amid the flash of lightning and the crack of thunder, she heard Bennet shouting.

Julianna turned and stared out through the viewing window.

Bennet had broken free from his father's grasp, took to chasing the carriage down the long winding drive, oblivious to the sharp gravel beneath his bare feet. But the vehicle picked up speed, the distance between her and her beloved friend stretching, stretching. Soon it would be miles.

Julianna pressed her palm to the glass.

Promise you'll find me when you're old enough.

But she knew she would never see Bennet Devereaux again.

CHAPTER 1

Hart Street, London, 1824
Townhouse owned by the Order

JULIANNA EDEN HAD her ear pressed to the drawing room door, trying to catch a hint of who the prospective new client might be. He was wealthy and powerful. That much she'd heard from Mrs Gunning—the woman paid to keep house and ensure the smooth running of the Order's business premises. He had a voice as rich as fine wine, that much Julianna had discovered for herself. A voice that stirred the hairs on one's nape, seduced the senses. A voice a lonely lady should avoid at all costs.

"Mr Daventry will summon you if he agrees to take the case," Mrs Gunning whispered when she came to see if Julianna was still waiting in the hall.

Mr Daventry was the master of the Order, a group of enquiry agents who helped victims of crimes, those without the funds to fight for justice. The gentleman's latest project involved hiring ladies who all, for one reason or another, might have ended up in debtors' prison, the workhouse, or flogging their wares in Covent Garden. Intelligent and insightful women who may be of help on certain cases.

"Won't you reconsider?" came the deep masculine voice sounding somewhat irate. "I know the men work for the poor and needy, that only your female agents accept wealthy clients, but this is a serious matter. Can you not make allowances for a friend?"

Mrs Gunning patted Julianna's arm. "Don't be offended, dear. Mr Daventry's agents have a reputation for getting the job done. I expect the marquess is embarrassed to find himself in such an awkward position, and notable men don't want to appear vulnerable in front of a lady."

"The marquess!" Julianna almost choked on the words.

By her calculation, two dozen peers in England carried the title. Most of them were doddery old men living uneventful lives. The man on the other side of the drawing room door was most definitely young and virile, which narrowed the odds considerably.

"You must have misheard." Julianna prayed the housekeeper had forgotten to remove the cotton plugs from her ears. "Why would a marquess need to hire an enquiry agent?"

Mrs Gunning clutched her chatelaine to prevent the keys rattling and shuffled closer. "It has something to do with death threats," returned the sturdy woman in a quiet voice. "That's what I heard him say before you arrived."

So, Julianna wasn't the only one who'd listened at the door.

"Did you manage to hear his name?"

Please don't let it be Devereaux.

Mrs Gunning shook her head. "He's handsome, though. Shoulders so broad and strong he could work as a packhorse. And he had that devilish twinkle in his eye one often sees in confident men."

Julianna breathed a small sigh of relief. Confident men were often immoral. Mr Daventry would not place a female agent with a rakehell. Not without the support of a gentleman agent, and they were all busy leading their own investigations.

"The ladies of the Order are as skilled as the men," Mr Daventry said bluntly.

It was an exaggeration. Julianna's skills would hardly inspire faith. She was light on her feet, could disappear from a room unnoticed. She could withstand a barrage of insults and scathing criticism, bear it all with good grace. She could smile, make the world believe she was blissfully happy when inside her heart might be breaking.

"Skilled in combat?" returned the delectable voice. "Because that's what we're talking about here. It's only a matter of time until the devil succeeds, and I'm too bloody angry to make sense of it myself."

"Why don't you meet her, decide if she's suitable? Explain your dilemma. See if she has any logical suggestions as to where she might begin."

The lord's deep sigh rang with desperation now. "Women gossip and spin stories. I'll not have the *ton* knowing my private business. That's why I came to you. I'll not have people think I'm too damn weak to handle my own affairs."

"The ladies who work for me have experienced hardships. They're not spoilt and pampered and are above the pettiness one associates with the *ton*. Trust me, Devereaux. If I've picked an agent to work on your case, it's because I know she's competent enough to get the job done."

Devereaux!

Merciful Lord!

Julianna might have felt a flutter of pride upon hearing Mr Daventry's praise, but her world suddenly shifted on its axis. Shifted to such an alarming degree, her knees buckled. She stumbled backwards, three steps ... four ... until she hit the wall.

"Goodness. What's wrong, child?" Mrs Gunning hurried forward and gripped Julianna's shaky hands. "Are you feeling unwell? You look like you've seen a ghost."

Promise you'll find me when you're old enough.

"I should go. There's been a mistake. Tell Mr Daventry I'm not ready for a case of this magnitude. Tell him I'm sorry, sorry to embarrass him in front of a client, sorry I'm not as strong as he thought."

Julianna continued with her mumbling apology. She would rather find herself alone and destitute, rather beg outside St Paul's than have her treasured memories disintegrate to dust.

But Mr Daventry opened the drawing room door and

stepped into the hall. The master of the Order was a man of thirty whose commanding presence unnerved most people, yet he looked upon Julianna with sympathetic eyes.

"Lord Devereaux would like to meet you, to decide if you might prove suitable, if you're the right person to take his case." Mistaking her shock for fear, he lowered his voice. "Devereaux is a good man beneath the bravado. You will be safe in his employ. Nonetheless, I shall warn him to treat you with the utmost respect."

There wasn't a man in London who would cross Lucius Daventry.

An immense sense of gratitude surfaced. He had rescued her from the steps of the Servants' Registry, given her a chance to earn a decent living, provided a home with three other female agents, all under the care and supervision of Miss Trimble. Unlike her mother, Julianna did not sneer at the hand affording every basic comfort. She should offer an explanation. Tell him that working for the Marquess Devereaux would be like tearing open an old wound.

But then Bennet Devereaux appeared, filling the doorway with his impressive shoulders, the sleeves of his fashionable black coat clinging to his muscular arms. She tried to look beyond his manly physique for the boy she remembered. Yes. Daylight caught the golden flecks in his brown hair. His amber eyes still seduced the senses with their rich, autumnal hue.

"Ah, Devereaux." Mr Daventry turned to his friend, who stood openmouthed and rooted to the spot. "This is the agent I mentioned. Allow me to introduce—"

"Miss de Lacy. I know."

"Mrs Eden," Mr Daventry corrected.

"Mrs Eden!" The marquess flinched. "You're married?"

"Widowed," she said but did not sound at all like herself.

Mr Daventry frowned. "You know one another?"

The marquess gripped the door jamb. "We were good friends."

Bennet had been her only friend until she'd joined the Order.

"Childhood friends," she managed to say. "But that was a long time ago. Indeed, I'm surprised you recognised me."

His gaze seemed to drink in every inch of her all at once. "I would know those wild red curls anywhere."

She coughed to halt the onset of tears. The boy she'd held in her heart was no more. In his place stood this attractive man with an aura of arrogance. This stranger had consumed the mind and body of the only person she had ever truly loved.

Julianna straightened. She would grieve for Bennet in her own time, as she had done before, when she was old enough to know he was not about to appear like a knight errant on his trusty steed and save her from a living hell.

"Under the circumstances, my lord, perhaps you might prefer to work with another agent." She glanced at Mr Daventry, hoping he could read her silent plea. "Perhaps Miss Gambit might prove a suitable replacement."

Mr Daventry rubbed his sculpted jaw while considering her suggestion. "Mrs Eden is interested in history and archaeology. I thought you could say you've hired her to write a book about the ruins of Witherdeen Abbey."

Julianna sucked in a sharp breath. "The position means moving to Witherdeen?"

Lord Devereaux nodded. "Hopefully, your explorations will take you further afield than the understairs cupboard." He sounded amused, but his eyes were like those of the ladies in the paintings lining Witherdeen's walls—downcast and doleful.

Mr Daventry cleared his throat. "Perhaps we should take tea in the drawing room, Mrs Eden. Discuss the matter at length, decide if you are the best person to help Lord Devereaux with his pressing affair."

Her heart screamed for her to run. The damaged organ would not withstand the torment, the pain. But Bennet Devereaux's allure was as strong now as it was then, and she longed to see Witherdeen again.

"I would be interested to hear of his lordship's dilemma."

"Excellent." Mr Daventry invited her to step into the drawing room, one as elegant as any in Mayfair, though in Hart Street they spoke of theft and murder, not of ribbons and lace.

Mrs Gunning hurried to the kitchen to make tea.

Awkwardness descended like a dense fog, so palpable it took

effort to breathe. Lord Devereaux lingered. He seemed unable to decide if he should wait for her to sit, if he should treat her as an old acquaintance or a woman soon to be in his employ.

Julianna sat in the chair while the gentlemen settled on a sofa positioned around the low table. Mr Daventry opened a leather portfolio, removed a handbill and placed it down in full view. It was not a printed notice. The words had been cut from a broadsheet, arranged neatly and stuck onto the paper.

"Devereaux, you may speak in the strictest confidence. Mrs Eden is sworn to secrecy and will discuss the case with no one but her colleagues."

"Confidentiality is of paramount importance."

Julianna swallowed down her nerves. "You may have faith in my integrity, my lord."

She saw the challenge in his eyes, alluding to the promise made and broken. She might have hurled her own accusations. Why had he not looked for her? Why had he not written? It would not have been difficult. Everyone knew of Giselle de Lacy's conquests, knew she had died of a laudanum overdose in a flea-infested pit in Paris.

Mr Daventry pushed the handbill towards her. "Study this for a moment."

Julianna retrieved the fabricated notice, though performing the simple task took effort when done under the weight of Bennet Devereaux's stare.

The bold heading leapt from the page—*The Reckoning.*

It sounded like the name of a novel or play—a story of vengeance and retribution. A victim's tale. She raised her gaze and considered the marquess. Had the kind boy grown into a heartless devil? Had his father beaten the goodness from his soul and left this insensible peer in his place?

Bennet Devereaux watched her intently as she read his obituary. Assembled on the single sheet of paper was an ugly collage of words, an account of the terrible accident that had occurred at Witherdeen, a tragic and abrupt end for the young Marquess Devereaux.

She looked up and frowned. "It says you were killed by falling masonry."

"A grotesque gargoyle, to be exact."

"Days after receiving the handbill, Devereaux found a stone gargoyle smashed to pieces on his front steps," Mr Daventry explained. "His steward inspected the building and found no damage. Someone staged the scene to unnerve him."

Julianna studied the page. "The fact it's entitled *The Reckoning* says we're looking for someone you've wronged, my lord. A mistress perhaps?"

He shifted in the seat. "Perhaps."

"We'll come to suspects in a moment." Mr Daventry removed another handbill from the leather portfolio and handed it to her. "Again, read the obituary."

The report carried the same title and stated that the marquess had died of syphilis in the Lock Hospital on Hyde Park Corner. That he was to be buried amid the abbey ruins at Witherdeen.

"Someone erected a gravestone during the night," the lord informed her, "though my death is recorded as being March 1824, two months hence. It's clearly a threat. Now you understand my urgency in finding the devil responsible."

"The woman responsible," she corrected. "Only a woman would act with such malicious intent." Giselle de Lacy had resorted to devious tactics to hurt her lovers. "Based on my experience, it should not take long to find her, though you will need to share details of your personal affairs. The names of the women you've bedded this last year. A list of those you elevated to the role of mistress."

Lord Devereaux gulped. A brief look of embarrassment passed over his handsome features. "Perhaps there are men who would like to see me suffer. Men my father wronged. It would be unwise to assume this amounts to nothing more than an ex-lover's spite."

And what of the men Bennet had wronged?

"Devereaux has made it known he's in want of a wife," Mr Daventry said calmly, though the news hit Julianna like a vicious blow to the stomach. "As you can imagine, many powerful men would like to align with the house of Devereaux, so we could be looking for a jealous debutante, a disgruntled father or jilted suitor."

"Is there a particular reason you've decided to marry now, my lord?" Julianna fought to maintain a professional air amid a flurry of odd emotions. "It may not be a coincidence."

"I have a duty to wed, Mrs Eden." He spoke bluntly, the last two words carrying a hint of contempt. "As daunting as that may be."

"A duty to your father?"

"To king and country. A duty to raise sons with the strength to carry us forward into a new, modern age. An age of scientific advancement."

Her snort echoed her disapproval. "I pray you've not told your prospective brides that's the reason you wish to wed. Some ladies like to imagine a marriage based on love."

"My father insisted romantic love was for the lower classes."

"I must disagree," Mr Daventry interjected. "Despite being the son of a duke, albeit an illegitimate one, I am deeply in love with my wife."

"Then you're one of the fortunate few, Daventry." Bennet turned to her, those brandy pools for eyes taking in her wild red curls and simple green day dress. "Am I to understand you were deeply in love with your husband, Mrs Eden?"

The question caught her off guard. "My personal affairs are not open to scrutiny, my lord." She refused to discuss her marriage with anyone. Ever.

Mr Daventry's curious gaze shifted between them. "We're digressing and should return to the matter at hand. Do you have an idea where you might begin, Mrs Eden?"

Yes, she might begin by gathering her skirts and bolting for the hills.

"I would compile a list of suspects, observe those who work at Witherdeen, interview the keepers of every coaching inn within a five-mile radius. Then I would return to town and work through his lordship's list of conquests. As the daughter of a woman who wangled her way into every lord's bed, it shouldn't be difficult to gain his mistress' trust." She paused for breath. "Shall I go on?"

"No, that seems sufficient." Mr Daventry turned to the marquess. "Well, will you hire Mrs Eden to uncover the identity of the person who sent the handbills?"

Hire? The thought left a nasty taste in Julianna's mouth. Giselle de Lacy had been nothing more than a body for rent. The fact Bennet Devereaux would pay for her services roused a deep unease. But Mr Daventry intended to use the funds to help other impoverished women, so she could not forgo her fee.

"And we would say you're at Witherdeen to study the abbey?" the marquess asked, but did not wait for an answer. "There's an empty cottage near the ruins that you could use for the duration of your stay. I wouldn't expect you to sleep in the servants' quarters. And if I grant you a chamber in the house, everyone will assume we're lovers."

Lovers!

The word dripped off his tongue so smoothly heat flooded her cheeks. Despite the fact she was not remotely interested in this man, she couldn't help but feel drawn to him in some inexplicable way.

Mr Daventry cleared his throat. "Mrs Eden will visit Witherdeen in a professional capacity. I expect you to treat her with the utmost respect."

The marquess' gaze softened. "As children, we formed a bond, helped each other through a difficult time. Regardless of what Mrs Eden may think of me when she delves into my affairs, I would never do anything to hurt her."

And yet, just by sitting there—a magnificent specimen of masculinity—he had unwittingly cut out her heart and destroyed every cherished memory.

CHAPTER 2

THE MEMORY of them huddled in the cupboard, scared to the marrow of their bones, of Julianna being ripped from his grasp, haunted Bennet to this day. If he closed his eyes, he might see her dainty hand pressed to the viewing window as the carriage charged down the drive. He might feel the sharp stones digging into the soles of his feet, experience the gut-wrenching pain that followed their separation.

Promise you'll return if you can.

He'd had many friends since—no one like Julianna.

And while Bennet had come to accept he would never see her again, understood they walked different paths now, like an angel of light she'd appeared unexpectedly. It had taken every effort not to hug her, stroke that wild hair from her face and beg to know where she had been for the last seventeen years. Anger had bubbled to the surface, too. Why had she not come to visit him at Witherdeen? But then he had not tried to find her either.

"We should make a list of suspects." Lucius Daventry handed Julianna a pencil and a small brown notebook. "Mrs Eden will record their names."

Mrs Eden!

Her husband was dead, yet Bennet wanted to wring his damn neck.

"Be honest with us, Devereaux," Daventry added. "No one is here to judge."

Thankfully, the housekeeper arrived with the tea tray and set about pouring three cups. Bennet helped himself to a shortbread biscuit but would need a stiff brandy if he were to reveal intimate details of his affairs.

"We should start with the name of your current mistress." Julianna seemed mildly annoyed. "I doubt it will mean anything to me, but Mr Daventry might like to offer an opinion."

Hell, Bennet felt as if he'd been dragged before the quarterly assizes. Surely every virile man of twenty-seven sought meaningless liaisons.

"Miss Isabella Winters," he said begrudgingly.

Julianna's hand shook as she scribbled down the name. "I assume you pay Miss Winters a monthly allowance."

"If you're asking if I pay for Isabella's *affections,* then the answer is yes."

Disappointment flashed in her vivid blue eyes. "Does Miss Winters know you are in want of a wife? Perhaps she fears she may lose the coveted place in your bed, my lord."

"No, I've not told Isabella I intend to marry."

"May I ask why not?"

"Does it have any bearing on the case?" Daventry interjected, as he must have sensed her hostility. "With your upbringing, you can guess why he has not been forthcoming with the information."

Bennet did not wish to be reminded of how Giselle de Lacy had mistreated her daughter. "Mrs Eden wants to know if I intend to keep a mistress when I'm married."

"Do you?" She turned to Daventry. "Lord Devereaux is fooling himself if he believes Miss Winters doesn't know of his desire to marry. Women who earn a living warming rich men's beds keep abreast of the gossip. Either she is seeking his replacement or doing her utmost to keep her position. Therefore, it is relevant to the case."

Daventry inclined his head. "Of course."

"I've not inherited my father's habits, Mrs Eden." He was not an arrogant reprobate who collected mistresses as if they were trophies. But he needed female company like every other man. "I shall be faithful to my wife and will expect the same in return."

"A task made more difficult if you're not in love with her, I might add."

Daventry sighed. "We are not here to advise his lordship on the pitfalls of marriage, Mrs Eden, even if I wholeheartedly agree with you. Now, I assume Miss Winters had a predecessor."

Bennet contemplated telling them both to mind their own damn business, but there was no one else he could trust. And while he had given Daventry two handbills, he'd not given him the third note, not told him about the hauntings.

"Before Miss Winters, I was involved with Mrs Bancroft."

Daventry frowned, and Bennet knew why. "Captain Bancroft's widow?"

"Indeed."

Both women had silky red hair, though not as vibrant as that of the siren currently sitting opposite. Both women possessed blue eyes and pale complexions, had bow-shaped lips that were nowhere near as alluring as Mrs Eden's. A man had a vision of what he liked in a woman, but despite meeting his physical criteria, they both lacked that special something.

"I see." Daventry sat back in the chair and steepled his fingers. "I wonder if your past connection to Mrs Eden might cause problems. I wonder if Miss Gambit might be better suited to the case."

Panic seized Bennet by the throat. In his mind, Julianna was back at Witherdeen, within arm's reach, there to talk to when he couldn't sleep, his only friend and confidante. Fate had thrown them together again. Though he prayed they were not destined to be torn apart under tragic circumstances.

"Mrs Eden knows my housekeeper," Bennet urged. "Surely that gives her an advantage." But the voice of reason said Miss Gambit might be the better choice. Miss Gambit wouldn't stir old feelings. Miss Gambit wouldn't look at him with disdain when he spoke about past lovers.

Julianna looked confused, for she couldn't know that every woman Bennet had bedded bore a likeness to her. He'd been looking for Julianna de Lacy for seventeen years, but in all the wrong places.

"Forgive me if my forthright approach has caused offence, sir," she said, oblivious to Lucius Daventry's concerns. "But if I am to help Lord Devereaux, I must know every intimate detail of his life."

Every intimate detail? The prospect of discussing his liaisons proved as daunting as the silence that followed.

"I'll be honest," Daventry began after some thought.

Bennet held his breath.

"You were close as children. I fear your connection may hinder your progress." Daventry's eyes flashed in silent warning. It was suddenly evident why most men feared this bastard son of a duke. "As an agent of the Order, Mrs Eden is under my protection. Her safety is paramount. I cannot have her distracted."

Julianna sat forward. "Sir, we're no longer those children. We're so far removed it's as if we're strangers."

Strangers!

Bennet firmed his jaw.

If suddenly struck blind, he could find her in a crowded room. Those unruly red curls would still feel like silk against his cheek. The scent of her skin and hair would evoke visions of an apple orchard. He would know her sweet cadence amid an orchestra of voices.

"I don't know this man." Julianna gestured to him as if he were a vagabond she'd stumbled upon in the street. "And once I have narrowed down the suspects, there'll be no need for us to spend time together."

Even as a child, Julianna had been logical while Bennet was prone to flights of fancy. Now, there was little point imagining something that could never be. He had a duty to marry the daughter of a duke. Duty did not permit a friendship with a courtesan's daughter.

"Do you think you can solve this case, Mrs Eden?" Daventry said.

"Yes, sir. I understand your concerns but assure you I shall treat his lordship like any other client."

Daventry considered her reply. "Then you may go to Witherdeen, but you will take Bower." He turned to Bennet. "Bower is a trusted servant and an ideal companion when one needs a man skilled in combat. He will assume the role of coachman and assist Mrs Eden where necessary. Having a spy amongst the ranks will prove useful, too."

Yes, and the fellow would be there to ferry Mrs Eden back to London should Bennet overstep the mark.

"I shall ensure there's a bed ready for him in the coach house."

"If Mrs Eden is to remain at Witherdeen beyond a week, I shall have Miss Gambit visit for a few days."

Anger flared, but Bennet held his temper. "Mrs Eden's well-being will be a priority, I assure you." He snatched another biscuit from the tray and stuffed it into his mouth, lest he tell Daventry what he really thought.

"Now that's settled," Julianna began, seemingly unaffected by the implication that Bennet might ravish her once he had her alone at Witherdeen, "we should continue making a list of suspects. I'm sure his lordship's time is precious, and our tea will be cold if we continue to digress."

At the mention of tea, they took their respective china. With an unsteady grip of the sugar tongs, Julianna dropped three lumps into her beverage. Bennet might have drawn attention to the fact she still had a sweet tooth, but didn't wish to provoke Lucius Daventry.

"Have any of your mistresses reacted irrationally when you gave them their *congé*?" came her blunt question as she absently stirred her tea. "Are any of them capable of murder?"

Murder? Hell, Isabella could barely rouse the energy to climb out of bed. She had a footman perform the arduous task of buttering her toast and lacked the mental capacity to think of anything but her next modiste appointment.

"No. But we're talking about four or five women, not a harem." He wasn't a complete reprobate.

"Which is it, my lord? Four or five?"

He huffed. "Five."

She scribbled that in her damn notebook.

"And what about prospective brides?" Daventry said. "Have

you entertained any prominent families in town or at Witherdeen?"

Bennet explained he'd invited three notable families to Witherdeen for a few days last November: Lord Pilkington, Lord Ledbury and Lord Addison. "I've spoken privately with the Duke of Pembridge. While he discussed his eldest daughter, I made no mention of forming an alliance."

Julianna did not look up from her notebook, but continued writing more than the names of the peers Bennet had mentioned. "Do any of the ladies have reason to think you might offer for them, my lord?"

"No, Mrs Eden. It was purely a social gathering to become acquainted with those ladies on the marriage mart."

She nodded, unaware that another teasing curl had escaped her simple coiffure. "May I ask who will inherit the marquessate should you die before siring an heir?"

The heir presumptive had been the first person on Bennet's suspect list.

"My cousin John Devereaux, but he's currently in the Bay of Bengal serving as Post-Captain on his Majesty's frigate *The Argyle*. I dined with Lord Melville—First Lord of the Admiralty —last night. He confirmed what I already knew."

"Is John Devereaux married?"

"I believe so, but I have never met his wife." Before she could ask the most obvious question, Bennet said, "My father despised his brothers. When he inherited, he refused to entertain either of them again. He feared Charles would murder him in his sleep and claim the title. And so he set about secretly ruining both men. I had the unfortunate pleasure of reading my father's journals after he died. The written word has a way of revealing the depraved depths of a man's mind."

Reading of his father's delusions, of his hostility and imagined conflicts, went some way to explain the lord's sudden acts of aggression. Perhaps John Devereaux had taken a commission in the navy because he wished to be as far away from England—as far away from the marquess—as possible.

"May I read the journals?" Julianna asked. "The threats made against you seem deeply personal. Vengeance is the obvious motive. But the perpetrator may have had a grievance against your father."

Had anyone else asked, Bennet would have refused. But Julianna had lived at Witherdeen for a year. During that time, she had witnessed his father's vile temper, had seen the violent outbursts, knew he had a grandiose sense of self-importance and blamed everyone else for his failings.

"I shall make them available to you when you arrive at Witherdeen but must insist you discuss the contents with no one but me."

"Of course."

She continued writing in her notebook, and Bennet couldn't help but wonder what impression he had made. Was the vision before her a terrible disappointment? Had she thought about him often during the last seventeen years? Or, like Giselle de Lacy, was Julianna oblivious to the devastation caused by her departure? Had she made a new friend, found Bennet's replacement?

"What of you, Devereaux?" Daventry's voice pulled Bennet from his reverie. "Was there not an incident with Mr Mullholland some months ago?"

Bennet gritted his teeth. Mullholland was the youngest son of a viscount, but had the arrogance of an eldest son. The man made his money breeding thoroughbreds and betting on the Turf.

"Mullholland called me out over an issue of race fixing when my horse beat his at Cleeve Hill, Cheltenham. We settled the matter there and then, choosing a bare-knuckle brawl in the stables, where my timely uppercut to his jaw put him out for two minutes."

"Mr Mullholland has every reason to despise you," Julianna stated.

"Yes, he lost a substantial sum that day."

"And was the race fixed?"

Daventry's sharp inhalation reflected Bennet's shock. Ladies rarely questioned a gentleman's honour, not openly at any rate.

Sensing the sudden shift in mood, she added, "Honest men may find themselves victims of blackmail or duped by a corrupt jockey. Men are made and broken at the racecourse, my lord. The question has no bearing on your character. I merely ask if Mr Mullholland had good reason to assume he'd been cheated."

"Mullholland's colt beat mine by a furlong in a race two days earlier. My horse won on the day, at greatly raised odds. Accusations were made against me and my jockey, but the Club ruled in our favour and could find no evidence of race fixing."

"Having lost a significant sum, Mr Mullholland must be bitter."

"One would imagine so."

Silence ensued, though her constant pencil scratching grated.

She studied her notes, absently tapping her lips with the tip of the writing implement. Bennet might have told her it was an unladylike habit, but he welcomed the opportunity to stare at her mouth.

"My lord, does anyone else have a grudge against you?"

Only you, he thought.

Did she blame him for breaking his promise?

"Not that I am aware."

She took to rubbing her finger over her lips as she thought. "Assuming Mr Daventry agrees, might I come to Witherdeen tomorrow? I would like to observe the staff and examine your father's journals. I would prefer to have a clear picture before investigating Mr Mullholland and making friends with your mistress."

Bennet's heart raced. "You need to befriend Isabella?"

"If I am to find the culprit without discussing the threats made, I will need to work covertly. Trust me. Those with a motive will reveal themselves."

Bennet stared. It should come as no surprise that a courtesan's daughter possessed such a calculating mind. Giselle de Lacy's greatest skill had been manipulation. And yet, he refused to believe Julianna had inherited her mother's wicked traits.

"While you're at Witherdeen, I shall make enquiries into Mr Mullholland's background," Daventry said. He leant forward, gathered the handbills, slipped them into the leather portfolio and handed it to Julianna. "And I shall take tea with Lady

Perthshore. She is always abreast of the latest gossip and may know if anyone else has a gripe with you, Devereaux."

Lady Perthshore often invented tales. No doubt Daventry was skilled enough to distinguish between lies and truths.

"Then I shall return to Witherdeen and await Mrs Eden's arrival."

The memory of him standing on the gravel drive as a ten-year-old boy flashed into his mind. For an hour, he'd waited in the rain, his sodden nightshirt clinging to his shivering body, praying Giselle de Lacy would have a sudden change of heart. That Julianna would come back to him, back where she belonged.

"Excellent." Daventry focused his attention on Julianna. "I shall ensure Bower is fully briefed and will expect your return within the week."

"I cannot imagine being at Witherdeen for more than two days," she said in the indifferent manner of a Bow Street constable. "But will send word if I'm delayed."

Two days wasn't enough.

Enough for what?

Enough for him to plead for forgiveness?

Enough for him to pretend they might still be friends?

She rose from the chair. "If you will excuse me, I have much to do if I'm to leave for Hampshire in the morning." She looked at Bennet, a ghost of a smile gracing her lips. "Until tomorrow, my lord."

"Until tomorrow." He couldn't bring himself to say Mrs Eden.

Bennet watched her as she spoke to Daventry, continued watching her until she left the room. The old feelings surfaced. The flutter of panic that he might never see her again. The ache in his chest at the thought of losing his one true friend. Feelings he had buried long ago. Feelings stamped down by the weight of responsibility, the pressures of his position.

Daventry crossed the room. He glanced into the hall before closing the door and returning to stand with Bennet. "Beneath Mrs Eden's confident facade lies a fragile woman who has endured many hardships. I trust you know how her mother died."

Of course he knew. "Of a laudanum overdose."

Lord Denver's son had told him one night at White's. Giselle de Lacy had lived like a pauper, selling herself like a backstreet whore. Bennet had asked about Julianna, and the fop had shrugged.

Such women are meant to be used and discarded.

Denver had echoed the sentiment shared by most men. It had taken immense effort for Bennet to keep his fists at his sides and not pummel the living daylights out of the cad.

"They say her body was so emaciated she was like a bag of bones."

"Giselle was sick long before she became addicted to laudanum," Daventry said with some vehemence. "When she exhausted her funds, she sold Julianna de Lacy to the highest bidder."

"Sold her!" Bennet covered his mouth with his hand as his stomach roiled. He should have tried to find her. But what could a ten-year-old boy do?

"Thankfully, Mr Eden treated her well enough, or so she tells me." Daventry suddenly gripped Bennet's shoulder. "It's obvious she meant something to you once. Her work for the Order is a way to earn an honest income and improve her prospects. I trust you will bear that in mind when she visits Witherdeen."

Bennet shrugged out of Daventry's grasp, annoyed at the man's hypocrisy. "You fear for her safety, yet place her in precarious situations. There are better ways to earn a living than chasing criminals."

In a half-mocking tone, Daventry said, "Do not mistake me for a fool, Devereaux. I knew of your history with Mrs Eden before you arrived today. Just as I knew you had a penchant for women with red hair. The last hour has been about helping Mrs Eden settle into her new role. Why do you think I chose her to help with your dilemma?"

"Because she's the obvious candidate given her background."

"And because you're intelligent enough to solve this matter yourself, were you so inclined. I suspect you will work with her to find the culprit, and that means I'll sleep easier at night." Daventry's hair might be as black as Satan's soul, but his heart brimmed with compassion. "It's unfortunate she bears an uncanny likeness to her mother, though that's where the similarity ends."

"Julianna is nothing like her mother," Bennet echoed.

"People would disagree. I found her sobbing on the steps of the Servants' Registry. The wife of her last employer recognised her and threw her out. No one wants Giselle de Lacy's daughter playing governess to the *ton*'s little lords and ladies. The wife complained, and they barred Mrs Eden from the Registry."

The sad story caused a tightening in Bennet's chest. How many times had Julianna been the object of people's disdain? "I would offer her a position at Witherdeen if I thought she might accept."

"A position as what? Housekeeper? Mistress? Governess to your children when you marry? I'm sure your prospective wife would have something to say on the matter."

Bennet threw his hands up. "Then what the hell do you want from me?"

"Help her solve the case. Help rebuild her confidence. Put her needs before your own. Perhaps be the friend you once were."

He wanted nothing more than to rekindle their friendship, to dance with her in the great hall, picnic in the ruins, talk as they used to all those years ago. Helping her would ease the guilt he felt for not caring enough about her welfare.

"I will assist in any way I can, though she seems determined to keep me at bay. I'm not the sweet boy she remembers." No, the years had hardened him, made him cynical. "One imagines she's developed a distrust for all men."

"People have abused her trust so many times over the years I doubt she will have faith in anyone again."

"Is mistrust not an advantage in your line of work?"

"It's a strength when investigating cases, a weakness when it comes to Mrs Eden finding true happiness."

Bennet considered the powerful man standing before him. Perhaps Lucius Daventry was a mender of broken hearts, not just the master of a band of ruthless enquiry agents.

"It won't be easy," Daventry added.

"What? Finding the devil responsible? Mrs Eden seems to think she'll have the matter concluded within the week." Though how she would get the culprit to confess was anyone's guess.

"No, being friends with a woman you'd like to bed. One only need look at your mistresses to know you're attracted to Mrs Eden."

Bennet inhaled sharply. He might have closed his eyes to shake the thought, but knew his mind would conjure an image of them writhing passionately in bed. The innocent love of a child had quickly become the lustful urges of a man.

"I made a promise seventeen years ago, a vow I failed to fulfil. I said I would find her when I came of age." At the time, he'd meant every word. "But—"

"The months stretched to years, and it's easier to dismiss a pledge given when one is too young to know better."

It was a reasonable excuse but did nothing to ease Bennet's conscience. "I shall do what I should have done years ago. Befriend Mrs Eden in the hope of rescuing her from her tragic past."

Daventry arched a brow. "You mean to restore her faith in humanity?"

"I mean to show her I'm the one man she can trust."

CHAPTER 3

MANY TIMES OVER THE YEARS, Julianna had imagined herself astride Bennet's horse, his arms wrapped around her as he nudged the mount along the winding drive back to Witherdeen. She had been but a guest in the sprawling mansion, yet everything about the place carried the comfort of home.

It wasn't memories of bricks and mortar that left her heart glowing, but memories of happy times spent with Bennet. The picnics by the lake. Slipping off the rope swing and plunging headfirst into the water. Them running away and hiding amid the abbey ruins, pretending it was their home. A sanctuary away from the constant bickering. A delightful fantasy that fed their minds and nurtured their souls.

But dreams were figments of the imagination, stories constructed to chase away the darkness and banish despair. The cold, hard reality was that Julianna had never belonged at Witherdeen. Bennet Devereaux was no longer her beloved friend but a grown man of wealth and title. Were it not for Mr Daventry's benevolence, Julianna would be slaving to the bone at Bethnal Green workhouse, where the only visitors were the anatomists queuing to claim the dead.

The differences between them were stark amid the light of day.

They had always been worlds apart.

Somehow she had to find the strength to live alongside him for the next two days. But she would work from the cottage, only venture to the house when necessary. There was no need to spend any length of time in his company.

Besides, had Bennet Devereaux not inherited his father's attitude for casual affairs? Did that not give her every reason to despise him the way she did most men?

Still, her newfound fortitude did not stop her heart lurching the moment she passed through Witherdeen's wrought-iron carriage gates. Nor did it stop tears springing to her eyes or destroy the memory of Bennet standing cold and wet in the rain.

Promise you'll return if you can.

When she made the vow, she never dreamed she would return as an enquiry agent, one trying to establish who wanted to murder the master. She'd never expected to see Bennet again.

But fate had intervened.

She caught sight of the ruined Augustinian abbey to the west of the house. The grey gothic transepts soared high above the barren winter landscape. The vast arched window no longer held the intricate pieces of painted glass—the religious depictions designed to uplift and inspire. It stood empty, neglected, the soul ripped out to leave but a stone shell. The grimness of the January morning provided the perfect backdrop, for Julianna could not help but draw parallels between her mother's tragic life and the splendid structure that had suffered a swift demise.

And then Witherdeen Hall came into view—a majestic building built by Bennet's great-grandfather—with its sweeping stone staircase and huge loggia supported by impressive Tuscan columns.

Julianna swallowed deeply.

It was as if she were a girl again, terrified the new lord would banish her to a cold corner of the sprawling mansion. Still, it was the thought that Bennet might be overly welcoming that left her most afraid.

She instructed Mr Bower to navigate the cobbled stable yard and deposit her at the mansion's rear entrance. The staff used the entrance to access the garden and to greet tradesmen and merchants delivering their wares. It would do her well to remember she was employed to perform a service, not befriend the marquess.

Mr Bower drew the carriage to a halt. Before he'd climbed down from the box seat, Julianna had opened the door and jumped to the ground.

"Eager to get started, Mrs Eden?"

The man smiled. Yet it was the scar cutting through his brow that captured her attention. With his dark hair and muscular physique, he resembled Mr Daventry and often acted as a decoy during investigations.

"I've but two days to conclude my business, Mr Bower."

It was nowhere near enough time.

"Then tell me what I can do to help."

Julianna kept her voice low. "I believe Mr Keenan is still in charge of the coach house and stables. Find out what you can about the mood of those who work here, but don't rouse his suspicions. Come to the cottage tonight, and we can discuss all you've learnt."

Mr Bower nodded and would have replied were it not for the sudden arrival of the housekeeper, Mrs Hendrie, who appeared at the service door somewhat breathless. Her ebony hair might be streaked silver now, the crinkles around her eyes more prominent, her slight frame more fragile, but her smile was just as endearing.

"Miss Julianna!" Mrs Hendrie abandoned all etiquette. She hurried forward and captured Julianna's hands. "My, how you've grown." She glanced at Mr Daventry's elegant coach, at Julianna's new green velvet pelisse, at the dratted red curls escaping her poke bonnet. "I cannot tell you how relieved I am to see you looking so happy and healthy."

Like the walls of Witherdeen, Mrs Hendrie knew all the family's secrets. She had disliked Giselle de Lacy, despised all women who hopped their way from bed to bed. And while she had performed her duties with the indifference befitting her station, behind closed doors, she had smothered Julianna with kindness and affection.

"It's good to see you again, Mrs Hendrie. I've thought of you often over the years." Memories of the woman's embrace proved there were loving people in the world. "A lot has happened since I left. I'm a widow now and have come to Witherdeen in a professional capacity."

"His lordship said you're to study the ruins, that he's commissioned you to write about your findings." Mrs Hendrie clutched her hands to her chest. "When he mentioned he'd met you by chance in town, my heart almost burst with excitement."

Guilt coiled like a serpent of deceit in Julianna's stomach. After Edward Eden's death, she had vowed never to lie again.

"My husband loved history, and we often toured old ruins." That much was true. "And there's something special about the abbey here." There was something special about all those who lived at Witherdeen now.

"You're a lady of some means. One must thank Mr Eden for that."

Julianna forced a smile. "Were it not for Mr Eden, I wouldn't have found my way back to you." No, she might have been sold to someone far worse. Might have had to ply her mother's trade or join the Covent Garden ladies and sell her soul for a pittance.

Mrs Hendrie shivered. "Best not stand out in the cold. I'll escort you to the study. Afterwards, we'll take a tour of the house." She cast a nervous eye over Mr Bower's hulking form. "Seek out Mr Keenan in the stable courtyard. There'll be a warm welcome there for you, too, I'm sure."

Mr Bower inclined his head and climbed atop his box.

"Come. Best not keep the master waiting." Mrs Hendrie hugged Julianna's arm as she led her into the house. "Milford is still the butler here. Do you remember hiding pine cones in his bed?"

Despite a sudden surge of emotion at being within Witherdeen's walls again, Julianna laughed. "Milford blamed it on the hall boy. Bennet felt so guilty he had to confess." And had spent the night in the understairs cupboard by way of punishment. Julianna caught herself. "Forgive me. I shall have to get used to addressing the marquess formally. We're not children anymore."

"His lordship's not the pompous sort who insists on rigid rules. His friends call him Devereaux, and I'm sure he'll afford you the same courtesy."

The only way Julianna would survive the brief visit was by keeping to strict boundaries. Her heart was already in her throat at the prospect of being alone with Bennet in a place that held many fond memories.

The narrow corridors widened as Mrs Hendrie led her from the basement into the main house. Julianna glanced at the entrance hall's chequered floor, at the stag heads and dreary paintings lining the wall, at the wooden panel disguising the old lord's torture chamber, and couldn't help but recall every harrowing detail of the night she'd left.

Part of her wanted to clap her hands with joy at being back at Witherdeen. Part of her wanted to take to her heels and run because her visit would surely end in heartache.

Mrs Hendrie knocked on the study door, and a deep masculine voice called for her to enter. "Miss Julianna has arrived, my lord. Do you wish to receive her now?"

The marquess sighed. "Mrs Hendrie, the girl we remember is a grown woman. We should afford her the courtesy of calling her by her married name."

"Yes. Forgive me, my lord. Mrs Eden has arrived."

"Then you may show Mrs Eden in."

Heavens. Julianna lacked the courage to cross the threshold. Her heart thumped in her throat. Everything seemed a little blurred, distant.

Wearing a beaming smile, Mrs Hendrie returned to the hall. "His lordship will see you now. Send for me when you're ready, and I'll take you to the cottage."

Julianna nodded. She touched the housekeeper affectionately on the upper arm. "It's so good to see you, Mrs Hendrie."

Mrs Hendrie gave Julianna's hand a reassuring squeeze, then gestured to the open study door. "Best hurry. His lordship likes to keep the room warm."

Julianna drew a deep breath and entered the study.

Had she found Bennet Devereaux dressed appropriately, consumed with the vast array of ledgers and papers spread over his imposing desk, she might have greeted him without her voice breaking. But he stood in shirtsleeves rolled to the elbows, displaying strong, muscular forearms. His gold waistcoat gripped his shoulders and clung to his chest like a second skin.

"G-good afternoon, Lord Devereaux."

"Mrs Eden." He did not reach for his coat or attempt to make himself presentable. He simply bowed. "Welcome to Witherdeen." A smile tugged on his lips.

"Thank you, my lord." The click of the door closing had Julianna's pulse pounding. It was so hot in the room she could barely breathe. "Everything is as I remember."

"Not everything," he teased. "We've both grown somewhat."

He'd grown considerably. She couldn't help but glance at the dark hair on his forearms. "Gone are the days when we might hide undetected behind the curtains."

"I don't know. Perhaps we won't giggle quite as much."

"Your laugh is contagious, my lord, and got us into terrible trouble."

His gaze slid slowly over her figure before lingering on the red curl bobbing against her cheek. "I see your hair is still wild and unruly."

"One learns to live with certain flaws."

"It's not a flaw."

She swallowed deeply. "You used to say I had a head full of piglet tails."

"It was a compliment." He laughed, but his amusement quickly faded. "I'm sorry, Julianna. Sorry for making a promise I didn't keep."

Oh, she'd hoped he would avoid discussing the past in detail. And why had he seen fit to use her given name? Panic ensued. Did he think that paying her a fee came with certain entitlements? She was not Giselle de Lacy. She could not be bought, not anymore.

"And I should not have promised to return knowing it was impossible. But we were children, consumed by heightened emotions." Although she was eager to know how long it had taken him to forget her. "A lot has happened since then. But we should remember I'm here to work, nothing more." While she had come to rescue him from his nightmare, that didn't mean history would repeat itself.

"Then forgive me again if I appear over-friendly." He sounded a little irate. "Am I permitted to ask if you've eaten?"

"I ate on the journey." Miss Trimble had made up a basket of delicious treats to keep in the cottage and a cold platter to have en route.

"Would it be inappropriate to ask you to dine with me this evening?"

Share a lavish meal in an intimate setting?

Had he lost his mind?

"Would you ask Mrs Hendrie to dine with you, my lord?"

"Mrs Hendrie has never been as close to me as you once were."

"*Were* being the operative word." She sounded cold, but it was the only way to protect her heart. "I have a duty to investigate the strange occurrences here. My future prospects depend upon me doing a thorough job. Let us leave our treasured memories in the past where they belong and focus on the pressing affair that led to you hiring an enquiry agent."

Time was of the essence. The longer she stayed at Witherdeen, the more she would grow attached to the place, the servants, the handsome master.

The marquess planted his hands on the desk and leant forward. "If you're asking me to treat you like a stranger, I cannot."

"Then you should have made that clear before I accepted the position."

"Devil take it, Julianna, we need to speak intimately if we're to find the villain sending the handbills. Am I to be the only one baring my soul?"

Good God! Surely he didn't expect her to reveal every harrowing detail of her life. Julianna swallowed past the lump in her throat. She would rather he remember her as a lively girl, not the emaciated young woman sold to feed her mother's addiction.

"My lord, I must insist you call me Mrs Eden." She hated the name. Her widowhood was akin to the understairs cupboard—a dark place full of horrible memories. But the sooner they focused on the case and not their past attachment, the better. "I must insist we concentrate on what's important, which is finding the person who sent the threatening notes."

He remained silent as he glanced out of the window at Witherdeen's grounds. A strange melancholy settled in the air, and it felt suddenly colder despite the fire roaring in the grate.

"Then you should sit, Mrs Eden. Make yourself comfortable, take notes. Allow me to present all the facts so you can make informed decisions."

All the facts?

"There are things you've omitted to mention, my lord?" Was this a ploy to gain her sympathy, to test her resolve?

"Just another handbill, and the ghost of a monk who walks the grounds after resting peacefully for three hundred years."

Intrigued, Julianna studied him for a moment. She'd learnt to look for the subtle signs of deception—exaggerated hand movements, a slight change in word choice or intonation—but noted nothing that might rouse her suspicion.

"Perhaps you can escort me to the cottage. On the way, you can reveal that which you failed to tell Mr Daventry. I trust you still have the handbill." If they walked, he would need to wear a coat, need to cover those strong forearms that proved equally distracting.

Bennet Devereaux took the small key hidden beneath the ink stand. He opened the desk drawer, removed the note and handed it to her.

Julianna tried to read the words pasted to the page, but her traitorous gaze drifted to the marquess as he rolled down his shirtsleeves and pushed his muscular arms into his black coat.

"The note arrived three days ago," he informed her as he rounded the desk.

As children, they'd been of similar height. Now, he stood almost a head taller, stood too close as he watched her read the obituary. His commanding presence proved a little suffocating, and so she turned to the window under the guise of concentrating on the words cut from a newspaper and assembled with care.

"This one reports that you died in a house fire." Her stomach twisted into knots as she reread the next line. "It says Witherdeen was reduced to rubble, that your charred body was found amongst the remains."

Julianna wasn't sure why the threat rocked her to her core. Stories of gargoyles and of gravestones found amongst abbey ruins were the constructs of gothic tales. Devices used to strike fear in the hearts of mere mortals. But houses of all sizes and descriptions had burned to the ground because of dirty chimneys and faulty candle wicks. Equally, one needed no skill to start a fire that could ravage a mansion house within hours.

She turned and met his gaze. "Has there been a fire?"

"Not yet."

The hint of sadness in his tawny eyes sent her hurtling back to the day she found him crying in the cupboard. The need to comfort him sparked anew.

"A coward sent this," she said, her voice full of contempt for the craven devil. "Someone without courage or honour. Someone too weak to seek satisfaction at a dawn appointment. Probably a jealous woman. Either way, I shall help you solve the mystery, help you any way I can."

He looked at her like he did the day he'd peeled back the napkin folds and found a slice of cake—with gratitude and wide-eyed wonder. "Though we hardly know each other now, Mrs Eden, having you here brings immense comfort."

Oh, why did every word from his lips stir such odd sensations?

Tears welled. She turned away on the pretence she may have left something on the seat. "Come, let's walk while we talk. It's sweltering in here. The fresh air will do us a wealth of good."

"We'll pass by the ruins. I shall show you where my steward found the gravestone."

She needed to inspect the grounds, discover who'd seen the ghostly monk. Indeed, there were so many lines of enquiry to explore, Julianna feared she would be at Witherdeen for a week.

A week?

Heaven help her!

She had been at Witherdeen less than an hour and was struggling against a range of emotions. No. She'd committed to two days and would have to work through the night if necessary. Besides, she could trust Mr Bower to perform certain tasks.

"We need to sit down and construct a timeline, my lord," she said as they moved from the study to the entrance hall. "Perhaps we might do that during our tour of the ruins."

The marquess seemed distracted. He came to an abrupt halt, took to glancing around the vast space as if witnessing the grandeur for the first time.

"My lord?"

Bennet Devereaux jerked in response. "Yes? Oh, you mentioned a timeline. I am at your disposal, Mrs Eden, and will give you any information you require." Stealing another glimpse at the broad oak staircase, he said, "Do you recall the last time we stood together in this hall?"

"With remarkable clarity." Sadly.

She could remember everything about that night. The patter of raindrops on the windowpane obliterated by the thud of footsteps on the landing. The rumble of thunder drowned out by the roar of angry voices. The taste of damp earth in the air, salty tears on her lips. And yet time and time again, it was the fear in Bennet's eyes that appeared in her dreams, her nightmares.

"One must question if we're at war with our memory."

"At war?" It wasn't such an odd phrase. Her inner battle began the moment she was reunited with Bennet Devereaux.

"Does the mind not spread propaganda?" he said. "Does it not ignore happy times and focus on painful memories?"

"We tend to cling to what we've lost and not appreciate all we've gained."

As a married woman, Julianna had gained respectability. And she didn't have to listen to her mother's harebrained plans or partake in her devious scheming. But in marrying Edward Eden, she had lost every shred of dignity, lost all hope of falling in love and having children. Had almost lost her sanity.

"The year spent at Witherdeen was the happiest of my life," she said without her voice breaking. "But I'm no longer that girl. Now I strive to make each new day worth living."

He held her gaze long enough for her to feel that spark of

connection. "Then come. You've never been inside the cottage near the ruins, and I think you'll find it rather charming."

Everything about Witherdeen held a certain allure.

That was the problem.

They left together through the huge oak doors, walked side-by-side down the sweeping stone staircase. It was impossible not to think of the last time she'd hurried down the steps.

The marquess offered his arm as they crossed the damp grass. "Grimley is attempting to fill the mole holes, and I'd hate for you to sprain your ankle."

"Would you afford Mrs Hendrie the same pleasure?" she said, feigning amusement, because the thought of touching him sent her pulse soaring.

"Are we to judge everything based on my treatment of Mrs Hendrie?"

"She knows your secrets yet still knows her place."

Indeed, Julianna would do well to take a leaf from the house-keeper's book. Somehow she had to immerse herself in Bennet Devereaux's world while attempting to remain indifferent.

CHAPTER 4

REKINDLING his friendship with Julianna proved harder than Bennet had expected. She insisted on erecting barriers, building giant walls no mortal man could scale. She hid behind imagined structures, used every excuse to leave him out in the cold. But every impenetrable fortress had a weakness. It was just a matter of locating hers and entering with caution.

"Daventry said you're interested in history and archaeology." Bennet guided her across the lawn and headed towards the grey, moss-covered walls of the old abbey.

The building had stood on the grounds since the thirteenth century. Once a place as inaccessible as Julianna's emotions, its crumbling walls were now open to the elements. The only living things seeking sanctuary were the wild plants growing in the gaps in the lime mortar and the oak saplings taking root around the perimeter.

"My husband toured the country, cataloguing buildings destroyed in the dissolution." Julianna's expression was as indifferent as her tone. "Other than history books, there was little else to read in the house. I couldn't help but take an interest in Edward's work."

"Did you accompany him on his excursions?" Bennet had no desire to speak about *Edward*, yet he wished to know everything that had happened since she'd been torn from his arms on that stormy night.

"Sometimes. Mostly he visited sites with a colleague, an artist."

Ah, he caught a hint of bitterness.

Did she resent the artist or resent being cast aside?

"It can be tiresome journeying from place to place." Surely a devoted husband sought any opportunity to spend time alone with his wife. "No doubt Mr Eden considered your comfort a priority."

"No doubt he did." Her tone rang with insincerity.

They fell silent and left the lawn to trudge along the dirt track. Gone were the days when they'd hold hands and race towards the ruins, laughing and talking incessantly. Now, their steps bore the burden of responsibility. His, from the pressure of inheriting a marquessate. Hers, from having to provide the basic needs, of surviving in a world where the odds were stacked against her.

When they reached the abbey's boundary wall, Julianna stopped. She removed her glove and pressed her palm to the mottled stone as if it held the propensity to heal her wounds.

"It's hard to believe these stones have been here for hundreds of years. Long before your great-grandfather built the house." She spoke with a sense of wonder. "Imagine all that has passed, yet they stand strong. A testament to faith."

If only people were as resilient, Bennet thought.

"It's so peaceful here," he whispered, as if the monks who once roamed the claustral buildings might chastise him for speaking. "Something about the air cleanses the soul."

She inhaled deeply, testing his theory. "Indeed."

Bennet opened the studded door in the wall and led Julianna into the old courtyard, now a sea of grass meandering through every damaged doorway and crevice. What remained of the abbey's walls looked to have burst up from the earthy depths below, a vast, awe-inspiring structure that dominated the landscape.

"All the lancet windows are intact and just missing the glass," she remarked. "They're perfect examples of bar tracery. If one looks at the huge clerestory window in the hall beyond, one can gauge the true height of the internal walls."

Was this how she spoke to Mr Eden? Cold. Formal. Did she impress him with her knowledge so he might appreciate the intelligence of the woman he had purchased for a pittance?

"When I come here, I don't imagine a place of worship." He saw a haven for childhood fantasies. Tended not to think of the abbey as being intact but a broken place for broken people.

Julianna glanced at him. "If you examine the architectural remains, it's not difficult to imagine how things used to be."

"If I wanted to remember how things used to be, I would take myself to what's left of the kitchen and light a fire in the hearth."

There, he could not say it plainer than that.

Her eyes brightened at the memory. "It's hard to toast bread without a roasting fork, though you did build an excellent fire. Shame the gardener saw the smoke and came running."

"Next time I decide to eat outdoors, I shall bring the correct tools and use seasoned wood. Warn Grimley that I can do what the hell I like now I own the land."

"As master of Witherdeen, why not have Cook prepare a basket?"

"Where's the fun in that?"

She scanned his face, her amusement fading. "Have you not found other ways to entertain yourself, my lord? I'm not sure Miss Winters will want to sit on the cold ground, eat burnt bread and inhale fire smoke."

"I hadn't thought of inviting Miss Winters." Isabella would never stoop so low. She'd need a gilded chair and servants to fan the flames. "Besides, I spoke to Miss Winters when I left Daventry's office yesterday. We agreed it was time to part ways." He'd not visited Isabella much of late. Entertaining a mistress now Julianna was back in his life seemed abhorrent.

"What? You've tired of Miss Winters already?" Julianna didn't wait for a reply but strode ahead. As she passed through the archway, she stroked the stone like it was a magical portal to the past.

Bennet caught up with her near the giant clerestory window,

a majestic frame for the heavens now. "You make me sound like all the lords your mother entertained."

"You do pay women to warm your bed."

"I pay for exclusivity. Should I remain celibate until I find someone I wish to wed?" He wasn't Isabella's first lover and wouldn't be her last.

"And what of Miss Winters?"

"Her generous settlement means she need never take a lover again."

Bennet thought Julianna would be pleased he'd taken his responsibility seriously, but she scoffed. "Settlement? You may have provided for her financial needs, but have you considered the negative impact on her emotions?"

Her emotions! Clearly Julianna did not know Isabella Winters. The woman boasted of having had offers from other lords and knew how to manipulate men.

"Would it please you if I wrote to her and asked about her health?"

Julianna shook her head. "You don't need to please me, Bennet."

She was angry, yet had spoken his given name with a familiarity that diffused the need to retaliate.

"I'm not perfect, Julianna. I've made mistakes." He kept calm. "As a marquess, people presume I have all the answers. That's not the case." He was an imposter. A simple man living a complicated life. "We all need love in one form or other."

She gazed up at the ancient window, at the clouds drifting idly by. The world kept moving, even if one felt they were standing still.

"Witnessing our parents' version of love has made us cynical." Her comment sounded like a veiled apology. "And you lost your mother at a young age. Such tragedies make us behave in ways that often don't make sense." She paused. "All I'm saying is, Miss Winters is likely using you to further her own ends. Don't mistake your liaison for love."

"I'm perfectly aware of the limitations," he said, equally aware that this was the only honest conversation he'd had in seventeen years. He decided now was the best time to ask the question gnawing at his insides.

"Did you love Mr Eden?"

The silence stretched to excruciating lengths until she eventually muttered, "I'm sure you've heard the tale of Giselle de Lacy's downfall. Heard how she sold her daughter into marriage to feed her laudanum habit."

"I have not heard it from you."

From her intense stare, he knew she was tempted to explain her sad story. But then a voice called out from beyond the ruined cloisters and Bennet's steward appeared.

Damnation!

"My lord." Branner approached and doffed his hat. "I saw you entering the ruins and thought to offer my assistance. I'm more than happy to give Mrs Eden a tour of the grounds."

Bennet wasn't sure what roused his ire most. The fact Branner had interrupted an intimate conversation, or that when the man smiled, one could almost hear a chorus of angels singing. Still, he kept his temper and introduced the steward.

"Do you know much about monastic history, Mr Branner?"

Julianna maintained a confident facade, but Bennet sensed her retreating to the safety of her fortress. He imagined most women would find the steward's charming manner and athletic build attractive. No doubt Julianna knew enough about cads to know when one was trying his utmost to impress.

Branner scanned the ruins. "This was an Augustinian monastery. They formed over a thousand years ago but only settled on English soil in the thirteenth century." He glanced at the crumbling walls towering forty feet high. "I'm familiar with the structural layout, know something of the demolition. Indeed, the dissolution deed is amongst the documents in his lordship's library."

Branner was being helpful, so why was Bennet so annoyed?

"You appear to be a fountain of knowledge, sir."

"Hopefully, I may be of use to you when you're gathering research for your book, Mrs Eden. Though one must ask, will it be a story of the abbey's historical background or a tale of the terrifying hauntings?"

Julianna glanced at Bennet. They had not discussed who amongst the staff knew about the threatening handbills. However, she knew the steward had dealt with the matter of the smashed gargoyle and would presume he knew about the grave-stone buried within the ruins.

Even so, she spoke with caution. "Are you trying to tell me you've seen a ghost, Mr Branner?"

"That depends. Do you suffer from a nervous disposition, madam?"

"I find the living more terrifying than the dead."

Branner laughed. "I'm not sure you'd say the same if confronted by a faceless monk swinging a thurible."

"Is that what you saw, sir?"

Branner pointed through the arched doorway where two huge fireplaces stood intact. "He passed from the kitchen to the refectory."

Julianna frowned. "If the ghost was faceless, why are you so certain it was a man?"

Branner jerked slightly. "Are monks not always men?" From his odd reaction, clearly he was unused to people contesting his wild tales.

"We're not talking about a monk, sir. We're talking about a phantom or a person out to cause mischief. Did you see the apparition at night?"

"Yes, sometime after midnight. Before you ask, I was in full possession of my faculties."

"I presume you live within the estate's grounds."

"Yes, in a cottage a half-mile walk from here."

Julianna gazed at the crumbling walls. "The ruins are some distance from your house. May I ask why you were here at such a late hour?"

Branner grinned. "You sound like the magistrate, Mrs Eden. Is it a crime to be out after dark?"

Despite the steward's mocking tone, her confidence did not falter. "While my research will focus on monastic life and the abbey's demise, a chapter about the hauntings will enchant the reader. I'm afraid I must ask many questions, sir, but please don't think it's a personal attack."

Bennet disliked the way Branner ogled Julianna Eden. The thirty-year-old steward was intelligent, witty, educated, and unmarried. He was assessing her, no doubt contemplating the possibility of them becoming friends, lovers, maybe more.

"Then forgive me, madam, if I sounded defensive." Branner slapped his hand to his chest to show he spoke in earnest. "Perhaps you might like to interrogate me at length once you've settled into the cottage."

The bounder made interrogation sound like seduction.

Bennet stood there like a blasted chaperone to a courting couple. He would have dismissed Branner, but Julianna needed to question him.

Branner turned to Bennet. "I shall leave last month's account ledger on your desk later today, my lord, along with the report detailing the necessary improvements to the stable block. I have an hour until I'm to meet with the tenant farmers and can remain with Mrs Eden while she inspects the ruins."

"That won't be necessary, but make yourself available this evening. Mrs Eden may want to question you at the house." Pleased that in a rare moment of jealousy he'd not told his trusted servant to sod off, Bennet added, "And if you could locate any old records of the abbey, it may save Mrs Eden some time."

"Certainly, my lord." Branner inclined his head. "I look forward to continuing our discussion this evening, Mrs Eden."

Julianna smiled. "I shall try not to bombard you with questions, sir." She watched the steward walk away, waited until he'd disappeared from view before facing Bennet. "Do you like Mr Branner?"

"I don't dislike him." Not until ten minutes ago, at any rate. "He's an excellent steward, trustworthy, meticulous in his work. Why do you ask?"

"How long has he worked here?"

"Two years. My father employed him before he took ill. Mr Branner replaced the light-fingered Mr Weaver." Who might never have been caught had Bennet not examined the estate's accounts.

"Mr Weaver stole from your father?" came the next abrupt question.

"Yes, over a period of years."

"Why didn't you mention it when discussing possible suspects?"

"The man is sixty and would have been strung from the scaffold had my father prosecuted. No, Mr Weaver wouldn't dare show his face in these parts."

Anger simmered. Like Branner, Bennet disliked the brusque questions. Not because he had something to hide, but because Julianna seemed so cold, so detached.

"And your father died eighteen months ago?"

"Yes."

"Was it of natural causes, or might—"

"That's enough, Julianna." Bennet could no longer hold his tongue. He hated seeing her like this, an empty vessel going through the motions. "I'm happy to answer any questions, but you're like an automaton firing at random without waiting to see if you've hit the mark."

Her eyes widened. "I'm here as an agent of the Order to ask questions, to determine if your life is in danger. Perhaps you're used to women pandering to your every whim."

Bennet stepped closer. "I'd rather hear your angry remarks than your cold questions, but one hopes you may stumble upon a more tolerable way of speaking."

She stood stiff, rigid. The Julianna of old would have stuck out her tongue, challenged him to a duel with sticks, thrown a mud pie. Instead, she darted away.

"Julianna!" He caught up with her near the boundary wall, grabbed her hand and swung her around to face him. "What the devil's wrong?"

"Please, Bennet, let me go." She tried to tug free of his grasp. "I can't stay here. It's too familiar. It brings back too many memories."

"Good memories, surely."

Eager to escape, she looked back at the open door. "Please, I must go."

"Don't leave." Hell, he sounded like his ten-year-old self. But he knew if he released her, she would have Bower ferry her back to London, and he would never see her again.

"Mr Daventry will send Miss Gambit to serve in my stead."

Miss Gambit? He didn't want Miss Gambit.

"I need you."

"No, you don't."

"What shall I say to the staff? That Miss Gambit wants to write a damn book about the ruins now? It will rouse suspicion." He caught hold of her other hand, held it as tightly as he had the night they'd hid in the cobwebbed cubbyhole. "What's wrong, Julianna? The girl I knew always faced her fears."

The comment hit a nerve.

She hung her head, dejected.

Bennet considered pulling her into an embrace but had already overstepped the mark. "Do you remember what you said to me the day my father tanned my behind and you found me sobbing? Do you?"

"Of course I remember."

"Well?"

She raised her head. Her eyes glistened with unshed tears. "I promised tomorrow would be a better day. I promised to make you smile."

She had done more than make him smile. Her impressions of the servants had left him rolling about the floor, crying with laughter. In some twisted way, he'd grown to like the crack of the cane across his thighs. Julianna had a way of turning his torment into moments of pure magic.

"Our friendship grew from strength to strength." He cared for no one the way he'd cared for her. "Yes, we're different people now, but I'm making you the same promise in the hope we can start anew. Become friends again." He squeezed her hands. "And if not, let us at least be kind to one another while trying to find the devil who wants to kill me."

She stared at their clasped hands and sighed. "You're right. Solving the case is important to us both. I need to prove my worth as an agent if I'm to support myself, and we must put a stop to these veiled threats."

Relief washed through him. "Then let us agree to put the past behind us and concentrate on working together."

Julianna nodded. An errant red curl bobbed in agreement, too. "I've made a terrible mess of things already, Bennet."

The fact she had used his given name spoke of progress.

"How so?"

"I've raced ahead, haven't written a timeline or asked the basic questions." She tried to draw her hands from his grasp. Reluctantly, he let go. "I'm much better suited to the role of governess, but there's not a family in London who'll have me."

He might have feigned ignorance, but friends didn't lie. "Daventry said the Servants' Registry struck you off their list."

"The pompous fool. Do you know how hard it is to find work without a reference?" She laughed as her gaze swept from his neck to his navel. "Of course you don't. You insist on employing the best."

A host of questions flooded his mind. The most prominent being why Mr Eden had failed to provide for her after his death. How had the man died? God, had he been old and decrepit? Bennet needed to make his own timeline, beginning with what happened to Julianna after she left Witherdeen.

"Most things can be bought for the right price." The stupid words tumbled from his mouth before he realised what he'd said. "You can purchase references easily, but I'd rather you work for Lucius Daventry than a profligate who abuses his children's governess."

Another weary sigh escaped her. "I do like living with the ladies of the Order. And it would be good to remain in the same place for more than a few months."

"It's settled then. I'll escort you to the cottage so you can unpack. Come to the house this evening, and I shall relate the events in chronological order, answer the basic questions."

She managed a faint smile. "Yes, I need to concentrate on gathering evidence. Forgive me. Being back at Witherdeen is overwhelming."

"I understand."

Their gazes locked. Bennet felt the same physical jolt he'd experienced upon first setting eyes on her again. God, how he wished he could go back and do things differently. But then he'd be in the same predicament he was now—not knowing how to help her.

"Do you remember how to find the cottage?" he said.

"Yes, you continue along the path for a few minutes."

"Good. First one there earns a privilege pass."

"A privilege pass! What?" She jumped to attention. "No! You can't expect me to run in long skirts."

Bennet grinned. "I'll give you a few seconds to gather your skirts, and then I'll start counting your ten-second lead. One. Two."

Panic had her gaze darting left and right.

"Hurry. I'm about to begin the proper count," he teased.

Flustered, she grabbed her skirts and dashed through the doorway in the boundary wall, laughing as she went.

Bennet had no intention of letting her win, not the first race. Holding a privilege pass meant she would have to agree to his choice of game. He needed it as leverage for the next time she decided to flee Witherdeen.

"Ten!" he shouted loud enough for her to hear.

He raced through the open gate, saw that she was a hundred yards ahead, though inwardly groaned when he caught sight of her trim ankles.

She clutched her bonnet to her head and glanced behind, squealed, laughed, then pushed harder.

Bennet waited until he saw the thatched cottage before breaking into a sprint. "You need practice."

"No!" She caught sight of him charging up the flank. "It's not fair. Your strides are much longer than mine."

"You had a head start." He eased back a little, wishing the moment might never end. He liked seeing her like this, so confident and carefree.

They were fifty yards from the cottage when he increased his speed and darted past her. He vaulted the low garden gate, much to her chagrin, for she had to stop to fiddle with the latch.

"Had I been wearing b-breeches," she paused to catch her breath, "I w-would have won."

"We shall test your theory tomorrow." He opened the cottage door and stepped back for her to enter. She edged past him. So close their clothes touched, so close his stomach muscles clenched. "I hope you like it here."

She entered the parlour and gazed around the small room. The oak-beamed ceiling and quaint stone fireplace made the space seem cosy, intimate. A man might imagine curling up on the sofa with a certain woman, not a book.

"There's a kitchen through the far door and two bedrooms upstairs." Bennet gestured to the open staircase. "Let me show you."

"No." Her nervous gaze moved swiftly from him to the staircase. "Honestly, there's no need."

"Don't make me use my privilege pass." He'd need it for another time. Like persuading her to stay an extra day, a month, a year.

She arched a challenging brow. "Then use your pass. Nipping upstairs will probably be less taxing than any game you have in mind."

She referred to his love of leapfrog, but that was not the game he wished to play with her now.

"Very well." Bennet raised his hands in mock surrender. "I shall save my pass and leave you in peace. Bower will bring your luggage down."

"Thank you." She seemed relieved as she escorted him to the front door. "One more thing. When might I read your father's journals? They could contain important information relating to the case."

Unease settled in his bones. His father's twisted account of his relationship with Giselle de Lacy made for uncomfortable reading. One needn't be an expert in human nature to know it stemmed from jealousy and heartache.

"I'll have a footman bring the trunk to the cottage and will give you the key this evening."

"The trunk? How many journals are there?"

"Twenty or so." He paused. "Please remember, they're the words of a bitter man who was often mistaken in his opinion."

"I understand."

He didn't think she did, but he touched her gently on the upper arm. "It's good to have you back, Julianna."

She shivered visibly. "It's good to be back."

Bennet hovered on the threshold. There was so much to say, so many questions he needed to ask, but he couldn't risk her fleeing again. Instead, he found the strength to step out onto the path.

Julianna closed the door gently behind him.

But as he walked away, he thought he heard her weeping.

CHAPTER 5

JULIANNA WASN'T sure how long she'd stood slumped against the door, crying. Long enough for her cheeks to sting and her breath to come in racking sobs. Long enough for her to heave from the strain, to realise they were the tears of a child, not an adult. Tears she'd suppressed the night she'd been dragged away from Witherdeen. Tears she had kept buried ever since.

Emotions belong to the weak!

That was Giselle de Lacy's motto. The sentiment drummed into Julianna from an early age. But one could not keep stuffing sad memories into a valise, keep lugging it from pillar to post. Eventually, the bag became so heavy the seams split, and everything tumbled out.

But what had prompted the emotional outpouring?

Racing with Bennet, laughing like they used to, had released something trapped inside. When had she last felt a rush of excitement? Too long ago to recall. When had she last stood alone in a room with a man and had to fight the irresistible impulse to touch him? Never.

Bennet's note arrived an hour later, slipped under the door while Julianna was busy unpacking and munching on Miss Trimble's millefruit biscuits. He had arranged for her to dine with Mr Branner and Mrs Hendrie at seven o'clock—an informal supper in the servants' dining hall where she could question them about the hauntings and the handbills.

The handbills?

So, both servants knew about the veiled threats.

Julianna had every faith in Mrs Hendrie, but had experienced a shiver of apprehension when listening to the steward's tale.

Indeed, she decided to leave the cottage before seven and spend a few minutes observing the ruins at night. If the ghostly monk carried a thurible and not an oil lamp, how had Mr Branner seen him in the dark? And why was the steward wandering about the estate when everyone else was tucked snugly in their beds?

She shrugged into her pelisse, snatched the lit lantern, and left the cottage.

The night was so cold and crisp she shivered beneath the thick velvet. The damp air, the eerie silence, the blackness creeping ever closer reminded her of the nights she'd slept under the stars, not in the bedchamber next door to her husband's.

She followed the path to the ruins. Her heart thumped wildly as she drew closer to the monstrous structure that looked like Satan's palace at night. Most ruins were hideaways for highway robbers. Whoever laid the gravestone within Witherdeen Abbey was just as devious.

Swallowing past her trepidation, Julianna opened the door in the boundary wall and spent a nervous few minutes scouring the darkness. Even while holding her lantern aloft, she saw nothing but the flicker of shadows amid an endless void.

"The intellect is less sharp at night; the vision grows dim," came the masculine voice that had her jumping out of her skin. "One might easily imagine seeing a spectre."

Julianna swung around so fast she almost stumbled.

"You fool!" she cried upon meeting the marquess' amused grin. "You could have warned me you were approaching. My poor heart almost gave out."

Bennet raised his lantern, sending light dancing across his handsome features. "Forgive me. I came to escort you to the house, but saw you enter the abbey. Is there a particular reason you're snooping about here at night?"

"I'm not snooping. I'm testing a theory. And you should have sent a footman to play escort, though I don't know why you would think I'm afraid of the dark."

As children, they'd often met outdoors at night.

"You should be afraid. A man buried the gravestone in the ground, not a ghost. A man bold enough to trespass on my land. How do we know he's not hiding in the shadows preparing another fiendish surprise?"

"We don't know a man laid the stone," she challenged. Mr Daventry said first assumptions were often wrong. One should not be fooled into believing the obvious. "You suppose it's a man because the object was heavy."

Bennet frowned. "A woman could not have carried the stone."

"Perhaps not on her own."

"You suspect an accomplice?"

As a complete novice, she suspected nothing, but Mr Daventry said the truth revealed itself as one uncovered the evidence.

"I prefer to keep an open mind," she said, trying to sound professional. "While we're here, perhaps you might show me where the blackguard buried the gravestone."

"Of course. It's through the courtyard and down a flight of steps." Bennet led her across the grass-covered courtyard and through a gap in the crumbling wall. "It's so dark you should hold on to my arm."

Beneath the glow of the lantern, Julianna studied the weathered steps. Streaks of light illuminated the loose stones and debris, confirming they were indeed a hazard.

She slipped her hand around Bennet's arm, instantly aware that it was no longer a boy's lanky limb. Strength vibrated against her fingers. Bennet Devereaux exuded raw masculinity, but his touch roused the warm, comforting feelings of home.

"This was the abbey's cemetery." He gestured to the mounds of overgrown grass. There wasn't a gravestone or marker in sight. "Though nothing remains above ground now."

Julianna shifted suddenly, aware she'd stood on someone's grave. "And this is where you found the stone carved with your name?"

Bennet pointed to a place a few feet in front. "Yes, with Devereaux and the date of my demise."

"Who found the stone?"

"Grimley. He alerted Branner."

She presumed the gardener was quite robust for a man approaching sixty. Could he have lifted the stone? But what gripe could he have with his master, and would he have sent the handbills? No, she dismissed the thought instantly.

"And where is the stone now?"

"In pieces. Branner smashed it with a sledgehammer and disposed of it in the rubble pit outside the nave."

Suspicion danced like the devil inside. Why would anyone want to destroy evidence of a potential crime?

"Did you order such an aggressive action?"

"Knowing of the incident with the gargoyle, Branner reacted angrily in my stead. He apologised for not consulting me first." Bennet paused and narrowed his gaze. "I know what you're thinking. You suspect Branner destroyed the evidence because he was the blackguard who placed it there."

Julianna gave a half shrug. "Intact, the stone would be heavy to carry. What if someone tricked Grimley into believing he saw a complete gravestone rather than assembled pieces? Do you have any reason to distrust Mr Branner?"

"None whatsoever."

"May I see the broken fragments?"

"Tomorrow, during daylight. It's not safe here at night."

"Because of the spectre?" Julianna teased.

"Because of falling masonry."

The comment drew her mind back to the first obituary. Perhaps the grave was a distraction. A means to get the marquess to spend more time amid the ruins. A place where he had a high chance of being killed by the collapsing stonework.

"I assured Daventry you'd have my full protection." Bennet softened his tone. "Promise me you won't wander the ruins alone."

How could she make a promise when the word carried little weight? "I've broken one promise. What's to say I won't break another?"

He faced her fully, the sad line of his mouth illuminated by lamplight while his eyes remained in shadow. "We outgrew our promises, Julianna. We didn't break them. You might think me foolish, but I believe you wanted to return to Witherdeen."

Oh, she coped well when discussing the case, not so when the conversation turned to the past. Still, she owed it to herself to tell the truth.

"If life were a fairy tale, I would have returned to a glorious fanfare. Your father would have welcomed me, and we'd have remained as we were, young and innocent and happy."

"If life were a fairy tale, I'd have fought them with every breath in my body. I would never have let Giselle take you."

She touched his upper arm briefly, her throat tight with emotion. "Now we've forgiven each other for not keeping our vows, we should make our way to the house. Mrs Hendrie hates tardiness, and I have many questions for Mr Branner."

Bennet opened his mouth to speak but only said, "Julianna—"

"On the way, perhaps you might explain what the staff know about the handbills," she said, desperately trying to concentrate on their present task. "If I'm to question them without arousing suspicion, I must ensure I'm familiar with the facts."

"Of course."

He captured her elbow and guided her towards the steps. The flutter of nerves stemmed from the fact she was unused to gentlemanly gestures. That, or just unused to the touch of a man so appealing.

"The hardest part will be extracting information while under the pretence of writing a book."

He gripped her hand and helped her climb the damaged steps. "That's why I told Mrs Hendrie I'd join you for supper. So I might help make your story sound plausible."

"You're dining in the servants' quarters?" Julianna was both shocked and relieved. Something about Mr Branner's friendly countenance made her uneasy. Then again, she distrusted most people. "Won't Mrs Hendrie think it odd?"

He closed the boundary door behind them. "I dined in Mrs

Hendrie's room many times during the weeks after my father's death, despite her finding it highly irregular."

Mrs Hendrie had doted on Bennet, more so in those early years. Naturally, during tragic times, he would seek those who cared.

"And I told her you felt uncomfortable dining alone with me in such lavish surroundings," he added. "She missed you when you left, and cried for days."

"She probably feared what would happen to me in Lord Denver's care. Although your father had a temper, he never took his frustrations out on me."

"Are you saying Lord Denver did?"

"No." Majority of the time, she was ignored. "But Mrs Hendrie always suspects the worst. Besides, I'm rather skilled at being invisible."

"Invisible?" he mocked. "With piglet tails for hair?"

She laughed again—this time with genuine delight. "You can't tame the devil. That's what Lord Carstairs used to say when insisting I wore a mob cap. That said, he did make me sleep with the maids."

Bennet muttered a curse. "I'll purchase Carstairs' vowels and make *him* don a mob cap the next time he dines at White's." His gaze came to rest on her red curls. "I can't be the only man who finds your hair attractive."

Heat gathered in her chest. He was the only man who'd ever treated her with respect. Mr Daventry and the other gentlemen of the Order did, too, but they didn't say things that stirred something warm and deep inside.

"You're the only man who skewers bread with a stick, not a fork. It's fair to say you're somewhat of an oddity."

He laughed. "I can always trust you to speak the truth."

"Always."

They walked to the house in companionable silence.

"So, Mr Branner and Mrs Hendrie know about the threatening letters," she clarified. "They know someone wishes to hurt you but don't know you hired an enquiry agent."

"Yes. Under no account should you reveal the true nature of your work."

"Is there anything else I should know before we dine with them?"

Bennet thought for a moment. "I saw the ghostly figure, too, but ask me about it during dinner. It will give you cause to probe them for information, and it's the reason I gave Branner for dining with you in the servants' quarters. The staff are protective of their private space, and I don't want mutiny in the ranks."

Bennet had seen the apparition!

She'd assumed Mr Branner had invented the tale.

Questions bombarded her mind. But Bennet was right. It was better to wait and use the information to interrogate everyone about the ghostly goings-on.

Bennet escorted her to the servants' entrance and along the cold corridor to the dining room. Numerous times he touched her arm or placed a guiding hand on her back. As children, she often took charge. Everything was different now.

Mr Branner and Mrs Hendrie were standing outside the servants' dining room, conversing in irate whispers. Both jumped to attention upon hearing the clip of footsteps.

"My lord. Mrs Eden." Mr Branner inclined his head while Mrs Hendrie dipped an elegant curtsey. The steward stepped forward. "Allow me to take your lanterns."

"Thank you, Branner."

Mr Branner took the lanterns to the scullery while Mrs Hendrie led them into the dining hall. A roaring fire warmed the chilly basement room. The closed shutters kept out the draughts. Mrs Hendrie had lit more candles than would usually grace the servants' table.

"Are you sure I can't summon a footman to serve, my lord?" Mrs Hendrie fidgeted nervously. She liked order and routine. Having the marquess dine with the staff clearly set her on edge.

"Please, there's no need to stand on ceremony tonight. And I'd like Mrs Eden to feel comfortable asking questions about the abbey."

Mr Branner returned.

Bennet waited for Julianna and Mrs Hendrie to sit—which left the housekeeper in more of a tizzy—before taking his seat at the head of the table.

"Shall I serve the soup, my lord?" Mrs Hendrie's chair creaked as she shifted uncomfortably.

"We will serve ourselves, Mrs Hendrie," Bennet said. "We're here purely to facilitate Mrs Eden's research. It will save time if she can question us about the abbey. She plans to return with an artist, but we must give her any information that might help with the writing of her book."

With that, Bennet stood. He removed the tureen lid and ladled white soup into his dish. Everyone followed suit, and soon they were discussing the mole problem and the tenant farmers' gossip.

"Flaxman and Brown are still squabbling about the dry stone wall." Mr Branner's blue eyes gleamed when he laughed. No doubt the self-assured steward was a favourite with the maids. "They've agreed to settle their dispute with a bare-knuckle brawl."

"You might find a bout between the men entertaining, but I'll not have the tenants fighting on my land." Bennet's tone rang with aristocratic confidence. "Find a compromise. Else I shall visit them myself."

"Might it be worth speaking to the tenant farmers about the abbey?" Julianna decided it was the perfect time to broach the subject of the apparition. "The locals always have a tale to tell and might know if the ruins are haunted."

Mr Branner dabbed his mouth with his napkin. "I'd be happy to play escort and assist in your research, Mrs Eden." He glanced at Bennet. "With your approval, my lord."

Bennet stared at his steward for strained seconds while imagining wringing his neck. "Mrs Eden may do as she pleases."

Desperate to ease the crackle of tension, Julianna said, "May we discuss the hauntings, Mr Branner? I'm intrigued to know if you did see something or if fear caused you to hallucinate."

"Hallucinate?" Mr Branner scoffed. "I have a vivid imagination, but I'm not the only one who saw the ghost."

"I saw the shadowy figure of a monk," Bennet confessed on cue.

Julianna feigned surprise. "You did? When?"

"Two weeks ago."

Mrs Hendrie cleared her throat. "Beg your pardon, my lord, but it was three weeks ago. The night before your friends came from town."

"Three weeks? Yes, Mrs Hendrie, you're right."

His friends had been at Witherdeen recently? Obviously, Bennet trusted these men and thought their visit irrelevant to the case.

"Perhaps we should begin with Mr Branner's sighting." Julianna wished to examine the steward's version of events and would question Bennet later. "Can you describe the apparition, sir?"

Looking somewhat unnerved by the terrifying topic, Mrs Hendrie set about clearing the dishes and laying clean plates while Mr Branner began his tale.

"You asked why I was out so late at night," the steward said. "What with all the strange occurrences lately, I thought it prudent to check the house before retiring."

"Strange occurrences?"

The steward cast a nervous glance in his master's direction. "Just estate business. Poachers and the like. They have no bearing on what I saw that night."

Bennet turned to Julianna. "If you wish to write about the ghost, you should be fully apprised of the recent threats."

Mr Branner straightened, wariness marring his affable expression. "My lord, I must advise against mentioning the matter. Though I do not wish to cast aspersions on Mrs Eden's character, the recent machinations would prove a welcome addition to her book. I doubt you want the *ton* learning of the odd goings-on."

Evidently, Mr Branner believed all women were merciless gossips.

"Thank you for your words of caution, but I trust Mrs Eden implicitly." Bennet held her gaze, a look that was more a caress, a need to appreciate every facet before she disappeared from his life again. "She lived here as a child, and I consider her family."

Family?

The word should have brought immense comfort, but it roused a pang of alarm. Did Bennet Devereaux see her as a sister? Did he feel a familial obligation? She could accept him as a friend, but never as a brotherlike figure.

"You lived here?" Mr Branner seemed shocked by the news. "Then you already knew Mrs Hendrie."

"Miss Julianna was like a daughter to me all those years ago." Mrs Hendrie's affectionate tone could warm the coldest heart. "I never expected to set eyes on her again."

Mrs Hendrie took to serving fillet of venison from the simple fare, while Bennet relayed all that had occurred concerning the handbills, the smashed gargoyle and gravestone.

Julianna gasped and frowned and feigned surprise. "Is it fair to say you saw someone dressed as a monk? Someone whose intention it was to cause alarm?"

"It's possible."

Mr Branner was quick to contest the theory. "A person cannot glide over uneven ground with such ease and grace."

"Glide? You could not see the monk's feet?"

"No, Mrs Eden. It was dark, and he wore a brown habit."

"Brown? You're certain?" Julianna was thankful she'd listened to Edward's ramblings. "Augustinian monks always wore black."

Mr Branner's bottom lip quivered. "It was so dark it might have been black."

"The monk I saw wore brown," Bennet said. "The figure passed through the open door in the boundary wall. When I went to investigate, I found no one lurking in the abbey's grounds."

"And this was three weeks ago?"

"Yes."

"Was the monk carrying a thurible?"

"Yes."

Realising her questions sounded abrupt, she modified her tone. "So you both saw the same vision. When did you see the spectre, Mr Branner?"

"Four weeks ago. Just after the first obituary arrived, and two days before I found what looked like the remains of a gargoyle smashed on the front steps."

Julianna made a mental note of the timeline.

Bennet laid down his cutlery and dabbed his mouth with his

napkin. "There's a sequence to the events. I received the obituary, then saw the monk, then Branner found the gravestone."

How interesting.

People were methodical, not ghosts.

"Having received the obituary, how many days passed before you saw the apparition?"

"Two," Bennet and the steward said in unison.

By Julianna's calculation, and based on the fact Bennet had received another handbill three days ago, the monk should have appeared last night.

"And no one saw the monk last night?"

"No," both men said.

"Why would the third note be different?" she mused aloud.

Mrs Hendrie's cutlery clattered against her plate. It wasn't an accident. The woman's hands shook with a fear she couldn't contain. "I may have seen something last night, but I can't be sure."

Bennet sat forward. "Why did you not mention it before?"

"Forgive me, my lord. My eyes aren't what they used to be. I never spoke about it because ... because I didn't see a monk." She cast a nervous glance at Julianna. "I saw a woman."

A tense silence settled in the room.

"A woman?" Bennet eventually said.

Mrs Hendrie nodded. "It was during my last inspection of the night. I stand on the front steps and scan the gardens before locking the main door." She bit down on her lip. "That's when I saw her, my lord. On the lawn, near the oak tree."

Bennet's eyes narrowed. "Might it have been a maid?"

"No, my lord."

"You believe you saw a ghost?"

Mrs Hendrie shrugged. "I thought it was Mrs Eden come early."

"Me?" Julianna's heart missed a beat. Heat rose to her cheeks even though she knew she'd been tucked in her bed in Howland Street until six o'clock this morning. It didn't help that Mr Branner's tight expression spoke of mistrust.

"The woman had vibrant red hair. I thought it was Mrs Eden

because she wore her mother's gown." She faced Julianna. "The scandalous gold silk one with the long train."

Julianna remembered the gown because it barely covered her mother's breasts. "She left that gown at Witherdeen."

"The woman looked just like you, Mrs Eden. But she had such a horrible presence I realised it must be a ghost. Indeed, I came inside to get a lamp. When I returned, she'd gone."

The housekeeper's confession roused a terrible sense of foreboding. Was Giselle de Lacy's ghost haunting Witherdeen? Was her presence a bad omen? The third note spoke of a fire. If the villain followed the same pattern, it meant something would happen at Witherdeen tomorrow.

Something dreadful.

Something that might cost Bennet Devereaux his life.

CHAPTER 6

HAD Giselle de Lacy faked her death? Had she returned to Witherdeen to punish Bennet for his father's sins? Those were the questions dominating Bennet's thoughts as he listened to Mrs Hendrie's confession.

Logic pushed through the chaos.

"Mrs Hendrie, what happened to Giselle de Lacy's possessions when she fled Witherdeen? She left with nothing but a valise." Not just a valise—she'd taken something infinitely more precious.

In the aftermath, he'd watched his enraged father hurl a mountain of gowns over the balustrade. Amid the turmoil, Julianna's clothes were left folded neatly in the armoire, the silver bangle given as a Christmas gift, one too big for her to wear, abandoned on the nightstand.

"They're in the attic, my lord. Your father wished to keep them."

Julianna glanced at him, for she must have arrived at the same conclusion. No, not that his father's obsession with Giselle had lasted long after she'd left, but that anyone might have stolen a gown from the attic.

Not anyone.

Isabella Winters.

Though their parting had seemed amicable, had she followed Bennet from town, intent on causing mischief?

"Who has access to the attic?"

Mrs Hendrie stiffened. "All the staff, my lord."

"And you have every faith Giselle de Lacy's clothes are there?"

His housekeeper hesitated. "No, my lord. During your house party last summer, you permitted your friends to root through the trunks. They took clothes for the masquerade. I presume they returned them."

Mr Branner coughed into his fist. "My lord, if you recall, Miss Winters wore a gold silk gown while in the guise of Cleopatra. After consuming too much champagne, she made the servants kneel at her feet and threatened them with her homemade asp."

"Indeed." Bennet swallowed deeply to curb his embarrassment. He glanced at Julianna, convinced she must think him thoroughly dissolute. "Miss Winters behaved appallingly and was forced to make a grovelling apology."

Julianna's gaze remained fixed on her plate as she sliced the venison. "Your father hosted similar parties. I remember watching the guests' outrageous behaviour through the balusters."

The implication that he was anything like his father left a sour taste in Bennet's mouth. Nothing horrified a man more than realising he'd inherited traits he despised.

"Maybe they'll not be so rowdy this time," Mrs Hendrie chirped.

This time?

Julianna raised her head. "His lordship is expecting guests?"

"Yes." Mrs Hendrie frowned. "You have remembered your friends are arriving from town tomorrow, my lord?"

Tomorrow!

Hellfire!

What with the threats and ghostly sightings, it had slipped his mind. "They usually visit at the end of the month."

"Miss Winters suggested coming a week early." Mrs Hendrie sounded panicked. "We spoke about it this morning, my lord, when we discussed the dinner menu."

This morning he'd been going through the motions while consumed with thoughts of Julianna's arrival. Having her at Witherdeen required his undivided attention.

"It's not too late to postpone their visit. I'll have a man ride to town with a note for Lord Roxburgh. He'll inform the others."

Julianna sat quietly, her thoughts a complete mystery, though she looked in some discomfort.

Then she straightened and gave a resigned sigh. "Please, don't cancel your party on my account. Tomorrow, I shall visit the tenant farmers with Mr Branner and spend the rest of the day studying the ruins."

Damnation. He'd hoped to spend the day with her, examining the evidence, discovering more about her life with Edward Eden.

"I shall call at the cottage at ten o'clock, Mrs Eden." Branner grinned like a cat who'd found the cream. "If anyone knows about the hauntings and ancient curses, it's the tenants. Some families have farmed the land for generations."

"Ancient curses?" Julianna's countenance brightened. "Do the tenants believe the land is cursed? It would make an interesting addition to my book."

Branner shrugged. "I have no notion, but I've heard whispers that anyone desecrating the abbey brings about a curse that lasts for a hundred years."

A curse that lasts for a hundred years!

Bennet had never heard anything so ridiculous.

It was another story to impress Julianna.

"Such threats shouldn't be dismissed," she said, pandering to the fool. "But if you believe that, Mr Branner, one wonders why you smashed a gravestone on consecrated ground."

The muscle in Branner's cheek twitched. "Sometimes anger takes precedence over logic, Mrs Eden. In hindsight, it was foolish. Not because of any supposed curse but because an examination might have helped find the devil who buried it there."

"Were you aggrieved on his lordship's behalf?"

"Naturally."

Julianna pursed her lips. Clearly she had more questions for the steward but chose to focus on her meal rather than bombard him again.

They all ate in silence—lost in their thoughts.

Tension thrummed in the air. More from Bennet's frustrations at having to entertain guests tomorrow. He didn't want them at Witherdeen, but in all likelihood, it was too late to postpone.

"Is there a particular goal you wish to achieve during your visit, Mrs Eden?" Branner said. "It strikes me it would take months to complete a full inspection of the site. Take days to read through the documents in the library."

Julianna seemed unnerved at the prospect of staying at Witherdeen for any length of time. "Tomorrow, I shall focus on the refectory, look for evidence of an undercroft. Do a quick pencil sketch if I can."

"No doubt your colleague will visit soon."

"My colleague?" Julianna frowned.

"The artist."

"Oh, yes. Mr Cole may accompany me on my return."

Branner continued discussing the ruined abbey. He questioned Julianna about the precepts of monastic life. Thankfully, she knew enough about the monks' rigid rules to appease the steward. Bennet listened intently, grateful for an opportunity to study the woman he hadn't seen for seventeen years.

A deep sadness lingered behind her magnificent blue eyes. Lord knows what horrors she'd witnessed over the years. He'd need to penetrate her steely reserve if he had any hope of rescuing their friendship, and there was no time like the present.

"When you're ready, Mrs Eden, I shall escort you back to the cottage." Bennet offered before his steward charged ahead like the gallant hero. "Until we've captured the devil responsible, it's not safe to wander the estate alone."

She made no protest. "I'm ready to leave now, my lord. I have notes to write before I retire, and I can talk to Mr Branner tomorrow."

Perhaps she wished to discuss aspects of the case privately.

Indeed, his theory proved correct. She bid his staff good night, promised to take tea with Mrs Hendrie, who had barely closed the servants' door behind them when Julianna asked her burning question.

"Were your friends in attendance when you found the smashed gargoyle on the front steps?" She stopped walking, fastened her pelisse to the neck and shivered as the chilly night air set her teeth chattering. "I p-presume they were still here when Grimley found the gravestone."

"No, they were in town when the first incident occurred."

"But you don't know that for sure. You can only testify to the fact they were not staying at Witherdeen."

"Then let me rephrase. To my knowledge, they were in town."

She muttered something about speaking to the local innkeepers.

"You suspect one of my friends might be involved?"

Bennet had known Roxburgh and Lowbridge since school and trusted them implicitly. Both men had brought their mistresses to Witherdeen to celebrate the new year. Hell, he'd not informed them he'd severed his attachment to Isabella, and the ladies were to accompany them again.

"Everyone is a suspect until proven innocent." She rubbed her bare hands together to chase away the cold. "The fact they're visiting days after you received the third note may not be a coincidence."

Bennet found himself in reluctant agreement. "You mean one of them had ample opportunity to bury the gravestone in the abbey." She meant one of them might attempt to raze Witherdeen to the ground, as proclaimed in the third obituary.

"We cannot rule it out." She came to an abrupt halt on the gravel path and faced him. "Don't send word to Lord Roxburgh. Let your friends come. But we must be vigilant. Perhaps have two footmen guard the corridors at night. And Mr Bower can help, of course."

Bennet inwardly seethed. The thought that a friend had sent the threats, had inflicted such torment, sent blood surging through his veins. He might have released the raging tempest had Julianna not shivered and taken to rubbing her upper arms briskly.

"We should keep walking," he said, yet placed the lantern on the ground. "First, let me warm your hands. You should have worn gloves. Have you no pockets in that pelisse?"

"Bennet, there's no—"

He snatched her hand, cocooned it in his and rubbed gently back and forth, generating heat. Heat journeyed up his arms, flooded his chest, spread south to his groin. Strange how a simple act of kindness stirred his desire. Strange how his childhood infatuation had quickly become a grown man's obsession.

He captured her other hand and continued his ministrations.

Julianna glanced up but struggled to hold his gaze.

"The cold wind sweeps in from the north," he said, hoping idle conversation would banish all amorous thoughts. "And it's mostly open ground here."

"I don't usually feel the cold." She glanced up at the array of stars twinkling in an inky sky. "Having spent many nights sleeping beneath the heavens, I thought myself hardened to the elements."

A heaviness settled in his chest as he imagined a young girl made homeless by her mother's selfish actions.

"Could your mother not have sold her jewels to provide a home, security?" Giselle had died penniless. A pauper. Surely she hadn't spent all her money on laudanum.

Julianna blinked in surprise. "My mother was never short of options, not until her latter years. There was always a gentleman willing to give us a room for a while."

"Then why sleep outdoors?" Was her husband a bully, a mean devil of a man who'd tortured the woman he'd bought? Did he treat her like a slave?

She flinched, though he suspected it was from a past memory, not the cold. "I would rather hear the soft hum of the night than the tormenting sounds indoors."

"You speak of life with Edward Eden?"

"It was no life."

"Daventry said your husband treated you well."

She stared at the ground, her shoulders sagging.

Bennet captured her chin and forced her to look at him. "Did he mistreat you?"

"Not in the conventional way."

What the hell did that mean?

"Julianna, I shall go out of my mind if you don't tell me what he did." Though he would be fit for Bedlam if he discovered she'd been beaten while he'd been indulging every vice. "Did he hurt you physically? Was he a rake who flaunted his conquests?"

"Edward was never violent."

"Then what in blazes did he do?"

She shook her head repeatedly, her silken curls whipping about her face. "I swore I'd never tell a soul, and I've kept that vow. More out of shame than loyalty."

Bennet recalled her bitter tone when she'd spoken about her husband. "Does it have anything to do with his colleague?" Had the man discovered Julianna's history and thought her free with her affections? "Did he make advances?"

"Lord, no!" Pain flickered across her face. "Justin had a distaste for women. He preferred men, preferred men in every regard."

"Men?" That shed light on the problem. "As did your husband." For it all slotted into place.

"Yes." A single tear trickled down her cheek, and Bennet wiped it away with his thumb. "Edward told his parents we were in love. But he married me so they would not learn of his relationship with Justin."

She exhaled—long and heavy—as if she had been holding the secret since her wedding night.

"Did Giselle know of his predilection for men?"

"Yes, but in some warped way, she thought it a good thing."

Probably because Edward Eden needed to play the dutiful husband to secure his wife's silence. And Giselle had always been tempted by a man with a bulging purse.

"Why the hell did you agree?"

"At first, I refused to be a part of her scheme to find me a husband, but her constant complaining wore me down. I hated watching her suffer." She dashed her hand across her face as more tears tumbled down her cheeks. "Edward was so kind to me, so attentive in the beginning. I truly thought he cared. And marriage was my only means of escape."

Bennet drew her into an embrace. Sod restraint. Lucius Daventry could go to hell. Could a man not console a friend who'd suffered? But it wasn't her tears or the way she nestled close to his chest that made his heart swell. It was the feeling that she was exactly where she belonged.

"Did you hope you might learn to love your husband?" He closed his eyes and breathed deeply, inhaling the intoxicating apple scent of her hair. "Did you hope he might return your affections?"

"I sought freedom, respect, a little tenderness. But it was so awful." Her shoulders shook as she sobbed. "Night after night, I had to listen to them in the chamber next door. Day after day, I had to witness the outpouring of love, love I've been denied my entire life. It was pure torture."

He wanted to say that he cared about her, but that would make him a damn hypocrite. If he'd cared that much, would he not have moved heaven and earth to find her? Would he not have ignored his father's vile threats and words of warning?

"People have manipulated me my whole life," she continued. "It cut deep to know I married a man who wished to exploit me, too. Having me in the house meant no one questioned his relationship with our lodger."

"Lodger? Justin lived with you and your husband?"

"They were barely apart."

Good Lord. It must have been unbearable.

The sudden crunching of gravel on the path behind forced Julianna to dart back. Bennet felt the loss instantly. He suspected Branner had left the house not long after their departure, and he'd not have the man jumping to the wrong conclusions.

Indeed, the steward gave a polite cough as he appeared from the shadows. He doffed his hat and bid them both good night. From his knowing smile, it was evident he'd witnessed the intimate clinch.

Julianna mumbled her frustration as soon as Branner was out of earshot. "Now he'll think I'm here to explore more than the ruins."

"I shall speak to him tomorrow. Explain how fond you were

of the place. How it's overwhelming to be back." Bennet didn't want his staff thinking Julianna was anything like her mother.

"Make it clear I am not here to replace Miss Winters."

"Of course." He gestured to the path. "We should continue before the chill settles into your bones."

She nodded and fell in beside him as they walked.

"You seemed suspicious of Branner during dinner. Your comment about the curse and him destroying the gravestone was particularly clever."

"I doubt Grimley wanders the grounds with a sledgehammer. Mr Branner must have left the abbey, hunted for the tool, and then smashed the stone. It couldn't have been committed in a fit of rage and was premeditated."

It was Branner's job to prevent trespassers. He saw it as a blatant attack on his character, or so he'd said when he burst into Bennet's study and gave an angry explanation.

"Branner prides himself on doing an excellent job and took it as a personal insult. While he pretends he acted in my stead, he confessed to being annoyed at the intruder's arrogance."

Julianna thought for a moment. "Bower can speak to Grimley. Determine exactly what happened that night."

They fell into a companionable silence, though Bennet's mind whirled with suspicion. In all likelihood, someone he trusted had betrayed him. The burning question was, why?

Julianna cast him a sidelong glance. "How many guests are arriving tomorrow?"

"Five, I believe. Lowbridge asked to bring his cousin who's visiting from Brighton. Roxburgh will bring his mistress. There's a chance Lowbridge will too."

Julianna raised a disapproving brow. "Then I doubt I shall see you before I leave."

"You're leaving?" He couldn't disguise the mild panic in his voice. "But there's so much to do. Did you not say we should be on our guard tomorrow?"

"I shall stay tomorrow night. Once I've spoken to the tenants and examined the remains of the gravestone, my investigation will take me back to town."

"Why town?"

"There are so many lines of enquiry, I need the help of the Order."

"Daventry is investigating Mullholland."

She pursed her lips as if reluctant to speak.

He drew the obvious conclusion. "You mean to investigate my friends."

"I must delve into the backgrounds of those in attendance the night someone laid the gravestone in the ruins. I'll need their names, Bennet."

He hesitated. "And what if they discover you're prying into their affairs, learn I'm the one who hired you?" He'd not skulk in the shadows like a damn coward. "I'd prefer to question them directly."

"You're missing the point. Devious people hide behind masks. They create convincing facades. Working covertly is the only way to gain the truth. At least until we have solid evidence."

Again, she spoke logically while he was ready to throw Roxburgh in the pillory and pelt him with rotten apples.

"Then I should return to town, too."

A twitch of alarm marred her pretty face. "How can I befriend Miss Winters if you're hovering in the background? I must make her think she has an ally, convince her I detest you, too."

"You'll not find that so difficult," he teased.

But she didn't smile. "I could never detest you, Bennet. Childhood friends remain in one's heart forever. But you're a marquess who must marry well. I'm the notorious Giselle de Lacy's daughter and must work to earn a living. The reality is we can never be friends, not publicly."

"We *are* friends. I'll not dance about in secret. The *ton* can go to hell."

She made no reply but probably doubted his word.

They arrived at the cottage. Seeing the house shrouded in darkness set Bennet's nerves on edge. What if the devious black-guard lurked amid the shadows? What if the scoundrel wished to punish Bennet by hurting the one person he cared about?

"Perhaps I should find you a room in the house."

She glanced at the thatched cottage. "Why? I like it here."

"I don't like the thought of you being here alone."

She laughed. "I've spent most of my life alone. My mother left me in some wretched places while gallivanting about town with her lovers."

"Then at least let me come inside and light the fire."

Bennet stepped forward, but she placed a staying hand on his chest. "I shall go straight to bed and begin reading your father's journals. I trust you have the key to the trunk."

He did, but her fingers flexed against his fine silk waistcoat in a gentle caress. Moving would break the enchanting spell that left their breathing shallow, their mouths slightly parted. The desire to lower his head and taste her plump lips proved overwhelming.

"The key?" She swallowed repeatedly and snatched back her hand. "Don't say we have to walk to the house."

Bennet reached inside his coat and removed the ornate brass key. Their fingers touched as she gripped the metal, and with it came the profound spark of recognition.

"Thank you. I shall stay out of sight tomorrow and will have Bower bring news should there be any developments."

He considered inviting her to dine with his friends, but what if they noticed her likeness to Giselle? Curious, they'd make the wrong assumptions, presume Bennet had inherited his father's obsession. And he'd not have them think so little of Julianna.

"I shall visit the cottage to discover what you've learnt."

She nodded. "Good night, Bennet."

"Good night."

He waited until she'd closed the door and drawn the bolt, stood staring for a while longer. When he eventually walked away, he found the irony of his situation amusing. His mansion house afforded every luxury, yet he would sell his soul to spend a night in that cottage.

CHAPTER 7

JULIANNA leant back against the wooden door, her trembling hand pressed to her heart, her eyes closed tight. Could Mr Daventry not have found another way to test her fortitude? Could Bennet Devereaux not play the arrogant rogue so she might hate him the way she did most men?

So much for keeping her distance.

In true Giselle de Lacy style, she'd permitted certain liberties, had let him warm her hands and draw her into an embrace. It hadn't helped that she'd blubbered like a babe. A courtesan's job was to bolster a man's confidence, and she'd certainly done that.

Bennet's touch had always brought comfort, but this new sensation was like a ravenous hunger she couldn't sate. Desire unfurled like spring blooms whenever their eyes met. Heat swirled in her stomach as the urge to know him intimately obliterated all rhyme and reason. Numbing her feelings was nothing new, but it had been easier with Edward. She had never cared a sot for him.

Still, she had broken a vow and given Bennet an accurate account of her marriage. He would ask more questions. She would be forced to explain how the crippling loneliness had robbed her of her sanity. How Edward had known he was dying yet still left her destitute.

She inhaled deeply to clear her head, but the smell of Bennet's cedarwood cologne teased her nostrils. The man invaded her thoughts, seduced her senses. His scent clung to her clothes. In her prayers, she had begged to see him again, just to gaze upon his face once more. Now, she would rather wallow in ignorance than know they could never be friends.

Releasing a groan, she unbuttoned her pelisse and draped it over the chair. Then she set about lighting the candles, though her hands were so cold it took six strikes to ignite the tinder.

A chill air circled the room, and she hurried to the window to draw the curtains, annoyed at herself for not letting Bennet come inside to light the fire.

Outside, all was dark except for the faint streaks of moonlight stroking the path. Julianna was busy tugging one curtain over the other when she heard the garden gate creak. She froze. Listened. The heavy pad of footsteps preceded the loud knock on the door.

Parting the curtains a fraction, she peered at the shadowy figure looming amid the blackness. The caller turned slightly, revealing his profile. Relieved to find it was Mr Bower, not Mr Branner, she went to welcome him.

Even a man with Mr Bower's brawn felt the cold. He knelt to light the fire while Julianna lit the stove and made tea. She spoke to him from the kitchen, relayed the events leading to the steward smashing the gravestone. Having Mr Daventry's man about the place forced her to focus on the task and not her conflicting feelings for Bennet Devereaux.

"Discover anything you can about the night Grimley found the gravestone," she said, settling on the sofa. "Did the gardener examine the stone? Where was the sledgehammer? See if any of the staff have ever seen the ghostly monk." She sipped her tea, hoping the beverage would warm her bones. "Did the coachmen or grooms say anything about the marquess?"

"Everyone respects his lordship." Bower's voice was as deep as the scar cutting through his brow. His hulking frame filled the chair, and his fists were the size of mallets. The teacup looked like it belonged in a doll's house when gripped between his thick fingers. "No one here bears him any ill will, ma'am."

"And what about Mr Branner?"

Julianna had met men of Mr Branner's ilk before. Beneath his portrait of affability lay a consummate seducer. The lecherous look in his eyes was often at odds with his polite discourse. Despite being educated, he'd behaved like a thug from the rookeries the night he found the gravestone.

"Most folk like Mr Branner. He's firm but fair. That's what they say." Bower drained his teacup. "Mr Keenan remembers your mother. He said it was a shame when she snatched you away, said that's the only time the master's ever been truly happy."

Julianna gulped. "The master? You speak of the old marquess?"

"No, ma'am. Mr Keenan spoke of the current Lord Devereaux."

"Oh, I see." Hastily, she moved to the topic of Bennet's friends. "I know I've asked a lot of you, Mr Bower, but I'm keen to know what the staff think of his lordship's friends."

"Pay it no mind, ma'am. I'll help in any way I can. I know they're none too fond of Miss Winters."

Yes, she got that impression from Mr Branner.

"Do you know why?"

The answer was obvious. Miss Winters took liberties, lacked breeding. She belittled those beneath her because she feared they might notice she was of less than average stock. Indeed, Mr Bower confirmed that the woman's arrogance and derogatory comments proved too much to bear.

"When we return to London, I'll befriend Miss Winters." The thought made her stomach churn. "Perhaps she has a different tale to tell."

"Mr Keenan is a friendly chap who only wants what's best for the master. He seems to think you being here is an omen. A sign the master's luck is about to change."

Heavens above! No doubt the servants thought the whole writing-about-the-ruins was a mere story, and she'd come to replace Miss Winters in the master's affections.

She told Mr Bower about the third obituary note, that she feared the villain might resort to arson tomorrow night, and he was to report to the marquess for further instruction. He took another cup of tea, then stoked the fire before retiring to the coach house.

It was so warm downstairs, Julianna decided to read the first journal before heading to bed. The footman had deposited the walnut trunk in the space beneath the stairs, and she unlocked the latch and lifted the lid. Dust and the musty smell of old paper assaulted her nostrils as she examined the mound of dog-eared journals. Evidently, the late marquess had much to say.

Bennet had placed the books in date order, something Julianna discovered as she rummaged through the top layer. When she read the first page in the journal dated 1797—the year Bennet's father inherited the marquessate—she realised the extent of the mammoth task ahead. The heading written on the recto page summed up the entire case.

They'll not rest until I'm dead!

●

"Thank you, Mr Branner." Julianna was about to part from the steward after a lively few hours spent with Bennet's tenants. "It's been an education. By all accounts, ghosts are averse to water and sage. If I meet one, I mustn't run but should ask how I might be of service."

Mr Branner laughed. "And don't stare at a looking glass for too long, else a spirit will possess your soul."

"Yes, I must not forget that, though I imagine it's an old wives' tale warning about the dangers of vanity."

At some time or other, every one of his lordship's tenants had seen a ghost. There was the demon crow that stalked fields and cursed crops. The ghoul who robbed graves—though she suspected they should look for a man down on his luck. And the mad monk of Witherdeen Abbey who'd escaped confinement and murdered three of his brethren.

"Their wild tales could fill an entire chapter." Mr Branner's amused grin seemed genuine. "I'm glad I could be of assistance, Mrs Eden. But if you'll excuse me, I must find the records of the tenants' boundaries before Mr Flaxman takes a sledgehammer to the dry stone wall."

"Of course. Someone must settle their grievance."

Guilt surfaced as she watched the steward stride towards the house. Perhaps she had misjudged him. Today, he'd been polite and helpful. The tenants treated him like the prodigal son. The children followed behind like ducklings, showing him their bruises and missing teeth.

Was his loyalty to Bennet the reason he'd lost his temper and smashed the gravestone? It seemed quite likely after what she'd witnessed today. Perhaps she might have Mr Bower pick the lock to the steward's cottage and search for anything incriminating. Yes, she would add it to her list of tasks, along with examining the handbills and hunting around the ruins for the broken gravestone. And there were still nineteen journals left to read.

Bennet was right. There was too much to do.

Julianna was musing over where to start when the crunching of carriage wheels on the gravel drive captured her attention. In a panic, she ran and hid behind the oak tree, for it gave an ample view of the mansion's entrance. Of course, if Mrs Hendrie glanced across the lawn, the poor woman would squeal and swear she'd seen the red-haired ghost.

A shiver shot down Julianna's spine.

Was her mother alive?

She had not seen Giselle's body or visited the grave.

But she quickly dismissed the notion. Giselle would not waste time exacting revenge. She would be out hunting for a wealthy lover to pay for her jewels and laudanum tinctures. Besides, it had been Giselle's decision to leave Witherdeen and take up with Lord Denver, so there was nothing to avenge.

The elegant equipage rattled to a halt before Witherdeen's sweeping staircase. Two footmen in blue livery descended the stone steps to assist the new arrivals. Bennet Devereaux appeared looking devastatingly handsome, his grey trousers and dark blue frock coat clinging to his impressive physique like a second skin. He brushed his hand through his hair, smiled at his friends as they alighted, though Julianna would stake every morsel she owned the smile failed to reach his eyes.

A hundred yards separated her and the unfolding scene, yet it felt as vast as an ocean. Julianna did not belong in their world. So why did everything about Witherdeen feel like home?

Two gentlemen, both prime specimens of the haut monde, emerged from the conveyance. They fussed with their clothes while the footmen assisted their female companions. The women's overtly affectionate gestures and excessive flounces marked them as courtesans.

After briefly exchanging greetings, Bennet paid scant attention to the women, though they made their presence known by continually touching his arm.

Jealousy burned inside like the devil's inferno. Unable to stomach the thought of Bennet entertaining these people, she slipped away and hurried back to the cottage. There was plenty to do indoors, but she resorted to eating all the biscuits from Miss Trimble's basket and daydreaming on the bed.

Confidence is a state of mind—and you are in control.

Mr Daventry's wise words jolted her from her reverie. She shot up and scanned the room, fearing the man had come to check her progress.

"Oh, pull yourself together," she mumbled, dragging herself from a mire of self-pity. "You're an agent of the Order, not a worthless wife."

The stern words did the trick, and with renewed faith in her abilities, she headed to the ruins.

●

"They keep the sledgehammer in an outbuilding a ten-minute walk from here." Mr Bower stood in the deep pit outside the remnants of the nave, rummaging through the dusty old stones.

"Did Grimley shed any light on what happened that night?" Julianna peered into the hole and pointed to a large brown stone. "What about that one? Can you see any chisel marks? We're looking for letters or numbers."

Mr Bower gripped the stone between his mighty paws and turned it over. "No, ma'am."

Julianna straightened and massaged her aching back. "Perhaps it's my suspicious nature, but I believe someone has removed the stones." Or Mr Branner lied, and they were never there in the first place.

"I'll keep looking, ma'am." Mr Bower wiped his sweaty brow with his coat sleeve. "Grimley said he saw the tombstone carved with his lordship's name and alerted the steward."

"He did? Did he say what he was doing here at night?"

"Looking for ghosts. But then I noticed someone had dug up the grass inside the chapter house, and I wonder if he's not secretly looking for treasure."

"Treasure!" Yes, there must be a wealth of items buried underground.

"Treasure?" a masculine voice echoed. Julianna turned to find an elegant gentleman with thick black hair watching her with bright-eyed interest. "Pray, have no fear. I'm happy to split the loot three ways. Just don't tell Devereaux."

Julianna forced a smile but silently cursed.

Dissipated rakes played billiards, drank copious amounts of brandy, and tried to tup the maids in the broom cupboard. They did not roam around historical buildings examining the architecture.

The gentleman bowed and presented himself as Lord Roxburgh. On her part, no introduction was necessary because the dratted footman had mentioned she was staying at Witherdeen.

"The staff should know better than to gossip, my lord." She'd been foolish to think they would keep her identity a secret.

He delved into a silver snuff box and inhaled a pinch. "The poor fellow was eager to please. The fact Giselle de Lacy's daughter was here writing about the abbey made his country-loving master seem less of a bore."

The lord was teasing, but the urge to defend Bennet burned in her veins. "There is no man more interesting than Lord Devereaux. No doubt the footman prayed the information would earn him a sovereign, my lord."

Lord Roxburgh laughed. "I must admit, the news came as a pleasant surprise. A much greater surprise to Miss Winters, of course, who arrived with Mr Granger mere minutes ago."

Isabella Winters had come to Witherdeen!

What the devil was she doing here?

Julianna almost choked in panic. Had Bennet lied about ending their relationship? And if so, why did it feel like the worst betrayal? She had no reason to feel anything but indifference. Having Miss Winters at Witherdeen gave her ample opportunity to befriend Bennet's mistress. Indeed, it was a welcome development.

"Forgive me, but I don't know Miss Winters."

"She's a friend of Lord Devereaux's, though I fear she's fallen out of favour."

"Is Miss Winters interested in monastic life, my lord?"

"Ha! She would find much enjoyment in an abbey full of men."

"Abbey life was about spiritual devotion."

"Ah, then we may have a problem. Miss Winters suffers from delusions of deity. I imagine the monks would have made a bonfire and burned her for heresy."

While his peers probably found his nonchalant wit entertaining, Julianna disliked anyone who belittled courtesans.

"One day, we may live in a world where Miss Winters can express her opinion without fear of castigation. But for now, I would be happy to give her a tour of the ruins."

Lord Roxburgh glanced at the abbey's dilapidated walls. "This place is a perfect example of how opinion has changed over the years."

"It's a perfect example of how a king's desire divided a nation. Every action has a consequence, my lord. Love and hate are sides of the same coin."

The lord stared at her as if she were a box of delicious confectionary. "I'd be interested to hear more about your work here, Mrs Eden."

No. Lord Roxburgh's only interest was of the salacious sort.

"Sadly, I must return to London tomorrow. Lord Devereaux's steward is extremely knowledgeable. Shall I arrange for him to give you a detailed tour?"

He found her comment amusing. "Is the steward as engaging as you are?"

"He gives a captivating account of the hauntings."

She studied the lord closely to see if he blinked excessively or avoided eye contact. Might he have donned a monk's robe to frighten his friend? No. Most definitely not. She suspected this arbiter of fashion wouldn't be seen dead wearing anything so crass.

"Hauntings?" he mocked. "I believe in science and the laws of nature, Mrs Eden. Uncanny events are merely the musings of a weak mind."

Did he know Bennet had seen the ghost of a monk?

Quick to change the subject, Lord Roxburgh turned his attention to the burly figure of Mr Bower. "Is there a reason your man is rooting through the stones?"

"We're looking for specific markings. A stonemason often leaves a symbol to identify his work."

"How interesting." His tone suggested he found the notion dull. "If your man grows tired and you need a helping hand, come and find me at the house."

Julianna smiled. "I would not wish to draw you away from your companion, my lord. And I think you would soon tire of my forthright opinion." He needed to know she was not mistress material.

"I doubt that, my dear."

Before she had a chance to reply, Bennet appeared, breathless and agitated. "There you are, Roxburgh. You disappeared from the drawing room without a word."

Being as sharp as a new tack, Lord Roxburgh glanced at Julianna and grinned. "You see, Mrs Eden, you have Devereaux flustered because I am stealing your attention."

"Lord Devereaux knows any distraction will cost him another day's pay."

"Mrs Eden must complete her work before returning to town tomorrow," Bennet confirmed.

"Then there is a simple solution." The lord gripped Bennet's shoulder in a firm gesture of friendship. "Mrs Eden will dine with us tonight so that I might quiz her about her fascinating hobby."

Julianna inwardly groaned. Why did the gentleman not speak

bluntly so she might refuse his advances and continue with her work?

"Society ladies have time for hobbies, my lord. I'm afraid I must work to earn my keep. Indeed, I have much to do before I leave tomorrow and will barely have time to take supper."

"Nonsense. Surely you can spare an hour out of your schedule. No doubt you're dying to meet Miss Winters."

Bennet frowned. "Miss Winters?"

Lord Roxburgh's teasing eyes widened. "Did she not arrive with Granger?"

"Granger came alone."

"Did he?" Lord Roxburgh seemed to enjoy feigning stupidity. Did he suspect Julianna was at Witherdeen to study more than the ruins and thought to prove his theory? "Forgive me, my dear. Travel arrangements were made earlier this week, and I presumed Miss Winters accompanied Granger."

Bennet's gaze drifted past Julianna's shoulder, and he rolled his eyes.

"So, this is where everyone is hiding," came a woman's teasing purr.

"Ah, my dear," Lord Roxburgh began, his eyes twinkling with mischief. "If you wish to see a strong man flex his muscles, you've come to the right place."

Julianna turned to meet the newcomer, both disappointed and relieved to find it wasn't Miss Winters. The auburn-haired lady observing Julianna with a hawk-like stare sidled up to Lord Roxburgh.

Bennet made the introductions. "Mrs Thorne, allow me to present Mrs Eden. She's researching the history of the abbey and intends to publish her findings."

"Devereaux is rather forward thinking, is he not?" Mrs Thorne's mouth was so small it formed a permanent pout. "To employ a woman to do what is invariably a man's work."

So, the lady was prickly by name and nature.

"Is it a man's work?" Julianna replied politely. "Did a woman not write the theoretical paper on combustion and invent the concept of catalysis? Was Catharine Macaulay not a highly respected historian who published her work almost sixty years ago?"

"Mrs Eden is equally respected in her field," Bennet added.

Mrs Thorne's counter-attack came in the form of a sneer as she considered Julianna's dusty old day dress. "I suppose hard work means you must neglect the usual feminine pursuits."

"I have never found discussions of frills and flounces at all entertaining."

Lord Roxburgh laughed. "I imagine you could wear a grain sack, Mrs Eden, and still attract a man's eye."

Julianna might have challenged the lord, too. Attracting a man's eye was not on her list of ambitions. She might have continued her verbal spar with Mrs Thorne, but she had to befriend these people if she hoped to solve the case.

"Mrs Thorne is right. Working hard means I rarely have time to consider my appearance. But when earning a living, one must make sacrifices."

Mrs Thorne narrowed her gaze and stared at Julianna. "Have we met before, Mrs Eden? In town perhaps? You look most familiar."

"Not that I recall." Not unless Mrs Thorne had taken to weeping on the steps of the Servants' Registry.

The woman continued pondering the possibility, then arched a neat brow in surprise. "That's it! There's a painting of you in the attic, though some devil has slashed the canvas, straight across your pretty face."

Bennet cleared his throat. "The painting is of Mrs Eden's mother."

"Her mother?"

"Mrs Eden is Giselle de Lacy's daughter," Lord Roxburgh chimed.

Mrs Thorne stared in stunned silence. "You're Julianna de Lacy? Devereaux speaks of you with such fondness. You're the sister he never had."

Sister?

The word cut like a sharp blade to the heart.

Julianna fought against the onset of tears. "We've been separated for so long, yet still feel a familial connection." She didn't dare glance at Bennet.

"All the more reason you should dine with us tonight," Lord Roxburgh added.

Perhaps the urge to flee was in the blood. Julianna imagined stuffing her clothes into her valise, abandoning Witherdeen and its confounding master.

But she could not abuse Mr Daventry's trust. The only way to achieve her goal was to don a mask and mingle with people she would rather avoid. To enter the world she loathed to the marrow of her bones.

CHAPTER 8

"Mrs Eden, my lord." Milford stepped aside.

Julianna entered the drawing room and Bennet's heart lurched. She'd styled her hair in a simple chignon, wore her mother's bronze silk gown that Mrs Hendrie had taken from the attic, aired and pressed. Most women would have thrown a tantrum and remained abed than wear the outdated style, but Julianna carried herself with elegance and grace.

Captivated, Bennet drank in her heavenly form. Candlelight sparkled in her blue eyes like sunlight on a calm sea. Her vivacious smile held him spellbound, despite it being a mask to hide her disdain for a society that was anything but polite.

If only life were a fairytale and one snap of his fingers could make them all disappear. All except her—Julianna de Lacy. The woman he'd presumed lost to him forever. The only person in the room he trusted with absolute certainty.

Indeed, he was wary of his friends' motives now.

Had one of them sent the obituaries? Had one of them come to Witherdeen armed with a tinderbox to raze his home to the ground?

Roxburgh reached the door first, Mrs Thorne scuttling behind to ensure she was not about to receive her *congé* in favour of this red-haired beauty.

Bennet stood. His gaze cut through those people surrounding

her and locked with Julianna's. The flash of panic in her eyes had him crossing the room to come to her aid.

"Let Mrs Eden catch her breath. You can hound her about the hauntings during dinner." Bennet barged through the group and offered Julianna his arm. "Come, Mrs Eden, let me pour you a sherry."

"Thank you, my lord." She took hold of his arm, gripped his sleeve as if she were teetering on a precipice, about to fall a thousand feet to her doom. "A sherry might settle my nerves."

"You looked like you needed rescuing," he whispered when they reached the drinks table. He removed the stopper from a crystal decanter and poured her a sherry.

"I'm not sure I can do this." She kept her voice low, and accepted the proffered glass. "With Lord Roxburgh's razor-sharp intellect, he's bound to recognise a fraud. Miss Ponsonby has already asked for my address in London, and I had to lie."

"You're more than a match for Roxburgh. But give the word, and I shall send them away. They can be gone from here within the hour." Yet he feared she wouldn't be far behind them.

"No. The gentlemen of the Order never miss an opportunity to question suspects. It's too early in the battle to wave a white flag and surrender."

Bennet stared at her, a little in awe. After everything she had been through, she had the courage and strength to soldier on.

"I shall support you in any way I can."

"You might regret saying that when I beg you to converse with Miss Ponsonby." She grinned, giving him a glimpse of the mischievous girl he remembered so fondly.

Bennet clasped his chest as if mortally wounded. "Please, no. I'd rather stick pins in my eyes than suffer her constant chattering."

Were she of noble birth, Miss Ponsonby would be a diamond of the first water. With hair like spun gold and a figure that left men drooling, Lowbridge found the benefits of having her for his mistress outweighed her obvious impediment.

As if party to Bennet's silent musing, Miss Ponsonby invaded the private moment. "My lord, you cannot monopolise Mrs Eden's attention the entire evening. We're all desperate to hear about this book of ghost stories she's writing. A monk wandering the ruins of Witherdeen! Who can believe it? Surely there's a logical explanation."

Bennet made a mental note to throttle his loose-tongued footman. "Mrs Eden is writing about monastic life, not the hauntings."

Hauntings was not a word one should use when dealing with an excitable woman whose constant chatter sounded like aviary squawk.

Miss Ponsonby pressed her fingers to her brow as if she might faint. "Oh, did you hear that, Lowbridge? There's more than one ghost. What next? Are we to meet a headless horseman in the stables, a drowned governess by the lake? Oh, oh, I shall die of apoplexy."

"Hmm." Lowbridge barely glanced in the lady's direction.

However, his cousin Terrance Granger stared with fascination. "Perhaps we should extinguish the lamps and call on the spirits of the dead."

Roxburgh groaned. "Good God, Granger, don't encourage her."

"I'd rather hear about life with a famous courtesan than ghostly nonsense," Mrs Thorne said, nestling next to Roxburgh on the sofa. "Was it as exciting as one imagines?"

Julianna's feigned smile wavered. "Yes, if one likes spontaneity."

Giselle de Lacy was undoubtedly a woman of impulse.

"Perhaps the ghost brings a message, Mrs Eden." Miss Ponsonby caught Julianna's hand and drew her to the sofa where they sat opposite Granger. "More often than not, they come to exact revenge for a past misdeed or to warn of a tragedy."

"Oh, do be quiet, Pony," Lowbridge uttered.

Roxburgh snorted. "I'm no mystic, my dear, but I'd wager my racing curricle you've got a gothic novel on your nightstand."

Lowbridge laughed and slapped his thigh. "By Jove, she has! Someone give the man a guinea."

Bennet observed the scene, silently acknowledging that he'd been living a lie since his father's passing. Filling one's house with fake friends did nothing to ease the loneliness. If left penniless and destitute, who out of this group would come to his aid?

No one but Julianna.

Even so, it was hard to believe any of his friends bore a grudge.

"Can we talk about something else?" Mrs Thorne complained.

Granger tutted sympathetically. "Are you afraid of ghosts, madam? Are you scared of things that go bump in the night?"

"One cannot fear what one cannot see. Mrs Eden must consider whether she is to publish a book based on historical facts or one filled with gibberish."

Julianna sipped her sherry. "While it's unwise to label the unknown as gibberish, Mrs Thorne, one must question why ghosts are only seen at night. In the dark, a tired mind might confuse a spectre with a peignoir draped over the armoire door."

"Precisely, Mrs Eden." Roxburgh looked at Julianna with such admiration, Mrs Thorne shuffled closer to her lover until they were practically conjoined.

"Ghosts have been known to kill people." Lowbridge spoke in a sinister voice to scare his mistress. "There's the tale of the man haunted by a woman in a blood-stained shroud. He tumbled down the stairs in a fright."

Miss Ponsonby's eyes widened in horror. "Did he break his neck?"

"No, Pony. He dropped his candlestick and set the house ablaze."

Roxburgh and Granger chuckled.

Bennet didn't.

Set the house ablaze?

Was Lowbridge the villain? Guilty people did not openly discuss their crimes. Still, Bennet glanced at the devil, unable to decide if he was remarkably clever or downright stupid.

"Then we must be vigilant tonight." Bennet observed Lowbridge's reaction with interest. "I suggest you all stay abed and lock your chamber doors lest one of you trip over the ghost and burn the house to the ground."

Julianna snatched a glance at him but quickly changed the

subject. "Lord Devereaux told me of the masquerade last summer. I wondered if someone had found a habit in the attic and thought to scare the host."

Mrs Thorne sneered. "The only garments we found were your mother's tired old gowns."

"What a pity." Julianna appeared unperturbed by Mrs Thorne's spiteful tone. "My mother was so petite, I doubt they'd have been useful."

Quick to bite the bait, Mrs Thorne exclaimed, "Nonsense! I was able to squeeze into one of them. Miss Winters took the other. She's such a vivacious young woman. With her lovely red hair, she looked remarkable in gold silk."

"Yes, you stole the gold ensemble," Miss Ponsonby said snidely, "but turned up your nose at the beautiful gown Mrs Eden is wearing this evening."

Julianna simply smiled. "Gold would have been my preferred choice, but it seems both gold gowns are missing."

"Missing?" Miss Ponsonby looked horrified. "Missing? How can they be missing? I assure you, Mrs Eden, we returned all your mother's items the day after the masquerade."

Everyone shot a curious glance at Mrs Thorne.

"Don't look at me!" Affronted, she clutched her hand to her chest. "I left my gown hanging in the attic. The housekeeper insisted on packing everything away. Apparently, we're all dreadfully untidy."

It was a lie. Mrs Hendrie hadn't taken note of the items borrowed or returned, though it was unlike her not to be pedantic about such things.

"Mrs Hendrie gets a little confused," Julianna said, though the fib had to be a ploy to gain more information. "She confessed to seeing the ghost twice."

"You see!" Miss Ponsonby clapped her hands four times in rapid succession. "A monk is haunting the abbey. Hurrah! We may actually get to see a ghost. Did you hear that, Lowbridge?"

"Hmm."

"Mrs Hendrie saw the ghost of a woman, not a monk." Julianna spoke matter-of-factly, but Bennet knew she was assessing everyone in the room.

Roxburgh tossed back his brandy. "Must we continue with this tedious topic?" He turned to Julianna. "Devereaux said you lived here when your mother was his father's paramour."

"Yes, my lord. I spent a year at Witherdeen."

"You were close as children," the devil pressed, "like siblings."

"Indeed." Julianna swallowed. "We were inseparable."

Bennet fought the urge to jump from his chair and shout, "No!"

Yes, they were inseparable. As close as children could be. But he'd never thought of her as a sister, just a dear, dear friend.

"I never said we were like siblings." Bennet hoped to God Julianna didn't see him as a brother. The flash of desire in her eyes, the hitch in her breath whenever they were close said otherwise.

Roxburgh smirked. "Did you not?"

"No."

"Mrs Eden said she thought of you as a relative."

"No," Julianna protested. "I said we were close as children."

"Enough about that," Miss Ponsonby interjected, moving to warm her hands by the fire. "Do you believe the housekeeper saw a ghost, Mrs Eden? She seems like quite a reliable woman. Oh, it's all so fascinating."

"Who can say?" Julianna's shoulders relaxed. She seemed more comfortable discussing ghosts than her complicated relationship with him. "I shan't be convinced until I see an apparition."

Annoyed that all talk had returned to the supernatural, Roxburgh decided it was time to meddle. "Tell me about your husband, Mrs Eden. Have you been widowed long?"

Bennet silently groaned.

Roxburgh spoke with polite interest, but his objective was to pry into Julianna's affairs and discover why she had really come to Witherdeen.

"A year, my lord."

Roxburgh's keen stare slid over Julianna's silk gown. "So you're not long out of widow's weeds. A woman so spirited shouldn't wear black. May I ask how Mr Eden died?"

"Of consumption. Tragically, he wasted away to nothing."

"Was he old?"

"Thirty-eight."

Did she know her tone lacked emotion? Bennet tried to catch her attention, but she seemed lost in the memory.

"It must have been terribly painful watching him suffer."

"Edward wished to die in the arms of the one person he loved." She spoke of Justin, of course, and avoided saying anything more.

"Ah, *l'amour*—a rare and precious commodity. A man may be as rich as Croesus, but still love eludes him."

"Love cannot be bought or traded," Julianna said.

"Nor can trust or loyalty." Bennet prayed he had no reason to distrust this man. "Are they not equally precious?"

Roxburgh's brow furrowed in curious enquiry. "Come, Devereaux, what would you choose? A woman who trusts you or one who loves you implicitly?"

Blast.

Bennet glanced at Julianna, and their eyes met. "I'd choose a woman who loves me because she knows there is no one she trusts more."

Julianna's gaze softened. "What of you, Lord Roxburgh?"

The lord laughed. "I'm a cynic, and people are fickle. As you rightly said, Mrs Eden, love and hate are sides of the same coin, and I never bet on anything with such frightful odds."

Thankfully, the clang of the dinner gong proved the saving grace.

With dinner being a relaxed affair, Julianna had asked to sit next to Roxburgh and Mrs Thorne. But Miss Ponsonby tossed manners aside, barged through the group and stole the woman's seat. Bennet remained at the head of the table with the insipid Mrs Thorne to his right—the wealthy widow's support of Roxburgh's gambling habit proved the only attraction—and Lowbridge to his left.

Having consumed the contents of Bennet's brandy decanter, Lowbridge took to dozing off between courses. Like Bennet, Mrs Thorne was so absorbed with the lively conversation further down the table she only picked at her food.

Granger clearly admired his cousin's mistress, for he'd taken to calling her by her pet name, too. "Pony, admit it. You'd die if you saw a ghost."

"Really, Granger, there are no such things," Roxburgh countered.

"I challenge anyone to meet me in the ruins at midnight." Julianna's eyes were bright with amusement. "The sight of the ghostly monk would soon have you whistling a new tune, my lord."

Roxburgh laughed. "If the monk burst into the dining room and perched on my lap, I'd likely believe myself sotted."

"What are we to do with him, Mrs Eden?" Miss Ponsonby batted Roxburgh on the arm. "I warrant we should tie him to a chair amid the ruins and leave him there all night."

"And I'll happily permit such mistreatment if Mrs Eden agrees to accompany me."

Was Roxburgh being intentionally provoking?

They continued laughing while Mrs Thorne scowled at her pheasant, and Bennet silently seethed.

"And what of your parents, Miss Ponsonby?" Julianna asked, reminding Bennet she was simply playing a role, digging for information. "Your family cannot be as scandalous as mine."

"Oh, they were simple country folk who lacked ambition. My brother and I made a plan to escape. He used to hit me on the head if I broke into a Somerset accent." She laughed and then continued her bird-like chirping about the ghost.

They all removed to the drawing room, though Roxburgh complained that he'd like to take his port without listening to Miss Ponsonby's inane chatter. And so the ladies remained while the men retreated to the library.

The next hour passed too slowly for comfort.

Terrance Granger left to smoke his cheroot outdoors, though he was gone so long he must have smoked five. Miss Ponsonby dragged Lowbridge away after begging him to walk to the ruins in the dark.

"Are you going to tell me what Mrs Eden is really doing here?" Roxburgh asked while they were alone. He relaxed back in the leather wing chair, cradling a brandy goblet between his long fingers. "I'm quite certain it's not to write about ghosts."

Hellfire!

"Is that why you've been fawning over her all evening?" Bennet said by way of a distraction. "Mrs Thorne has grown tired of your wandering eye."

Roxburgh swallowed a mouthful of brandy, savouring the taste as he studied Bennet. "Did you invent the tale of the ghost as an enticement? Did you hear about her work with her husband and use it as an excuse to invite her to Witherdeen?"

"She's qualified to write about the ruins. I didn't know Julianna de Lacy and Mrs Eden were one and the same until I met her in London to discuss the project." Both facts were true.

"But you're considering taking her for your mistress."

"No. I am hoping to keep her as a friend." Together they might decide where to go from there.

"And yet there is a definite attraction. The desire to please men is in her blood. After a year spent in mourning, she's looking for a virile fellow to fill the void. One senses a wealth of passion just waiting to be unleashed. Hmm. She's most definitely ripe and ready for plucking."

Weeks of pent up anger erupted. "Say one more word about Mrs Eden, and I'll knock that damn smirk off your face! It's a bloody good job we've been friends for years because it's the only thing stopping me dragging your arrogant arse off that chair and slamming your teeth down your throat!"

God, it felt good to release his frustration. Sod the case. He was tired of dancing to everyone's tune.

Roxburgh smiled. "Finally, I get to see the Bennet Devereaux I know and love. I don't know what's really going on here or what you're plotting behind the scenes, but you're as miserable as a murderous Macbeth."

"I am not the one obsessed with stratagems." Damn, he'd not meant to say that aloud.

"You speak of Isabella Winters. The woman is a conniving devil. So, Granger told you she persuaded him to bring her to the coaching inn in Bramley. She said she has a friend in the area whom she'd promised to meet."

God's teeth!

Isabella had come to stay in the village?

"Whatever her reason for being here, I suspect it has nothing to do with her imaginary friend," Roxburgh continued. "I'll visit the inn in the morning and ferry her back to London. See if I can discover what's behind her ruse."

The morning might not be soon enough.

It took one spark to destroy a house full of guests.

Perhaps he would have Bower stay at the inn tonight and keep a watchful eye on the devious Miss Winters.

"It might be worth you all returning to town," Bennet began, fearing his friends could be caught in the blaze, but then Lowbridge returned, followed by a rather harried Mrs Hendrie.

"Forgive the intrusion, my lord. Might I have a moment of your time?" She hopped from foot to foot as if standing on hot coals.

Bennet excused himself. He ushered his housekeeper out into the hall and closed the library door behind them. That's when the woman had a sudden fit of hysterics.

"My lord, you must come quickly." Mrs Hendrie flapped her hands. "There's a fire. A fire in the stables. Hurry."

Good God!

Bennet darted along the hall and out of the front door, leaving his poor housekeeper trailing behind. He reached the stable block to find every man and boy filling buckets from the water trough, while Bower used his brawn to work the pump.

Like an army of ants, the men raced in single file to the north stalls, depositing the contents of their buckets and sprinting back for a refill. Mr Keenan stood amidst the men, barking orders.

He spotted Bennet and came hurrying over, wiping sweat and soot from his brow. "We've got the fire under control, milord. Praise be, no one was hurt."

"What happened?"

Had one of his friends crept out of the house to cause mayhem? Had Granger used his lit cheroot as a weapon of destruction?

"Young Povey had trouble securing the pulley. The rope snapped and sent the lamps crashing to the floor. Flames caught the dry straw in no time."

A new pulley system was on Branner's list of improvements. "We'll have it replaced as a matter of urgency. What about the horses?"

"The horses bolted at the first sign of the flames, almost trampled poor Povey to death. Saracen's got a nasty burn to his fetlock, but I've Mason tending the wound."

Saracen! The horse that beat Mullholland's at Cheltenham? Was Mullholland the culprit? Were his friends innocent of any wrongdoing? Hell, Bennet was as delusional as his father. Indeed, mistrust for everyone flowed in his veins. And where the hell was Branner?

"Question the boy again. Check his story. I want to know the whereabouts of all visiting coachmen and grooms. Have any of the guests been seen in the stables tonight?"

Keenan frowned. "Not that I know of, milord. But I'll check with Mr Bower. He's been mighty friendly with the coachmen."

"Don't trouble yourself now. Wait until things have settled here. And send the men to the house when they're done. Cook will feed them, and I'll have Milford bring up a few bottles of brandy from the cellar."

Keenan relayed his heartfelt thanks and returned to help the men. Bennet went to check the stalls, seeking reassurance that the fire posed no real risk.

Thoughts of Mullholland circled as Bennet made his way back to the house. Were the notes empty threats, merely a means to torment a man? Had Mullholland orchestrated events to exact his revenge?

What would Julianna make of this new development? Indeed, seeing her was Bennet's only focus as he charged into the hall and burst into the drawing room.

The room was empty.

He summoned Milford, who explained the ladies had joined the gentlemen in the library, except for Julianna, who had left for the cottage. "Mrs Eden wishes to discuss the notes she made this afternoon, my lord, and asks that you visit the cottage before you retire."

Excitement sparked. She wanted to discuss what she had

learnt in his absence this evening, but the thought of being alone with her in the quaint cottage heated his blood.

Bennet reminded Milford to post two footmen on the landing tonight.

Roxburgh, Lowbridge and Mrs Thorne were the only guests in the library when Bennet entered.

"Ah, the wanderer returns," Roxburgh teased.

"You look in need of a drink, Devereaux." Lowbridge shook his empty brandy goblet. "I'll have another."

Bennet didn't need a drink. He needed the company of one woman.

"There was a fire in the stables, an accident it seems." It wasn't a secret. The men's servants would inform them soon enough. "It's under control, but I must speak to my steward and have him assess the damage." Feeling a prickle of trepidation, he glanced around the room. "I trust the others have retired for the evening."

Lowbridge gave a sly chuckle. "Granger is on the hunt. He's left the house, has his sights set on a particular red-haired beauty."

So Granger had arranged to meet Isabella at the coaching inn.

"Presumably, he's off to the village. Why else would Isabella persuade him to bring her here? Perhaps she has her sights set on a trip to Brighton."

Lowbridge snorted. "Granger isn't interested in Miss Winters. The rake has set his cap for Mrs Eden."

CHAPTER 9

JULIANNA WAS NOT in the habit of inviting handsome men to visit her at such a late hour, but she couldn't shake the crippling feeling that something dreadful would happen at Witherdeen tonight, and she desperately needed to speak to Bennet. Hopefully, he already knew about Mr Granger depositing Miss Winters at the coaching inn in Bramley.

The woman was up to something.

Why else had she come if not to seek vengeance?

Nevertheless, it would be foolish not to investigate Bennet's other female guests. Both ladies had left the drawing room to use the pot. Mrs Thorne was gone for thirty minutes and must have ventured outside because she returned with blue lips and frost-nipped cheeks. But what possible gripe could she have with Bennet when her obsession began and ended with Lord Roxburgh? And Miss Ponsonby's constant chatter marked her as someone too simple to orchestrate the threats.

Upon her return to London, Julianna would have Mr Bower watch both women, so she might cross them off her suspect list.

Something Lord Roxburgh said during dinner flitted into her mind. While challenging Miss Ponsonby's belief in the supernatural, he had cited numerous criminal cases of people donning white robes and haunting their rich relatives.

"They torment their victims to such a degree they believe

they've seen an apparition, believe it disappeared before their eyes." Lord Roxburgh had spoken in his usual pompous drawl. "But I'd wager my wine cellar there's a logical explanation."

There were so many nooks and crannies amid the ruins it wouldn't be hard to hide. And the mind did play tricks. Julianna was so fearful of Bennet dying in a blaze she could smell smoke carried on the evening breeze.

She stopped walking, tightened her mother's silk shawl around her shoulders and glanced back at the house as if expecting to see a burst of orange flames licking the gables. All was quiet, but for the distant echo of voices.

She turned to the huge black shadow of the abbey marring the landscape. The ghostly monk had disappeared after passing through the gate. With it being so dark, the secret hideaway would be close to the boundary wall. Unless the villain knew the ruins so well he could navigate the crumbling walls blindly.

Deciding to take one quick look around the courtyard, she hurried towards the abbey's entrance, swallowed down her nerves and stepped inside.

During daylight, the ruin was a place of wonder. At night one imagined horned devils hiding in the cloisters, bats roosting in the belfry. Blackness swamped her like a shroud, so heavy and oppressive one might easily mistake the place for Satan's sanctuary.

A shiver rippled across her shoulders. A woman would not brave this terrifying place alone. The person dressed as a monk had to be a man. A man Miss Winters had come to meet at the coaching inn in Bramley.

Julianna stood amid the gloom, silently debating who'd want to hurt Bennet, when the shadows shifted. A tall, slender figure slipped out of the darkness and skulked across the courtyard like a wildcat stalking prey. A sliver of moonlight caught his angular features and golden blonde hair. His iniquitous grin marked him as Lucifer's lackey, not a man with pious intent.

"You came," uttered the masculine voice that had Julianna clutching her hands to her chest and gasping for breath. "I knew you would."

"Mr Granger." Every muscle in her body stiffened. "You

frightened me to death. I might ask what you're doing here at night, but I assume you've come ghost hunting."

"Oh, I've come hunting, darling, but not for ghosts."

Breathe!

"Have you not arranged to meet Miss Winters?"

"Why would I meet Miss Winters when we arranged to meet?"

Julianna tried to temper the rising panic. "You're mistaken. We made no such arrangement, sir."

He prowled closer. "During dinner, you challenged me to come to the ruins tonight. It was a novel way of arranging a secret assignation, but I heard your silent plea."

A secret assignation?

The fellow had taken to inventing stories. Dangerous people convinced themselves their fantasies were reality. She'd need all her wits to keep this viper at bay.

"I believe Lord Roxburgh offered the challenge, sir." It was a lie, but she had to buy time so she could shuffle closer to the boundary wall. "I am here to decide if someone has been impersonating a monk."

He tilted his head. "I understand. They say your mother played the coquette. Women of your ilk enjoy making men sing for their supper."

"Women of my ilk?" Heavens above! He thought her reservations were a ploy for attention. She had to keep him talking until she reached the boundary door. "Are you implying I've inherited a desire to entertain men?"

"You're Giselle de Lacy's daughter. Lust is in the blood." Mr Granger licked his lips while his lecherous gaze devoured her figure. "You've been staring at me all evening."

She had been staring at all the men, wondering if any of them bore a grudge against Bennet Devereaux. "And you've been staring at Miss Ponsonby. I assumed you'd taken a fancy to your cousin's mistress."

"I've taken a fancy to you, Mrs Eden." He shifted closer, so close she caught a whiff of his foul brandy breath. "Pony is a pest, while you're a sumptuous package."

How she wished the ghost would appear and scare the

dickens out of this devil. But there was no chance of that. Miss Winters was holding a secret meeting with her accomplice at the coaching inn in Bramley.

In the absence of a ghost or a weapon, Julianna had but one option if she hoped to calm this beast. "What will Lord Devereaux say when he learns you've propositioned his mistress?"

The blackguard's mocking laugh echoed through the cloisters. "Devereaux left the library an hour ago and failed to return. He's taken himself to Bramley to visit Miss Winters." He tapped his nose and winked. "It will be our little secret. What he doesn't know can't hurt him."

Julianna's stomach roiled.

Not because she believed the rogue.

But because she knew she had no option but to fight this fiend.

"Then let me make my position clear, Mr Granger, in the hope we may laugh about this silly misunderstanding." She edged left. "My loyalties lie with Lord Devereaux. I will never entertain another man in my bed." She felt the truth of those words as she spoke.

As expected, Mr Granger did not respond kindly. He pounced, his claw-like fingers grabbing her cheeks and squeezing her mouth into a painful pout.

"Let me make my position clear, Mrs Eden." Anger distorted his features. "Women do not refuse me, and certainly not a cheap whore following in her mother's shadow. I take what I want. Do as I damn well please." Droplets of spittle hit her cheek. "Play along nicely, and I'll not be so rough."

The man was like a feral dog, snapping and snarling just to intimidate. Julianna's only option was to run, to fight him with every breath in her lungs. Without further thought, she kicked him hard in the shins, followed it with a powerful punch to his gut.

Mr Granger cried out and doubled over.

With no time to lose, Julianna dropped her shawl and scooped up her skirts, took to her heels and darted through the boundary doorway. She left the path and crossed the grass, deciding it was safer to head to the house than the secluded cottage.

The slam of the boundary door and Mr Granger's cruel curses sent her heart leaping to her throat. She could not outrun him, but the closer she got to the house, the more someone was likely to hear her screams.

"Bitch!" Mr Granger yelled.

He was close now.

She couldn't risk glancing behind for fear she'd trip and fall.

"Whore!" The brute's ragged breathing and vile obscenities permeated the night air. He grabbed the back of her gown and yanked hard, tearing the silk.

"Argh!" Julianna tumbled back onto the damp grass. She kicked Mr Granger, but after a frantic tussle, he managed to sit astride her.

"Is this how you like it?" He captured her flailing arms and pinned them to the ground to stop her thumping his chest.

"Get off me!"

The stench of his breath made her retch.

"Help!"

Fear will make you weak.

Mr D'Angelo's words entered her head. As an agent of the Order, he had come to Howland Street to teach the new recruits how to defend themselves against the villains in the rookeries.

Keep your elbows tight to your ribs. Grab his wrist with one hand, his upper arm with the other, and a quick flick of your hips will unbalance him.

Julianna had listened intently, remembered every word. But with this disgusting devil looming over her, gripping her arms, it was impossible to act.

She screamed, screamed so loud someone must have heard her plea.

Consumed by anger and lust, Mr Granger collapsed on top of her. His weight crushed the air from her lungs. Then his filthy mouth slammed against hers, smothering her cries for help.

Memories of Edward Eden surfaced. Courage abandoned her, and the need to fight scurried away like a craven coward. She lay still on the cold ground, tears slipping down her cheeks, and prayed it would soon be over.

Then came the battle cry—the inarticulate roar of reinforcements.

Mr Granger seemed oblivious to the commotion and continued nudging her skirts higher with his knee. The attack, when it came, tore a shriek from the reprobate as he went hurtling through the air and landed on the ground with a thud.

"Get the hell off her!" Bennet snarled through gritted teeth. He dragged Mr Granger to his feet and punched him hard on the nose. "Is this how you treat women? Is this how you treat a guest in my home?"

Mr Granger clutched his face and howled in pain.

Amid a torrent of vitriolic curses, Bennet kicked the lout to the ground, climbed on top of him and hit the man about the face so hard Julianna winced with each loud smack.

"Bennet!" She scrambled to her feet, righting her skirts. "That's enough! Stop! Please!"

But he was like a man possessed. He yanked Mr Granger to his feet. "You spineless bastard. Let's see how you fare with someone your own size."

Despite the trickle of blood leaking from Mr Granger's nose and mouth, he found his arrogance. "Let's make a wager. The winner gets to bed Mrs Eden."

The comment left Bennet enraged.

A fight ensued.

Savage grunts echoed as the men threw punches. Bennet ducked to avoid Mr Granger's weak attack and countered it with a vicious blow to the man's stomach. The miscreant groaned and cradled his abdomen. He recovered in seconds, then growled and charged at Bennet, knocking him to the ground.

They continued wrestling and exchanging blows. Bennet was by far the most skilled in combat. Julianna begged them to stop, but her words fell on deaf ears.

Thankfully, Lord Roxburgh heard the hullaballoo and came charging across the lawn. He grabbed Mr Granger by the scruff of his coat and hauled him backwards, though the man continued flailing and spitting blood-stained insults.

Lord Roxburgh glanced at Julianna's torn, mud-splattered gown. Recognition dawned. In an uncharacteristic surge of anger, the lord released Mr Granger and slammed his fist into the man's jaw.

Mr Granger's head whipped left with such force he was left dazed.

Bennet fought to catch his breath. "Get this bastard off my land! Now! Tonight! I want them all gone. Do you hear? I want them out of my bloody house!"

Lord Roxburgh held up his hands in mock surrender. "I'll have the carriages brought round at once. We'll be gone within the hour."

But Bennet refused to let the matter rest. He charged at Mr Granger and punched him in the ribs. "I should call you out for disrespecting Mrs Eden. Indeed, name your second, and we shall meet at dawn."

Lord Roxburgh's dark eyes flashed with fear. "There's no need for grand gestures, Devereaux." He tugged Bennet's arm and pulled him away from the brute. "You've given the man a good beating. Mrs Eden wouldn't want you risking your life for this worthless ingrate."

"Please, Bennet. Let him go." Tears welled at the thought of Bennet wielding a pistol at dawn. "Mr Granger will leave. Let that be the end of the matter."

It would not be the end. She would conduct an investigation into the man's affairs and find some way to punish him. If only to prevent another woman from suffering the same fate.

Mr Granger remained tight-lipped, his bravado vanquished.

"I'll hear it from Granger," Bennet insisted. "Along with an apology for the deplorable way he treated Mrs Eden."

With obvious reluctance, the cad confirmed he had no desire to meet on the duelling field. He mumbled an apology. Agreed he would leave for Brighton immediately and remain there for the foreseeable future.

For Bennet's sake, she accepted his insincere offerings, and Mr Daventry would not permit anyone to treat his agents with disrespect. Lord help Mr Granger when the master of the Order discovered she had been assaulted in such a degrading manner.

"Escort Mrs Eden to her cottage." Lord Roxburgh grabbed hold of the bruised and bleeding Mr Granger. "I shall personally throw Granger into his carriage. We won't be far behind."

Bennet nodded. "We'll talk about this when I come to town."

"Perhaps then you might tell me what the hell is going on."

Bennet watched Lord Roxburgh drag the rogue across the lawn. Anger emanated from every fibre of his being, but when he turned to face Julianna, guilt marred his handsome features.

"Can you forgive me, Julianna?"

"There is nothing to forgive. It wasn't your fault."

"We should have stayed together."

"I encouraged Lord Roxburgh when he suggested retiring to the library." She'd thought it a perfect opportunity to question Mrs Thorne about the dresses stolen from the attic. "And you weren't to know of Mr Granger's questionable character."

Shock suddenly took command of her body. The trembling started in her shoulders and rippled violently to her toes. Vile images of the miscreant's face flooded her mind. The sickly stench of his brandy breath filled her nostrils.

"I cannot recall ever being so frightened," she admitted.

Bennet stripped off his coat, draped the garment around her shoulders and slipped her arms into the sleeves. "Come. This should keep the cold at bay until we reach the cottage. This time, I insist on lighting the fire and making tea."

"Do you even know how?"

"To light a fire?"

"To make tea."

He shrugged. "How hard can it be?"

The comment chased away the chill, as did his coat. The heavy garment enveloped her with his warmth, his scent, his unique essence that was entirely unforgettable.

"Do you want to tell me what happened?" he said, escorting her across the manicured lawn back to the cottage. "You used to tell me everything."

Yes, and she had not spoken to anyone in the same way since.

"If I tell you, promise you won't chase after Mr Granger and beat him senseless." Mr Daventry would make the reprobate pay for his crime.

"I've stopped making promises I cannot keep. Be assured I shall cross swords with Mr Granger soon." Bennet paused. "I presume he followed you from the house."

"He made the usual mistake. He believed Giselle de Lacy's daughter must be equally free with her affections." Lord, she suddenly recalled what she'd said to the brute. "Bennet, to discourage him I said I was your mistress."

He jerked to a halt. "You told him we were lovers?"

Lovers.

Heat coiled in her stomach. Heat journeyed south, pooling hot between her thighs. For the first time in her life, the word didn't sound dirty or disgusting. It sounded beautiful. Divine.

Julianna kept walking lest he notice the flush rising to her cheeks.

"Forgive me. I thought it might deter him," she said when Bennet caught up with her. "But he said you'd left Witherdeen to meet Miss Winters at the coaching inn. You do know Mr Granger brought Miss Winters to Bramley?"

"Roxburgh told me, but I had no knowledge of it until an hour ago."

She'd not doubted him for a second. "Evidently, she's here to cause trouble. The question is, who has she come to meet?"

"It cannot be anyone here. Miss Ponsonby retired for the evening. Lowbridge and Mrs Thorne were in the library when I left."

"Who else could it be?" Julianna hadn't seen Mr Branner all evening, although he would have no cause to come to the house at night. Miss Winters may have lied about meeting someone when really she had nefarious plans.

They reached the cottage.

Bennet opened the garden gate and stepped aside for her to enter. "It could be Mullholland. There was a fire in the stable block tonight. Mrs Hendrie called me from the library. I remained there until certain the blaze posed no threat. I should speak to Branner, but it can wait until tomorrow."

"A fire! Good Lord!" Panicked, she scanned every inch of his muscular body. "You're not hurt? Tell me you're not hurt." This fear of him dying, of losing him again, proved confounding.

He rubbed his jaw. "I may have a faint bruise from Granger's weak right hook, but my men have the blaze contained."

"Do you think Miss Winters started the fire?"

"No. The faulty pulley system seems to be the cause."

"Based on previous events, we were expecting a fire tonight."

"An uncanny coincidence, one might think." He sounded doubtful.

"Or a rather skilled deception."

The cottage stood in darkness but for a stream of moonlight illuminating the door as if it were a gateway to heaven. Logic said they should part ways here. Being alone with Bennet Devereaux for any length of time would arouse feelings best left buried. Only a fool would fall in love with a man destined to marry the daughter of a duke.

"Is this where we say good night, Julianna?" His velvet voice stirred her senses. "Am I allowed inside, or will you banish me back to the house?"

The need for his company ran deeper than the endless fathoms of the sea. Besides, should she not distract him until Mr Granger's carriage was clattering back to Brighton?

"And refuse a cup of tea made by the Marquess Devereaux?" she teased.

"You may live to regret it."

"Undoubtedly."

Julianna tried to keep her breathing even as she led him into the cottage. It didn't help that he lingered near the door, forcing her to brush past him to lower the latch and slide the bolt.

The darkness possessed the power to bring raw emotions to the fore.

The darkness gave one the courage to speak from the heart.

"Tell me you're all right," he whispered, gripping her arms gently.

She looked up at him. "I've suffered worse hardships."

"I swore you'd always feel safe here. I failed you again."

"I always feel safe with you."

He brushed an errant curl behind her ear. "How can I put things right? What can I do to make you laugh like you used to, make you happy?"

Oh, she'd not felt the glow of happiness for such a long time.

"You could let me win the next race," she said because giving a voice to her deepest desires would cause them both immeasurable pain. What was the point of wishing for something that could never be?

"Consider yourself victorious. Reach into my coat pocket and claim your reward."

"My reward?" Intrigued, she delved into his coat and withdrew a silver bangle. It took a few seconds to register the significance. Then the beautiful memories came flooding back. Happy memories of a perfect Christmas spent with Bennet.

"Oh, Bennet! Is it the same one? Is it?"

"It's the one from my mother's trinket box. The one I gave you as a gift. The one you were forced to leave behind when Giselle stole you away on that stormy night."

Tears sprang to her eyes.

A hard lump formed in her throat.

"Try it on." Bennet took the bangle and slid it over her trembling fingers. "As a boy, I prayed you would return to claim your gift. As a man, I'd lost all hope."

Julianna couldn't speak.

Not because she'd forgotten how it felt to be happy, but because the boy she held in her heart still lived in this magnificent man.

Grateful beyond measure, she came up on her toes and kissed Bennet Devereaux on the cheek. As children, they'd not shied away from demonstrations of affection, but as her lips lingered on his warm skin, she was suddenly overcome with a woman's lustful urges.

Bennet turned his head. Desire glinted in his tawny eyes, eyes so rich, so compelling, she could get lost in their majesty. He was so close his hot breath breezed over her mouth. The world around her faded. It was just the two of them, alone in the dark. Lost. Hurting. Seeking comfort.

"Thank you for helping me to remember."

Before logic took command of her senses, she pressed her lips to his. An innocent kiss to banish all thoughts of Mr Granger. That's what she told herself. But the mere brush of

Bennet Devereaux's mouth ignited her passions. The intoxicating taste of him, the power of his magnetic pull, left her hungering for his touch.

He returned her kiss with slow, expert strokes, luring her deeper, holding her under his hypnotic spell. With a gentle slide of his tongue, he coaxed her lips apart and slipped inside her mouth.

Mother Mary!

Her blood turned molten. The sudden pulsing in her core mimicked every deep plunge. Bennet cupped her cheeks, drank like he was dying, desperate to quench his thirst.

He broke contact. "Am I the first man you've kissed?"

Embarrassment dampened her desire. "Is it so obvious?"

"Then you've never known a man's touch?"

"Only my husband's on our wedding night. A physical act merely to ensure we were married in the legal sense, though I didn't know that at the time."

It was a quick, cold affair. The memory of her lying rigid in the tester bed, used and unloved, chilled her to the bone. She wrapped her arms around Bennet's waist and pressed her body to his, wishing she could crawl inside him so they need never part again.

"I don't want to think about that now, Bennet." She wanted to talk, to explore this undeniable passion that existed between them.

Hearing her silent plea, he kissed her again—a sensual melding of mouths and hearts that left her breathless.

She didn't want this moment to end.

Fate had determined it invariably would.

CHAPTER 10

Bloody hell!

Bennet couldn't kiss her deeply enough or passionately enough to satisfy his craving. He'd never wanted a woman the way he wanted her. They were connected. Their hearts and souls entwined in ways that defied logic. The need to cement their union with a rampant sexual act proved the driving force. Though he feared they would pay a hefty price for succumbing to their desires.

That didn't stop him from wanting to free her breasts from the sagging neckline of her gown and feast like a king. From wanting to feel her hugging his cock, to see her riding him senseless while he bathed in all her wondrous glory.

Destiny had brought them together again. Were they destined to become lovers? Or would one mindless night of pleasure ruin a friendship that might span a lifetime?

Ignoring his desperate need to have her—to know her in every way a man could know a woman—Bennet dragged his mouth from Julianna's and suppressed a frustrated groan.

"Something always prevents me from keeping my promises."

In her glazed eyes, he saw his own restless yearning. "You speak of agreeing to be my protector? Mr Daventry won't blame you for what happened tonight."

Daventry might not blame him for Granger's actions, but he would have much to say if Bennet bedded his agent.

He stroked her cheek with the backs of his fingers, wondering if her thighs were as soft, if she'd sigh in the same way if he touched her there. "I speak of promising to light the fire and make tea."

"It's too late to worry about fires and tea."

Too late because they were on the verge of stripping off their clothes and making love? Too late because they should part before they did something they might come to regret?

"I'll not leave you here alone tonight." A man would need the morals of a saint to stay. "Not when Granger might sneak back to Witherdeen and take his vengeance out on you."

Her breath caught in her throat. "But he'd be a fool to come back."

"Depraved men are undoubtedly fools." A vision of her writhing helplessly beneath the rogue flashed into Bennet's mind. He gritted his teeth. "I'll murder the devil if he lays a hand on you again."

"I shall murder the devil myself. Before Edward, I was used to fighting off lecherous louts and often turfed Giselle's drunken lovers out into the street. It's just a matter of finding my confidence."

"You shouldn't have to deal with degenerates."

"We're to have lessons in combat from Mr D'Angelo."

Lessons in combat!

Dante D'Angelo certainly knew how to pummel a man senseless. The best fighters took risks, didn't care if they lived or died. That's what made him a ruthless enquiry agent. Julianna did not possess the same indomitable spirit. The thought of her tackling thieves in the rookeries chilled Bennet to the bone.

"You haven't told me how you ended up penniless when your husband died. Eden must have given Giselle a substantial sum to purchase your hand in marriage."

"I'm glad I got nothing. I'd rather die a pauper than be indebted to him."

Edward Eden had hurt her deeply. The urge to know every

intimate detail of her married life, to throttle a dead man and stamp on his rotting corpse, left Bennet seeking a distraction.

He glanced at the mud stains on her gown. "Why don't you wash and change into your nightclothes, climb into bed? I'll come up and light the fire in your room, sleep in the chair."

"You don't need to stay."

"Do you want me to leave?"

"I'll be fine."

Did she honestly think he would abandon her after the terrifying attack? "You didn't answer my question. You don't need to pretend with me. And I can always use my privilege pass to force the truth from your lips."

"A man of your size cannot sleep in a chair." With evident admiration, she scanned the breadth of his shoulders. "We often shared a bed as children. We slept together in the tent you erected in the playroom, much to Mrs Hendrie's dismay."

The memory of those happy times rippled through him in pleasurable waves. He should remind her there was a second bedchamber upstairs, but remained tight-lipped.

"We're not children anymore, Julianna. The kiss we shared proved that." As did the swell of his cock straining against his breeches.

"We kissed more than once, Bennet."

"And the urge to kiss you again burns in my veins." The urge to do a host of other intimate things burned there, too. "Perhaps we should change the subject. Talking like this serves to feed my fantasies."

Her arresting blue eyes sparkled. "Then I shouldn't tell you I'm addicted to the taste of your mouth. That you're the only man I have ever wanted to kiss."

"Such talk is unwise." Hell, his heart thumped louder than a blacksmith's hammer. "Just as I shouldn't say I long to slip that gown off your shoulders, set my mouth to the swell of your breasts."

She smoothed her hand over his bicep. "I'll not tell you I'm desperate to know what you look like beneath these clothes."

"Most definitely not." He could be naked in seconds.

"You're the only man who has ever wanted me, Bennet."

His lust spiralled. "Then the world is full of imbeciles." He glanced at the cottage door. "Shall I go back to my cold, lonely bed, Julianna?" Restraint was for better men. "Or do you desire my company tonight?"

"Logic says we should abstain from anything but lighting fires and drinking tea." So why did she continue stroking his arm as if it were his cock?

"Living in the moment has a certain allure."

The temptress trailed her fingers over his chest. "Hard realities are best left for tomorrow." She turned away, climbed the first few stairs, and cast him a coy glance. "Stay with me tonight. Stay in my bed." He saw the promise in her eyes—a promise she intended to keep. "Come up in five minutes."

Hell, he almost dropped to his knees and thanked the Lord. "You may come to regret it, Julianna."

"I could never regret a moment spent with you."

Five minutes felt like five hours.

The creak of the upstairs boards preceded the creak of the bed.

Mindless with lust but not wishing to scare her, Bennet mounted the stairs slowly and entered the dark room. It was so damn cold he hoped the frigid air didn't hinder his performance.

"We should have lit the fire." She'd pulled the blankets over her shoulders, leaving nothing but a pale face and a mass of red curls visible above the coverlet. "But don't bother with it now."

A quick glance at the discarded garments on the floor said she was naked, but for the bangle he'd given her as a gift. "I doubt either of us will be cold for long." Her nerves were so palpable he shivered, too. "While I undress, tell me what happened after Edward died." He started slipping the buttons on his waistcoat.

"A week after our marriage, we moved to a small manor house near Hastings. I thought Edward owned the house but later discovered it belonged to Justin."

Bennet casually shrugged out of his waistcoat, though his blood pumped so fast he wanted to rip the damn thing off his back. "Did Justin ask you to leave?"

"Yes, on the day of the funeral. He said I'd been a burden for too long."

"And Eden made no provision for you in his will?" Bennet removed his cravat and tossed it onto the chair. "Not even a small allowance?"

"Nothing." She inhaled sharply when he dragged his shirt over his head. "Do we have to talk about Edward? Can we not talk about you?"

"I merely sought to distract you while I undressed." To distract himself, for he could think of nothing but pushing into her warmth, of having the only woman he'd dreamed of for God knows how many years.

"If you're embarrassed, I can turn my back," she teased.

"And yet the truth is you want to gawp and stare."

She did more than stare. Those brazen eyes widened as he stripped off his breeches and palmed his erection. Julianna raised the covers in open invitation, gave him a glimpse of her porcelain skin, the flare of her hips, the soft curve of her breasts.

"I don't remember ever being naked when we were children." He climbed into bed, drew the covers over them, and turned to face her. "We used to invent stories of running away from Witherdeen, and yet there is no place I would rather be than here with you."

Her palm came to rest on his chest, so light, yet so damnably arousing. "Your skin is so hot there was no need to light the fire."

"Then move closer, and I'll keep you warm."

She hesitated. "Whatever happens between us tonight, it's an experience we cannot repeat. It's one night. One night to forget the rest of the world exists, for I must leave tomorrow."

One night he would remember until he drew his last breath.

"One night," he echoed but wouldn't swear to it if prompted, and he would do everything in his power to persuade her to stay.

She bit down on her lip. "I don't know how to please you."

"If we did nothing but sleep, I'd be satisfied beyond measure."

She edged closer. "But you want to do more than sleep."

"A great deal more."

She cupped his neck. "Show me."

Hell, her sultry tone made his cock weep. She watched him beneath heavy lids. He took a few seconds to drink in the sight of her wild red curls splayed over the pillow, of those kissable lips parted in anticipation. Took a moment to say a prayer of thanks to fate, to God, the Devil. He didn't care who.

"You do want me, Bennet?"

"Love, I've never wanted anything more." Surely the raging erection nudging her thigh proved how much. He tried not to think about that bastard Edward Eden, hoped to erase the memories of her wedding night, of the tortuous sounds coming from Justin's chamber, even if he had to howl his pleasure.

Not wanting to rush, he kissed her slowly, his mouth gliding over hers in a sensual caress that left every muscle taut. The need to push inside her in any form had him tracing his tongue over the seam of her lips, teasing his way into her wet mouth.

God, he'd imagined this so many times it hardly seemed real.

She tasted sweet, like orchard apples picked from the tree-top. A man would risk life and limb to steal another. Unable to stem his hunger, he twined his tongue with hers, a seductive mating that soon became an insatiable need to plunder.

"Say you want me, Julianna. Say you want to feel me moving inside you." Hungrily, he dragged his mouth to the sensitive spot below her ear, took to raining kisses down her neck, across her shoulder. "Tell me now because my control is hanging by a flimsy thread."

"You're the only man I've ever wanted."

He locked gazes with her. "Say if you want me to stop."

She shivered as he drew his fingers across her collarbone, gasped when he caressed her breast. He slipped lower, down the soft swell of her belly, into the damp curls to massage her sex in a slow, teasing rhythm.

Her enchanting blue eyes widened. "Don't stop, Bennet."

He would make her come like this, watching with utter fasci-nation, listening to her little moans and pleas, loving her as no man had done before.

That would have been his plan had the minx not reached under the bedcovers and wrapped her hand around his shaft.

"Christ!"

"Tell me what to do."

"Just touch me, love. Grip me tight and tell me how you've longed to return to Witherdeen."

"I've visited many times in my ... my dreams." She arched her back, writhed against his fingers. "Oh! Being with you feels so good."

"Have you missed me, Julianna?"

"Yes! Yes! More than you know." She started stroking his shaft back and forth. The hesitant movements lacked experience, which made it all the more erotic.

Damn. He almost lost focus. But nothing was more important than being the first man to make her come. "Next time, when we're lying before a roaring fire, it will be my mouth devouring your sex. Next time, we'll be stretched naked, not be encumbered by bedsheets."

"One night, Bennet, that's what we s-said." She was panting now. "Oh! That's all we h-have."

Like hell it was!

Now he'd found her, he had no intention of letting her go.

The dainty hand massaging his manhood stilled.

"Come for me, love."

She closed her eyes. Her head fell back. Her mouth formed the perfect O. He felt her climax pulsing in her sex. She reached down and covered his hand, held him there while shuddering through her release.

God, she was beautiful. Watching her ride each pleasurable wave was a magnificent sight to behold. Sinking into her wetness could not come soon enough.

She opened her eyes and smiled. "That was divine."

"A man does his best." With luck, she'd want him again.

"I can barely catch my breath."

"We don't have to continue." His cock jerked in protest.

A smile, shameless and suggestive, touched her lips. "Make love to me, Bennet." Her words were like a potent aphrodisiac. She pulled him on top of her naked body, opened her legs so he would fit perfectly between her thighs. "You will be mindful of the fact I don't want a child?"

The question caught him by surprise. Not because he hadn't

considered making a timely withdrawal, but he needed to know her thoughts before proceeding.

He was two inches away from pushing home. "Don't you want children?" Or did she not want a child out of wedlock with him?

"Yes, but I don't want any child to suffer as I have." She gripped his back, opened her legs wider. "Just be mindful."

Not wanting to think about who would father her children, Bennet kissed her deeply, driving his tongue into her mouth the way he wanted to drive his cock into her sweetness.

When he pushed inside her, he almost expired from a rush of pleasure. The first slide to the hilt was heavenly. Warmth encompassed him from head to root. She was so tight, so wet. She was finally his.

Julianna clung to him, tilting her hips, holding him there—loving him. "I always knew we'd fit perfectly."

"Look at me, love. You'll feel every thrust more keenly."

Lust coursed through his veins, a raging hunger to slam into her so hard they'd rock the abbey's foundations. But the look that passed between them went deeper than mere physical desire. He made sure she felt the full depth of his devotion with each measured thrust. Pushed deep and long and hard, over and over and over, at just the right angle to make her come again.

She came apart, clawing his back, hugging his cock, crying his name.

A few fierce, frenzied thrusts, and he withdrew from her body, his seed exploding from him as if he'd abstained for years.

He fell back on the bed, his heart thumping wildly, and fought to catch his breath. Julianna threaded her fingers with his, brought his hand to her lips, and kissed him tenderly. He felt closer to her now than ever. The same thought that had been echoing in his mind since he climbed into bed surfaced again.

When it came to loving Julianna, one night would never be enough.

●

Bennet woke sometime later. It was dark outside, the room still bitterly cold. A wave of euphoria washed over him as he suddenly recalled why he lay naked in bed in the quaint little cottage.

God, she'd been magnificent. The sight of Julianna writhing beneath him, wearing nothing but his gift, had left him as stiff as a ramrod. The mere thought stirred his cock from slumber.

He contemplated the possibility of making love to her again, but the strange stillness captured his attention. He listened, expecting to hear her soft, rhythmical breathing, but heard nothing. The moment he sat bolt upright in bed, he knew he was alone. Through narrowed eyes he scanned the darkness, listened for any sign of movement downstairs.

Nothing.

Seized by a sickening sense of foreboding, he leapt out of bed, searched the drawers, the wardrobe. Empty. All empty. The torn gown lay in a puddle of silk, but the undergarments were missing, as was her valise.

Bennet quickly dressed and raced to the coach house. But he knew one thing with absolute certainty before he noted the absence of Lucius Daventry's coach.

Julianna had left Witherdeen.

And in all likelihood, she was never coming back.

CHAPTER 11

"ARE you going to tell me what happened with the marquess, or will you stare at the ceiling until your meeting with Mr Daventry? You've been abed since you crept into our chamber just after dawn, and Miss Trimble isn't of a mind to pry."

Julianna glanced at Rachel Gambit, who sat perched on her own bed in the room they shared in Howland Street. Sunlight caught her golden hair, and she looked like an angel come to relieve sinners of their burdens.

"If I speak I shall cry and I doubt you want me blubbering on your shoulder."

"Was it as you feared? Has the darling boy grown into an obnoxious oaf? Did he put paid to all those glorious memories?"

A rush of emotion brought tears to Julianna's eyes. "No. It was quite the opposite."

Their connection was as strong now as it had always been. And while the year she'd spent at Witherdeen had sustained her in the interim, the memory of making love to Bennet Devereaux would nourish her until the end of her days.

"I see." Rachel's tone carried the weight of the problem. "Your love for the boy has become a fondness for the man."

More than a fondness, she feared.

Rachel huffed. "I sometimes wonder if Mr Daventry is a devil in disguise. To send you there, knowing what happened all those years ago. It's tantamount to cruelty."

Julianna could not think ill of the man who had rescued her from the gutter. She didn't dare contemplate where she might be if Mr Daventry hadn't offered a helping hand.

"I believe it was an education in fortitude." And by God, she'd been tested to the limit. "We'll need emotional strength if we're to tackle cases objectively."

"Mine must be an education in patience."

"Has Mr Daventry not given you an assignment?"

"None of us have an assignment. That's what I find so baffling. Mr Daventry is so cautious, yet threw you to the lions and hoped you'd return unscathed."

She *had* come close to being brutally savaged.

Had returned with a few battle scars.

Julianna recalled something Bennet had said. "The marquess swore to protect me. I believe that's why Mr Daventry gave me the case."

Rachel arched a curious brow. "And yet something went terribly wrong. Why else would you spend hours crying into your pillow?"

Because they had crossed a line. How could she be friends with a man who roused her passions? How could she ever look at him again without recalling how he moved deep inside her? By now, she should be used to pain, but that would be pure torture.

"You may have to share this room with someone else soon." Julianna's heart grew heavy at the prospect of making her own way in the world. "Today, I must tell Mr Daventry I cannot work on Bennet Devereaux's case."

"What? No!" Rachel shot to her feet and deposited herself on Julianna's bed. "Cursed saints! Why? Are you in love with him?"

Julianna sat bolt upright. "Hush. You'll alert Miss Trimble. No, I'm not in love with him." She cared about him in ways she couldn't explain, and always would. "Let's just say my mother would be proud of the way I behaved. After all, he is paying me a substantial fee."

Recognition dawned. Rachel was no fool. Her mouth fell open and her eyes grew as round as saucers. "What was it like?"

"Rachel!"

"Sorry. I'm curious that's all."

"Promise me you won't breath a word about it to anyone. Promise me, Rachel. Please."

Her friend crossed her heart. "I know you find it hard to trust people, but you can trust me, Julianna." She fell silent for a moment. "All the gentlemen of the Order married the ladies they worked with on cases. Mr Daventry must have sprinkled love potions into their tea. Maybe he has some for Bennet Devereaux."

Love potions? Rachel rarely suffered moments of fancy.

"There's more chance of Mr Sloane cutting his hair than me marrying a marquess." If only Bennet were a simple man without wealth and title. "And you know how the agent loves his pirate locks."

Rachel laughed, but then her expression grew serious. "Could you not work on the case without returning to Witherdeen? Tell me what evidence you have so far and I might be able to help."

Julianna explained all that had happened during the two days spent at Bennet's estate, including the terrifying incident with Mr Granger.

"The blasted scoundrel!" Rachel gritted her teeth. "And I don't care if Miss Trimble hears me cursing. He lives in Brighton, you say? Perhaps a brief trip to the coast is in order. You do realise Mr Daventry will skin him alive."

"Trust me, I have every intention of punishing the cretin." He'd just caught her by surprise, and her fragile emotions had left her weak.

"I don't suppose the marquess will let the matter rest, either." Rachel clapped her hands. "Back to the case. If it were me, I would visit Miss Winters and accuse her of sending the handbills. She has motive and opportunity."

"Does she have a motive? Do courtesans not expect their lovers to marry, eventually?" And her threats would not deter Bennet from doing his duty.

Still, Julianna should have checked the trunks in the attic before leaving Witherdeen. She should have visited the innkeeper to enquire if Miss Winters had made other secret visits to Bramley.

"Perhaps Miss Winters is unbalanced."

"She does strike me as the vindictive sort."

"You see." Rachel gave Julianna a reassuring tap on the leg. "Focus on discovering if Miss Winters is guilty of threatening the marquess. I assume she returned to town."

Julianna silently groaned. The fact she hadn't stayed at Witherdeen long enough to find out proved she lacked the skills required of an enquiry agent.

Rachel must have read Julianna's strained expression. "Never mind. Mr Daventry will know where the woman lives."

The thought of meeting Mr Daventry in Hart Street made her shudder. He would think her completely incompetent. When life threw obstacles in one's path a de Lacy always bolted. Having spent a lifetime fleeing problems and misfortunes, perhaps it was time to stop and tackle what lay ahead.

She had no issue hammering on Miss Winters' door and demanding answers. But how would she fare when she saw Bennet Devereaux again? How would she ever feel whole when he owned a piece of her heart?

CHAPTER 12

Hart Street, London

"COME IN, Mrs Eden. Please sit down. I've asked Ashwood and Cole to join us." Mr Daventry gestured to the two agents seated on the sofa, who both stood and inclined their heads respectfully. "With their wealth of experience, they may provide valuable insight on your case."

Julianna pushed her nerves aside. "I welcome their opinion, sir."

The men waited for her to sit in the chair before dropping into their seats. Mr Ashwood's handsome countenance would leave any woman floundering, though she found Mr Cole's dark, brooding features more disconcerting.

"Perhaps you might begin by explaining what happened at Witherdeen." Mr Daventry retrieved a notebook and pencil from the low table and met her gaze. "Only those incidents relevant to the investigation."

Good Lord! Did he know of her intimate liaison with the marquess? Was he a mystic from the Orient with the power to read minds?

Julianna's heart thundered faster than a horse at the Derby. She told her tale, informed them of the third note and the ghostly sightings.

"There is still plenty to do at Witherdeen," she said while the men listened, though twice Mr Ashwood and Mr Cole took to whispering between themselves. "It strikes me that the person sending the handbills and staging these alarming scenes is a frequent visitor to the estate."

Namely Isabella Winters, though she needed substantial evidence before voicing her suspicions.

"Were the notes delivered to Witherdeen?" Mr Ashwood asked.

Relieved she could answer at least one question, Julianna said, "The person left the first two notes at the gatekeeper's lodge at Witherdeen. No one saw who delivered them. The marquess received the third note at his London address, delivered by a penny boy who ran off before anyone could question him."

"May we see the notes?" Mr Cole said.

Julianna handed the gentleman her portfolio, and while both agents examined the documents, Mr Daventry probed her about her sudden departure.

"Why return to town in the dead of night when you should have stayed to question Lord Devereaux's friends?" Though he spoke bluntly, his tone held a hint of compassion. So much so, she suspected he already knew about the terrible incident with Mr Granger.

Julianna raised her chin. "A guest mistook me for my mother and presumed I was as free with my affections. He refused to accept he'd made a mistake and so acted on his impulses. Thankfully, Lord Devereaux came to my rescue before the fellow followed through with his threat."

Mr Daventry's jaw firmed. "Had I known Devereaux was expecting guests, I would have cautioned you about walking alone at night."

"It was my own foolish mistake."

"The mistake was Mr Granger's. One that will cost him dearly."

So he did know! Had Mr Bower revealed the rogue's name?

"I trust the matter is in hand." Mr Ashwood spoke like a protective brother, while Mr Cole looked ready to rip Mr Granger's heart from his chest with his bare hands. "Should you need me to teach the man manners, just say the word."

"He will receive his education tonight," came Mr Daventry's sinister reply.

The ringing of the doorbell caught everyone's attention, as did the clip of booted footsteps in the hall. All the men pinned their gazes to the door and were evidently expecting someone.

A flutter in Julianna's stomach told her who that someone was before Mrs Gunning opened the drawing room door and presented the Marquess Devereaux.

The men stood and exchanged greetings.

Julianna gripped the chair to gain the strength to stand.

Bennet was dressed impeccably in tan breeches and a dark blue coat, yet she saw rippling muscles and firm buttocks. He smiled at the agents, though she remembered his open-mouthed moans of pleasure.

When he faced her, she dipped a curtsey and kept her gaze rooted to the floor. That didn't stop her core muscles turning traitor, clenching in a desperate hope he'd come to fill the emptiness.

Mr Daventry told everyone to sit.

Bennet sat facing her, on the sofa occupied by the master of the Order.

Heat pooled between her thighs when their eyes met. The corners of his mouth curled as he perused her slowly from head to toe. Was he imagining every naked curve? Was he remembering how she'd writhed beneath his hard body, gripped his sweat-soaked back and cried his name?

"Sorry I'm late. It's been an eventful few days." Bennet rubbed his solid thigh the way he'd palmed his manhood.

So, he must have visited Mr Daventry this morning, must have left Witherdeen before the cock's crow. She envisioned him waking, stretching his strong limbs, dipping his hand beneath the coverlet to massage his erection, hoping he might tempt her to sin again. He must have rolled onto his side and suddenly realised she was gone.

"Might we open a window?" Julianna was so hot her cheeks burned.

Mr Cole obliged and raised the sash.

A tense silence ensued.

Was this how it felt to be Giselle de Lacy, to have every man's eyes fixed intently on her person? She could cope with an inquisitive stare or two, but Bennet Devereaux's gaze slid over her like a sensual caress.

"Mrs Eden's work at Witherdeen is incomplete." Thank God for Mr Daventry's comment, else she would likely combust. "Experience tells me one of your friends has a part to play in this, Devereaux. I presume they've all returned to town, bar Granger, who'd better be in Brighton."

"That's why I'm late. To my knowledge, Granger journeyed south, though I cannot attest to the fact he reached the coast."

With luck, he'd broken his neck in a carriage accident en route.

"Everyone else is in town," Bennet confirmed. "I did what you asked and have spent the best part of two hours reluctantly making amends. I blamed Granger for my angry outburst and for banishing them from Witherdeen, though I begrudge entertaining any of them again."

"Sometimes, a man must accept he's been living a lie." Mr Cole sounded as if he'd once come to a similar conclusion. "Lowbridge is a self-serving prig. A man needs a friend who challenges him to be the best version of himself."

Bennet thought for a moment. "He wasn't always that way. People change. Sadly, human nature leaves us clinging to what's familiar."

Overcome by the urge to defend Bennet, she said, "Strong men admit their mistakes. What matters is how one moves forward. And I believe Lord Roxburgh is a good friend."

"Indeed," Mr Cole agreed.

"Did you call on Miss Winters?" Mr Daventry said.

Hearing the woman's name sent another rush of blood to

Julianna's cheeks. Miss Winters truly was the ex-mistress now, because Julianna had inadvertently taken her place.

Bennet shifted in his seat. "No one seems to know if she is in town, though I'd rather suffer more threats than be seen in her company."

"Because you believe she is guilty of tormenting you?" Mr Daventry glanced at Julianna. "Or is there another reason you wish to avoid seeing your mistress?"

"As you know, Miss Winters is no longer my mistress."

"May I ask what prompted the sudden change of heart?"

Bennet's brief look in her direction spoke volumes. "I meant to sever ties long ago. As Cole rightly pointed out, a man is often forced to accept he's living a lie."

"No doubt it's for the best," Mr Daventry replied. "You'll be looking to marry soon. Lady Perthshore said you can have the pick of the crop."

Jealousy twisted like knots in Julianna's stomach. Oh, she wished the ground would open up and swallow her whole.

"How did you fare with Mr Mullholland in my absence?" she quickly blurted. "A man who lost a substantial sum at the races might well set fire to a stable block."

"Mullholland is not our man."

"What makes you sure?" Other than Miss Winters, Mr Mullholland was the only one with any real motive. Who else had a reason to hate Bennet Devereaux?

Mr Ashwood snorted. "Are you sure you want to hear the details?"

"I bumped into Mullholland in the alley behind the Blue Jade." Mr Daventry's eyes darkened. "He was extremely forthcoming with information."

"But you said he's not our man." Bennet seemed confused. "And even if he was guilty, the scoundrel would never confess."

"Oh, he confessed. He spilt his guts and piddled his trousers. While he despises the ground you walk on, Devereaux, he is not the person responsible for the cowardly attacks. Mullholland paid his jockey to lose the race. His brother thought there was more money to be had betting on your horse."

Bennet shook his head. "The threats, the fight, it was all a ruse?"

"Indeed."

A sense of pride enveloped Julianna as she listened to Lucius Daventry's escapade. The man carried himself with such confidence, was so skilled at gathering information, he must have seen something worthwhile in her when he offered her the position.

That's why she could no longer remain silent. The life of an enquiry agent was not for her. Having lived with liars and deceivers, she wanted an honest means of earning a crust. Manipulating people to get to the truth might have appealed to her mother, but Julianna had a conscience.

She cleared her throat. "Sir, it has become apparent during the last few days that I am not equipped to work as an enquiry agent. I accepted the position in desperation, but it would be unfair to deprive someone else of the opportunity. Miss Gambit is eager to prove her worth, and I'm sure she will be of great help to Lord Devereaux."

"I have other plans for Miss Gambit."

Bennet sat forward. "I hired you, Mrs Eden, not Miss Gambit. I'll not waste time relaying the facts to a stranger."

Mr Daventry considered her through narrowed eyes. "Does this have anything to do with what happened at Witherdeen?"

Oh, it had everything to do with her loose morals. Not that she regretted what happened. She would throw herself into Bennet's arms in a heartbeat. But it was better to part now before she lost sight of reality altogether.

"I refer to the incident with Mr Granger," Lucius Daventry clarified.

"In my case, men will always presume the worst, but I cannot bear the lies."

"And where will you go?"

Far away from all temptation. "I have enough money to reach Paris and know someone who—"

"Paris! Good God!" Bennet shot out of his seat as if the cushion were ablaze. "Don't just sit there, Daventry. Put her mind at ease. Tell her she's wrong." He swung around to face her, confusion and panic warring in his handsome brown eyes. "They're not lies in the normal sense."

Mr Cole came to Bennet's defence. "We fight for the truth, for those who've suffered a great injustice. Lord Devereaux may be a man of power and means, but this deception is complex. I doubt he'll uncover the culprit without you."

"Three days," came Mr Daventry's cryptic reply. "Assist Lord Devereaux for three days. Do what is needed to solve the case, and then you may leave the Order with money enough to cover a year's rent in Paris."

Three days!

Heaven help her! During the two days at Witherdeen, she'd gone from pretending indifference to gripping Bennet's buttocks and panting his name.

Three days would be a true test of her resolve.

Like Mr Mullholland's horse, she would likely fall at the first hurdle.

●

Julianna had been torn away from him one stormy night, had escaped in the early hours the second time, but Bennet would be damned if he'd let her flee again. His heart still hadn't recovered after waking and finding her gone. This time, he wasn't restricted by age or lack of resources. This time, he'd been hot on her heels.

"You're confident we'll find the culprit in a few days?" he said.

"Less if we all work together." Daventry sounded optimistic. "It's imperative we solve the mystery before the villain discovers Mrs Eden is an enquiry agent."

In helping him, had Julianna placed herself in danger, too? Surely the culprit was out to torment him, not murder him in his bed.

"That's another reason why I think you should see this case to the end, Mrs Eden," Daventry continued. "If you're to leave for Paris, I'd rather you do so knowing no one bears a grudge."

"It seems I have little choice, sir." Julianna's shoulders

slumped with the weight of her burden. "I'll not spend the rest of my days fearing a reprisal."

"We do have a problem, one that might make you reconsider." Bennet had to be honest with her, though he feared she'd have every reason to run now. "Lowbridge told his sisters what happened with Granger. They cornered me when I arrived this morning and begged to hear how I thumped their cousin for attacking my mistress."

"Your mistress!" Daventry did not look pleased.

Julianna paled.

"You denied the fact, surely," Ashwood said.

"Of course. I explained we were old friends." Though after their rampant night of passion, his tone had carried a distinct lack of conviction.

"I'm afraid it's all my fault," Julianna confessed. "While attempting to deter Mr Granger, I said I was Lord Devereaux's mistress. It never occurred to me the devil would admit to behaving so disgracefully, let alone explain every sordid detail."

"When it comes to gossip, young ladies are rarely discreet," Cole said.

True. Lowbridge's sisters thrived on spreading tales.

"It may yet serve as an advantage." Daventry took up his notebook. "Let's begin again. Tell me everything that happened at Witherdeen, including the ghostly sightings."

The men of the Order listened to the tale. Bennet added relevant information regarding the third note, the clothes worn at the masquerade, of the monk he saw entering the abbey and how he beat Granger when in truth he wanted to murder the bastard.

"And you left Witherdeen after your encounter with Granger," Daventry stated. "Bower said you were crying when you woke him and begged him to bring you back to town."

Julianna failed to look Daventry in the eye. "Is that not to be expected after suffering a trauma?"

Bennet's heart thumped fiercely. Why had she not woken him? Had their lovemaking been so disappointing she'd decided to run? And yet she'd kissed him like he was the air she needed to breathe. Had writhed beneath him like she would die without his touch.

"Based on the facts, who do you think sent the notes to Lord Devereaux?"

Julianna thought for a moment. "Evidence suggests Miss Winters and an accomplice, a man. Her coming to stay at the coaching inn in Bramley rouses suspicion, yet her motive is weak. Too weak to make sense."

"People do foolish things in the name of love," Ashwood added.

Julianna glanced at Bennet, her mind most definitely occupied with thoughts of them naked together in bed. Had her love for the boy she'd lost caused her to behave recklessly with the man she'd found?

"Isabella Winters doesn't give a damn about me," Bennet said. The woman cared about money and grasping any opportunity to rise above her station. "While Granger confessed to bringing her to Bramley, I'm convinced my housekeeper saw her at Witherdeen two days before the guests arrived."

"Then we need to focus our attention on Miss Winters to either prove or disprove your theory." Daventry turned to Cole. "Ride to the coaching inn in Bramley today and find out how many times Miss Winters has stayed there during the last month. Ask if anyone came to visit her at the inn. And call at Witherdeen and inspect the ruins. Devereaux will give you a letter to present to the housekeeper."

Cole nodded.

"Say you're an artist, sir, come to sketch the abbey. Mrs Hendrie is expecting my colleague, and in a panic, I gave your name." Julianna paused. "There are two other possibilities I think deserve a mention."

"We are all ears, Mrs Eden."

Julianna shifted in her seat. Nerves saw her catch her lower lip with her teeth. Eventually, she said, "What if my mother is alive? What if her mind is so fractured she's come to punish her old lovers? It sounds far-fetched, I know, but when I questioned Mrs Hendrie about the ghost, the likeness to Giselle is uncanny."

Daventry frowned. "I am more inclined to believe the housekeeper has a vivid imagination. Or Miss Winters did not arrive with Granger as stated. How could it be your mother when she left the gold dress behind? I can send word to Paris, but it will take weeks to receive a reply." He paused. "I will send for confirmation if it will settle your fears."

"Yes, I would like to know for sure," she said so quietly and with such sorrow in her eyes, Bennet wanted to cross the room and hold her hand.

"And the second possibility?"

Julianna cleared her throat. "Mr Weaver, the steward who preceded Mr Branner, was dismissed due to discrepancies in his bookkeeping."

"Mr Weaver had been purchasing goods at inflated prices for years, splitting the profits with his supplier." Bennet had also discovered deliberate accounting errors, stolen sums amounting to a few thousand pounds. "My father chose not to prosecute. What man wants to appear foolish amongst his peers?"

"And where might we find Mr Weaver?"

"He had family in Farnborough, but that's all I know."

Silence descended while Daventry consulted his notes.

Bennet looked at Julianna. While part of him wished he could go back to the moment before she'd found the bangle in his coat pocket, wished he would have kept his cock in his trousers because it would have given him more time to forge a friendship, he longed to know her intimately again.

Now he feared it was too late.

How could they be friends when the need to touch her proved maddening? What was the point of trying when she would be gone from his life again in a few short days?

Daventry, in his infinite wisdom, decided to take charge of the problem. "Ashwood, where should Devereaux and Mrs Eden focus their attention?"

Ashwood cleared his throat. "They should spend the afternoon reading through the journals Mrs Eden brought from Witherdeen. Checking for anything that may seem pertinent. They need to provoke a reaction from Miss Winters and should do so by flaunting the fact Mrs Eden is Devereaux's new mistress."

Julianna inhaled sharply. "If Miss Winters doesn't care about the marquess, why would it matter?" She looked like she would rather do a stint in the Marshalsea than be seen about town on his arm.

"We need to know if that's true," Daventry said. "Men invariably underestimate women's emotions. What other motive could she have for visiting Witherdeen?" He gestured for Ashwood to continue.

"They should attend Lord Newberry's Winter Ball tomorrow evening. With the information you hold on Newberry's nefarious deeds, it won't be difficult to secure Mrs Eden an invitation. Devereaux should encourage his friends to join them. Mrs Eden can ply the women with punch, coax them for information about Miss Winters, Lowbridge and Roxburgh."

"Devereaux should confide in Roxburgh," Cole added. "Explain someone is trying to kill him and see how the lord responds. If Roxburgh is innocent of any wrongdoing, the evidence should support his claims. If he's guilty, he will try to throw Devereaux off his trail."

Daventry clapped his hands in agreement. "You will both attend Lord Newberry's Winter Ball tomorrow evening. Let the gossips have their day. Let everyone believe you are following in your father's footsteps and have taken Julianna de Lacy as your mistress." He raised a hand when Julianna opened her mouth to protest. "You'll be gone from London in a few days, Mrs Eden, leaving Devereaux to deal with the aftermath. Let's do everything we can to put an end to his torment."

After some thought, she sighed. "Yes. Lord Devereaux's happiness is of the utmost importance. I only hope it won't hinder his plans to find a wife."

Find a wife!

Did she honestly think that was his priority now?

Daventry rubbed his jaw. "There is a slight problem. I cannot have the villain following you back to Howland Street. With Devereaux's permission, you will move into his London home for a few days, until you leave for Paris. Protecting the ladies in Howland Street must be a priority. Surely you see that."

While Julianna blanched, Bennet resisted the urge to throw

himself at Daventry's feet and pay homage to the genius. He had three days to—to do what? Bury himself so deep in her body she'd never want to leave? Beg her to stay and become a permanent part of his life?

Either way, his plan was flawed.

He didn't want her as his mistress.

She was worth a damn sight more than that.

CHAPTER 13

CONFUSED, Julianna stood in the hall of Bennet's lavish town-house in St James' Square, trying to determine why she felt instantly at home. It had nothing to do with the luxurious surroundings. During her formative years, she had grown accustomed to living in grand mansions. Perhaps it had something to do with the lingering scent of Bennet's cedarwood cologne. A smell that roused memories of her kissing his neck, nipping his bare shoulder, memories of the only man who'd ever touched her heart.

"Lord Devereaux is expecting you, Mrs Eden. I shall inform him you've arrived." The hint of disrespect in the butler's tone soured her mood. He glanced at her shabby valise as if it were a mangy dog. "I'll have a footman take your *things* upstairs, madam."

He spoke of the box Mr Bower had deposited on the parquet floor. A box containing the journals she had stolen while Bennet slept naked in bed.

"Have a footman deposit the box in his lordship's study." Julianna spoke with a confidence belying her station. While it felt unnatural to be anything but kind, her stay would be unbearable if the servants thought her weak. To them, she was the harlot corrupting their master. A strumpet. A whore.

Beyond the grave, Giselle must be clapping her hands with glee.

Bennet appeared at the top of the stairs. "Julianna."

Two hours had passed since she'd left him in Hart Street. Still, it took an immense effort to calm her racing heart. She tried to keep her gaze locked on his face as he descended, yet stealing a glimpse at his muscular thighs proved too tempting to resist.

For the next three days, she would be living in purgatory. A torturous place where heaven was but a heartbeat away. A place for sinners to face their temptations and repent, repent, repent. But how could she fight these damnable cravings when Bennet gripped her arms and kissed her forehead as if she were his dearest treasure?

"Come, let me give you a tour of the house." His velvet voice melted her insides. "Let me show you to your room."

The butler presumed Bennet meant to spend the afternoon frolicking upstairs because he said, "Do you still wish to dine at seven, my lord?"

"Unless Mrs Eden would care to dine later."

"Seven is perfect." She turned to the sour-faced grouch. "We'll be in his lordship's study, examining historical text. Have a bath drawn at six, so I might wash and change before dinner."

"I shall inform the maid at once, madam." The butler inclined his head and probably couldn't wait to tell the servants that their master's mistress was a fussy trollop.

"Excellent." Bennet grabbed her hand and drew her upstairs. "Let me show you my bedchamber. Then you'll know where to come should you suffer a nightmare."

She was already living a nightmare.

At no point had she planned to become any man's mistress.

Before she could protest, he pulled her inside an overtly masculine room akin to the devil's boudoir. The second she glanced at the impressive tester bed, she imagined them writhing naked atop the counterpane.

Bennet closed the door.

With the click of the latch, all pretence slipped.

Wearing an arrogant grin that was almost predatory, he prowled towards her, forcing her back against the bedpost.

"Now we're alone, you'll tell me why you ran." He braced his hands above her head, caging her in a masculine prison. His hot breath breezed across her cheek, sending her mind whirling. "Why did you not wake me? I might have persuaded you to stay. You didn't even wait to say goodbye."

His sensual drawl penetrated her reserve. The raw power of his presence left her floundering. She swallowed deeply, remembering the hardness of his body, the mastery in every delicious stroke.

"Isn't it obvious?"

"If it were obvious, I wouldn't have asked."

"It seemed better to leave than prolong the agony." She hated how that sounded. Cold. Heartless. The need to soothe him surfaced. "Bennet, I'll reiterate what I said before. Being friends will only lead to heartbreak." That hadn't stopped her from succumbing to her carnal appetites or running away when, in truth, she'd wanted to stay. "The memory of being dragged away on that stormy night still hurts, and I cannot bear the thought of saying goodbye to you again."

"You presume the outcome will be the same."

"How can it be any different?"

The more time they spent together, the deeper she'd fall. Their lovemaking proved they had an undeniable bond. And even if in some far-fetched fantasy she might marry the only man who'd made her feel cherished, special, even if they could weather the storm—a marquess did not wed a strumpet's daughter—their children would forever bear the mark of shame. After all she had suffered, she couldn't inflict that indignity on another poor soul.

She saw the same conflict in his eyes. "Bennet, it was inevitable we'd end up in bed. We both craved the connection we shared years ago. But we're adults now with the sense to know what's right." And yet nothing about being with him felt wrong.

"What's right for us or society?"

"Your birthright means they are one and the same."

He touched his forehead to hers and sighed. "I can't stop

thinking about last night. The need to be close to you, to move inside you, is driving me insane."

Every muscle in her core throbbed. All she need do was look up, and in seconds his mouth would be ravaging hers. Instead, she pushed his chest with what little strength she could muster and forced him to straighten.

"We've work to do. Three days is no time at all. Let us focus on that."

Their physical desires would wane. Protecting their hearts mattered most. It was too late for her. She wanted him more than she could ever express in words. And she had been selfish enough already.

"Say I'm not the only one suffering," he pleaded. "Say it."

"Stop. Stop making it so hard. Direct me to my bedchamber. I shall meet you in the study in ten minutes to examine your father's journals. He must have left some clue. It's a shame the trunk is at the cottage." She had taken to babbling like Miss Ponsonby.

"I brought a handful of books with me. The evidence may lead us back to Witherdeen, and we can examine the rest of the journals then."

She could never go back to Witherdeen but didn't have the heart to tell him. Hopefully, Mr Cole would conduct a thorough investigation when he visited. She would be keen to hear his opinion of Mr Branner.

"Then let us start at once. If I could just have a few minutes alone in my bedchamber," to cry and console herself, to climb onto the bed, hug the pillow and pretend it was the master of the house, "and then we'll get to work."

Bennet inclined his head. "You can access your room through the adjoining door." He gestured to the right of the large mahogany armoire. "You'll find the key on your nightstand."

"You put me in the marchioness' suite?" Lord, no wonder the butler seemed aggrieved. "Bennet, you cannot put your mistress in a room soon to be occupied by your wife."

He arched a mischievous brow. "You're not my mistress, and I have no definite plans to marry. Does a dear friend not deserve the best chamber in the house?"

"Everyone thinks I'm your mistress. When the *ton* discovers what you've done, they'll think you've inherited your father's obsession."

"I don't give a damn what they think. It's a delightful room, and I want you to feel comfortable. Besides, we're already courting scandal. Most men provide houses for their lovers, not move them into their family home."

She supposed he had a point. But how in Lucifer's name could she sleep knowing he was naked in bed next door? The need to solve the case quickly suddenly became more important than ever.

"I'll visit the bedchamber later. Let's take tea in the study while we examine the journals. We've got two hours until I need to wash and change for dinner. We should be able to get through a few by then."

She left the room without waiting for a reply. Bennet followed behind. His butler kept an impassive expression when ushering the maid out of the study, but he must have wondered why they were not thrashing about in bed.

Seated on the opposite side of Bennet's desk, and after sipping a calming cup of tea, Julianna delved into the box and handed Bennet a journal.

"In the journal I read at Witherdeen, your father wrote about his father's passing and inheriting the marquessate. What's strange is the title on the first recto page."

Bennet settled back in the chair behind his desk. "You mean the one where he fears everyone wants to murder him in his bed?"

"Did he ever have cause to fear for his life?" Giselle always said she'd stab him with a letter opener should he ever darken her door again.

"Not that I'm aware. He severed contact with all family members when he inherited. That's when he started recording his feelings. Until then, I believe he kept his outrageous thoughts to himself."

Julianna reached for her notebook and pencil. "Tell me what you know about your uncles." She scribbled Charles Devereaux's name. "I recall you mentioning Charles was heir presumptive before you were born."

"Yes, Charles was a year younger than my father. John, three years younger. Charles had two sons who both died in infancy. Uncle John's only son is John Devereaux, the current heir presumptive serving on *The Argyle*."

"Did you ever meet them?"

"No. Uncle John came to Witherdeen once. My father threw him out."

"When was this?"

Bennet shrugged. "My father wrote about it in a journal. It was an argument about money. Uncle John invested in a scheme based on the word of a good friend. He lost a substantial sum before learning my father had paid the friend to lie."

The depth of the late marquess' deception was sickening. "How awful. To be tricked by one's own brother."

Bennet glanced at his father's elegant penmanship in the open journal on his desk. "I tried to love my father. At least, I tried to love the man I knew in those latter years. But he behaved despicably. His terrible deeds were driven by unfounded fears."

She remembered the awful beatings, the cruel taunts. Why would anyone want to love a monster? But she understood. For all the mistreatment she had suffered, she always hoped her mother would change. Besides, she had not lived Giselle's life or walked in her shoes and so could not judge.

"We tried to love our parents even though they struggled to love us in return." Surely that said a lot about their characters. "Neither of us inherited their bitterness. Each new generation should learn from the last, and we're certainly a testament to that."

Bennet's weary sigh touched her heart. "It might have been easier to fail."

"Much easier." Julianna had lost count of the times she had been offered an exorbitant amount of money to sleep with men. "But I admire your desire to raise strong sons, good men who will make a difference to the world."

"Privilege comes with a responsibility I cannot ignore."

"No. You have a duty to king and country." Thoughts of her future pushed to the fore. Would she ever be happy without Bennet? "Perhaps one day I will marry again, have spirited daughters who will defend their sisters' rights to freedom. Daughters who never have to beg at the Registry."

Bennet held her gaze. "Daughters as remarkable as their mother."

Heat rose to her cheeks. "You've always been kind to me, Bennet, though you're often prone to exaggeration. I never did see that giant fish you caught."

"It was so big it almost snapped the line."

They both laughed, fell quickly silent. She suspected his thoughts turned to their childhood, to that one blissful summer she would sell her soul to experience again.

They continued reading until the mantel clock chimed five.

"John Devereaux died not long after he lost a fortune in the mining scheme."

"Yes, in 1801. The year my mother died."

She had no wish to stir painful memories but had to say, "It was a riding accident, I recall."

Bennet responded by handing her the journal he had been reading. The pages bore his father's deluded suspicions and outpourings of grief.

"My mother fell from her horse and broke her leg. She'd told the groom she was heading across country to Bramley, but they found her the next morning in a field near Turgis Green. She died of exposure to the elements."

"And you were four?"

"Yes, I have vague memories of her."

Her heart sank. Loss tainted Bennet's childhood. The loss of his mother and the loss of his best friend. Had it affected him more deeply than she'd known?

"When we left Witherdeen, did your father bring another mistress into the house?" It could be pertinent to the case.

"No. As I said earlier, men rarely move their mistresses into their family home. Your mother was the exception."

"Giselle had rules. She refused to hide in the shadows. If a man wanted her, he had to declare it openly, treat her like a duchess." Her mother had oozed class and elegance until her latter years. Until the loss of her looks led to her addiction.

Bennet sat forward. "Then why did you agree to stay here, knowing people would assume you were following in her footsteps?"

"I owe Mr Daventry a debt I must repay. And I cannot leave England without knowing you're safe." She was destined to spend her life worrying about his happiness.

"You don't care that people will compare you to her?"

She would never be as beautiful as her mother.

Giselle de Lacy's allure drew men in droves.

"Moths don't become butterflies. But I shall play the role for your sake, and because Mr Daventry's generous gift will give me plenty of time to find my way in Paris. Who knows? I might enjoy teasing the *ton* for a while."

She expected an amusing quip about the upper echelons, but Bennet suddenly shot out of the chair. "Leave now, Julianna, before it's too late. Go. Take as much money as you need. I have a property in Scotland. It's yours. Do what is right for you, not for me or Lucius Daventry."

Stunned by his sudden outburst, she struggled to form a reply.

"What do you want, Julianna? I can tell you it's not to have the *ton* call you a whore or have people think I'm paying to bed you."

"We have been intimate. And you are paying me a fee."

"You know damn well there is no correlation between the two. I'm paying Daventry a fee. And we were intimate because ... because when we're together, the feelings are too powerful to ignore."

He was right on both counts. "It's too late, Bennet. Mr Lowbridge and his sisters will have told half a dozen people or more. By tonight, it will be the topic of conversation in most ballrooms. We have no choice but to see this through to the end." To the bitter end, for their parting would bring great sorrow.

"I'll tell them they're mistaken."

"The curtain twitchers have seen me entering your house

with my valise. And what if the villain decides to hurt me to punish you?"

The comment had him flopping back into his seat. "Then leave for Scotland, not Paris. It's a pretty shooting lodge on a loch overlooking glorious mountains. You'll love it there."

If she had learnt anything from her mother, it was not to become attached to beautiful places.

"And where is the nearest town? Fifty miles away, no doubt. Bennet, I'm tired of being alone and need to find work, meet new people. I like Paris." She glanced at the mantel clock, desperate for a distraction. "Heavens. Time runs away when we're together. We must finish reading the journals tonight. I cannot afford to disappoint Mr Daventry."

With a disgruntled sigh, he buried his head in another book.

It was no good. She couldn't concentrate, not when she could feel Bennet's burning gaze. Oh, she had to be the worst enquiry agent in living memory. If only she had Rachel's strength and determination. Rachel was as skilled and as quick-witted as the men and would solve her first case quickly.

"Did you leave the cottage the second I fell asleep?" Bennet's husky whisper captured her attention. "When I moved inside you, pushed so deep you cried out with pleasure, were you thinking about making your escape?"

Her sex pulsed at the memory. She couldn't tell him that she'd watched him sleeping for so long she'd almost stayed. She couldn't tell him that she loved him as much now as she did when they were children. Daren't tell him the feelings were more profound.

"I lay there not knowing what to do."

"You didn't consider how I might feel when I woke to find you gone?"

If she had, she wouldn't have left. "If I'd stayed, we would have made love again and—"

"Again and again because I could never tire of having you."

The room grew suddenly hot. Julianna looked to the mantel clock, wishing the hands would move faster, hoping the dour-faced butler would knock on the door, so she never had to think about her reply. Never have to acknowledge that his choice of words reminded her of her mother's stark warning.

Men are governed by their appetites. They confuse lust with love.

"I left because I don't want to hurt you any more than I have already. I left because we're different people from different worlds. In bed, those things don't matter. Tomorrow, at the Winter Ball, I suspect we will both receive an unwelcome dose of reality."

And he was wrong. He would tire of her, tire of the cuts direct, tire of being looked down upon by his peers. She had seen the game play out so many times she knew not to pin her hopes on a fantasy. When she drew her last breath, was it not better to remember those magical moments than die angry and bitter?

Thankfully, the butler knocked to say the maid was ready and waiting in the bedchamber.

Julianna informed him she would be along shortly, then gathered two journals. "I think it best I take a tray in my room this evening. After a hectic few days, an early night is in order. You must be tired, too."

"I doubt I shall sleep tonight."

She wouldn't sleep either. "Perhaps you can study the journals, and we can discuss our findings during breakfast tomorrow." At breakfast, she wouldn't drink too much wine and be tempted to straddle his lap.

"I'm to ride on the Row with Roxburgh in the morning and must visit Lowbridge to make sure he attends the ball. Daventry has arranged for you to visit his wife's modiste. The woman is said to work miracles, and I imagine you'll be out for most of the day."

Julianna inwardly groaned. She could wear a gown made entirely of jewels and would still walk in her mother's shadow.

"Mrs Sloane is to meet me at the modiste and take me to her house in Little Chelsea." Arriving separately seemed unnecessary, but Mr Daventry insisted it would create more of a stir and allow Miss Winters to speak privately with Bennet. "I shan't see you now until the Winter Ball."

He held her gaze, the few seconds stirring something deep inside. "You will save a dance for me tomorrow?"

She would save everything for him, every dance, every kiss. "Of course. We must make Miss Winters believe I have replaced her in your affections."

Again, he stared for the longest time. "Good night, Julianna. Should you change your mind about dinner, or anything else, don't hesitate to come and find me."

"Good night, Bennet."

She left the room, spent the night alone with his father's journals and the unbearable craving that gave her some appreciation for her mother's wretched plight.

CHAPTER 14

J ULIANNA HAD WITNESSED many wild parties from curtained hideaways and doors left ajar, though she had never wished to join the rowdy rabble. People behaved foolishly. Acted like buffoons. Lay comatose after consuming ridiculous amounts of punch and champagne.

Themed balls were the worst. Guests hid behind disguises to excuse their vulgar manners, to piddle in potted ferns, and explain why they'd climbed into bed with the wrong goddess Venus.

Lord Newberry's Winter Ball should have been the exception.

The ballroom glistened like a magical ice kingdom. Footmen wore silver coats and silver breeches, sported silver laurel wreaths in their hair. White chiffon cascaded down walls, and candlelight sparkled in crystal icicles hanging from huge chandeliers.

It would have been the perfect setting if not for the gentleman tearing his tongue from an ice sculpture while his drunken friend mounted a stuffed stag.

Despite the distractions, heads whipped in Julianna's direction.

"Pay them no mind." Vivienne Sloane clutched Julianna's arm

and gave an encouraging squeeze. "I imagine they're jealous of your magnificent gown. It fits you like a glove."

"It's a little tighter than a glove." Julianna placed her hand on her abdomen to calm her breathing. "And I never bare my shoulders."

She shouldn't complain. Under Mrs Daventry's expert supervision, Magdalena had spent eight hours sewing glass beads to the bodice, ensuring the silk skimmed every natural curve.

"What a shame you're not a courtesan," Vivienne whispered. "The way men are gawping, you could name your price." The lady caught herself. "Forgive me. I meant it as a compliment, though I imagine you see it as an insult."

Julianna smiled reassuringly. "My mother played one lord against another. No amount of money would induce me to do the same." There was only one man's attention she craved.

People spoke in hushed whispers as Julianna passed. Men ogled every inch of exposed flesh. Ladies lowered their handheld masks and stared at her wild red curls and elegant gold gown. Their sneers and sly grins spoke volumes, and the name *Giselle de Lacy* drifted through the room on a bitter breeze.

This was what Julianna had spent her life avoiding—the daggers of disdain, the lecherous grins, the judging, the snarls, the drooling.

"We're to stand near the fir tree with the frosted branches. Else my husband will never find us in the crush." Vivienne must have noticed the scornful looks hurled their way. "Hold your head high. It's that, or I draw my cutlass and show them what a pirate's granddaughter can do with a deadly weapon."

Julianna laughed. She was so grateful to have an ally. "I thought your grandfather was a privateer." Mr Daventry had given her a thorough briefing on his gentlemen agents and their wives.

"He was, but to this pompous lot, it still means pirate."

They waited near the fir tree for Mr Sloane to bring refreshments.

"Let's discuss the case before Lord Devereaux arrives. It can help to get a second opinion, and I love solving puzzles." Vivienne's eyes shone with barely contained excitement. "You can trust me, Julianna."

Vivienne and Evan Sloane had solved a complicated case orchestrated by their privateer grandfathers, and so Julianna had no qualms speaking of the strange events troubling the Marquess Devereaux.

"Evidence says Miss Winters has some part to play. But if there's one thing I know about courtesans, it's that they never form attachments to their lovers."

Enquiry agents shouldn't form attachments to clients either, but that hadn't stopped Julianna devouring Bennet Devereaux's mouth.

Vivienne nodded. "Is detachment not the primary rule of survival?"

"Indeed."

Yet Bennet was no ordinary man. He was intelligent, handsome, and kind. When he kissed her, all her doubts disappeared. A woman might easily fall in love with him. Julianna had.

"And you found nothing in the journals? Nothing to suggest a motive?"

"Nothing other than a delusional man's ramblings. The old marquess hated his family. He gave them grounds to murder him, yet neither brother sought revenge."

"And the only heir is five thousand miles away in India." Vivienne seemed to ponder that snippet of information. "What about his wife?"

"Mr Daventry mentioned her today when he came to speak to Magdalena about my gown." And to steal a few moments alone with his wife. "Mary Devereaux lives in Kent with her two young children. She's not left the village since her husband set sail for India over a year ago."

"Mr Daventry visited the modiste?" Vivienne was more interested in the gentleman's motive than finding someone with a reason to hurt Bennet. "What suggestions did Mr Daventry make regarding your fitting?"

"That the gown must be elegant, under no terms scandalous."

Vivienne's gaze skimmed the beaded bodice and modest decolletage. "It's a gown fit for a marchioness, not a mistress."

It was an exceptional dress. "Perhaps he felt guilty for persuading me to play Lord Devereaux's mistress and thought I should wear something demure."

"Guilty?" Vivienne scoffed. "Mr Daventry does whatever's necessary to solve a case. He's not shy about expressing his opinion."

Maybe he knew life in Paris would be difficult and wanted to show her the advantages of working as an enquiry agent.

"I assume you've named Mr Branner the prime suspect," Vivienne said.

Sadly, the steward was first on Julianna's list of those with opportunity and no motive. "He could have produced the obituaries, staged the scenes, and must have lied about the gravestone, but I'm baffled why he would bear the marquess any ill will."

After spending the morning with him in the village, she couldn't help but like Mr Branner. He was personable, had an aristocratic bearing. One might believe he was the illegitimate son of the marquess, but Bennet would have been made aware, and the old marquess had made no provision for Mr Branner in his will.

"Jealousy is often a motive. Jealous people torment their victims but rarely seek to murder them. It seems for all the threats, Lord Devereaux's life isn't in any real danger."

No, she supposed not.

So why did she feel an immense sense of dread?

"Jealous people are vindictive." Mr Sloane interrupted their conversation. With his long hair tied in a queue, he looked ready to plunder the high seas. He came bearing gifts—two frosted glasses of winter punch. "While they enjoy making their victims appear weak and foolish, one should never underestimate an opponent."

"Two opponents." Julianna took the proffered glass of punch.

"Mr Branner might be acting alone." Vivienne smiled at her husband and accepted her glass. "What evidence is there to suggest he has an accomplice?"

Julianna told them about Mrs Hendrie's ghost and that the third obituary was delivered to Lord Devereaux's London address. "Mr Branner has not left Witherdeen for two months."

"Miss Winters can't be the ghost. You said Granger brought her to Bramley. Mrs Hendrie saw the ghost two days before they arrived." Mr Sloane scanned the ballroom and gestured to a red-haired woman talking to two gentlemen near the grand fireplace. "From a distance, you look similar. Having heard of your imminent arrival, perhaps Mrs Hendrie imagined seeing you again."

Julianna caught Miss Winters' dismissive gaze. They looked similar, had the same porcelain skin and red curls, but it wasn't like staring into a looking glass. There was a noticeable difference. Miss Winters' arrogant bearing—the mark of any worthy courtesan—was so opposed to Julianna's quiet reserve.

"I'd be interested to know when Miss Winters returned to town," Julianna mused aloud. "Do you know when we might expect to hear from Mr Cole?"

"Cole will remain at Witherdeen until he secures the information he needs." Mr Sloane chuckled. "Let's hope his pencil sketches are up to par, else Branner may become suspicious."

The lively hum of conversation quietened. The crowd parted, and Julianna became the subject of backward glances and shared whispers.

Bennet appeared with his entourage. Miss Ponsonby gazed at the winter spectacle like a child witnessing her first snowfall. Mr Lowbridge left the group within seconds of entering the ballroom. Lord Roxburgh looked thoroughly bored, while Mrs Thorne stared upon the crass display with disgust.

Bennet craned his neck and scoured the room, disinterested in those trying to attract his attention. He was forced to converse with a matron who introduced him to a young woman with a dainty face and golden hair. She was graceful, timid enough to rouse faith in her character, a perfect wife for a powerful peer.

"Poor Lord Devereaux." Vivienne sighed. "He may reach us eventually."

"Hopefully before the supper gong," replied Mr Sloane.

A middle-aged gentleman stepped in Bennet's way and presented his daughters. Bennet smiled and spoke to both ladies, but continued to glance covertly over their heads.

Then Bennet saw her. Their eyes met across the crowded

room, and she struggled to catch her breath. Now she knew why her mother called love a sweet poison. Love radiated from her heart, warming every extremity. Love infused her being. But Bennet Devereaux could never be hers.

The reality was like a poison, a bitter and toxic thing slowly eating away at the happiness, the hope. The physical pain was almost unbearable.

Love is misery hidden in a bottle and passed as medicine.

The debutantes and courtesans didn't want Bennet Devereaux. They wanted his wealth and title, the power he wielded. Julianna wanted the man, wanted to hear his voice, feel his touch, talk to him until the early hours, laugh with him, make love to him, spend the rest of her days entwined in his embrace.

But they were two people from opposite ends of a spectrum.

Nothing could change that.

Julianna blinked when she heard her name. Lord Roxburgh appeared in her line of vision, looking elegant in black. He bowed as if she were of royal blood. "Mrs Eden, you look remarkable tonight."

Mrs Thorne's scowl slipped enough for the ice queen to say, "Gold suits you, Mrs Eden."

"Thank you. I'm like my mother in that regard. It's such a shame her gowns are missing." Not missing. Stolen.

Miss Ponsonby burst into the conversation and clutched Julianna's hand. "Mrs Eden, tell me you're well. How you've suffered at the hands of that dreadful beast. I knew there was something unsavoury about the devil. Thank heavens for Lord Devereaux."

"I'm perfectly well," Julianna lied. Every muscle in her body ached from the weight of this burden. The deceit, the battle to maintain a facade, it was all too much.

Julianna introduced Vivienne Sloane. Mr Sloane had crossed the ballroom to rescue Bennet, who had been waylaid by another swarm of admirers.

"We met at the circulating library," Julianna lied for the second time in as many minutes. "I had my head buried in a book about the dissolution."

Vivienne chuckled. "And I stumbled into her while engrossed in a tale of lost pirate treasure. X marks the spot and all that."

"How fascinating," Lord Roxburgh drawled in his usual languid fashion. "Unexpected encounters are always the best. Are they not, Mrs Eden?"

He knew! He knew she had been hired to help Bennet find a devious devil, not write tales about ghosts and a king desperate to seize assets. He knew every word out of her mouth was a lie.

"Everything happens for a reason, my lord."

"Life has a way of forcing us in certain directions, madam."

"I wish someone would force Lowbridge in this direction." Miss Ponsonby gestured to her lover, who stood with Isabella Winters. "The man cannot stay put for more than a minute."

Keen to stir up trouble, Mrs Thorne said, "Lowbridge has always admired Miss Winters. Perhaps you should hurry home and gather up your jewels, my dear. I hear our host is looking for a new paramour should you find yourself wanting."

It was Miss Ponsonby's turn to scowl. "You should hope Lord Roxburgh doesn't tire of his gaming haunts, else you will find yourself completely redundant."

Mrs Thorne's cheeks flamed. "Miss Winters came to Bramley to meet someone. Who's to say Lowbridge isn't dipping his toe in her pond?"

Had Isabella Winters come to meet Mr Lowbridge?

He seemed thoroughly bored of Miss Ponsonby's company.

Had Mr Lowbridge persuaded his cousin to act as the go-between?

"Miss Winters is warming the steward's bed." Miss Ponsonby beckoned them closer. "I saw her walking to his cottage when we were at Witherdeen in December. I believe she visits him often. If he were wealthy and titled, she'd be *his* mistress now."

The news came as no surprise. Julianna had suspected the couple were in cahoots. Loath to admit it, Mr Branner had to be Miss Winters' accomplice.

"Why dabble with a steward when you're bedding a marquess?" Mrs Thorne gasped as if she had made a terrible *faux pas*. "Forgive me, Mrs Eden. I should have spoken in the past tense. I hear you're Bennet Devereaux's current distraction. Though one wonders why he's chosen someone so similar."

Vivienne sucked in a breath. "You sound jealous, Mrs Prickle."

"It's Mrs Thorne," the woman snapped.

Julianna couldn't help but laugh at Vivienne's deliberate mistake. Even Lord Roxburgh pursed his lips to hide a grin. Oh, she would much rather spend time with the wives of enquiry agents than with these insipid women.

"Not jealous of you, Mrs Sloane. Who wants a pirate for a husband?"

"Yes, who wants a man who'd risk his life for one kiss? Perhaps it would be better to be ignored until the creditors come knocking."

Mrs Thorne gawped like a fish out of water and flounced off in a huff.

Lord Roxburgh's languid laugh confirmed he was shameless. "What I lack in funds, I make up for in wit, Mrs Eden."

"Let's hope wit is enough when it comes to securing a bride, my lord."

Roxburgh snorted. "Do I look like a man keen to wed?"

"There are many advantages to marriage. Soon, you might find yourself in need of a large dowry."

"Roxburgh, you'll have to marry at some point," Miss Ponsonby chirped. "Think of your poor sister. With your reputation, she'll never make a good match."

"Did I hear the words *Roxburgh* and *marriage* in the same sentence?" Bennet appeared, looking breathtakingly handsome in black evening attire. "I'd sooner believe in ghosts than the prospect of my friend exchanging vows."

"And I'll wager my diamond-encrusted pocket watch you'll be married within the month, Devereaux." Lord Roxburgh glanced over his shoulder and met a host of ladies' stares. "They're queuing up like prized ewes at auction."

Nausea roiled in Julianna's stomach.

Thank heavens she'd be in Paris. Truly, she didn't care for the place, but in Paris, there'd be no risk of seeing the newly crowned Marchioness Devereaux swollen with Bennet's child.

Bennet exchanged pleasantries with Mrs Sloane and Miss Ponsonby. And then it was Julianna's turn to face the man who made her knees weak.

"Mrs Eden." The name she detested sounded erotic from his lips.

"My lord."

His intense amber gaze left a scorching trail over her bare shoulders. "You could steal a thousand hearts in that gown. Let's hope mine is the one you cherish." A slow smile teased the corners of his mouth. "I hear the first strains of a waltz, and you promised me a dance."

She knew what to expect when she placed her gloved hand on his sleeve. The ache coiled low and heavy. The sweet poison flooded her veins, her heart, her sex.

Focus on the case, she silently told herself.

"I'm glad you suggested dancing." She gripped Bennet's sleeve as he led her onto the floor. Their audience increased in number, but she ignored their smirks and mocking whispers. "It will give us an opportunity to discuss the case."

Bennet slipped his hand around her waist and pulled her close, a little too close she feared. "We're to make it look like we're in love. Daventry said the ruse will reap results."

Ruse? She had no trouble playing a woman besotted.

She placed her hand on his shoulder, relishing the hardness beneath her fingers. "No. Mr Daventry said to let people believe I'm your mistress, not pretend we're in love."

"I thought we could improvise. It might rile Isabella if she thinks I'm in love with you."

"What? You can fall in love so quickly?"

He pinned her with his heated gaze. "I've loved you all my life."

Those words—those tender, heartwarming words that brought a rush of euphoria—caused her to misstep. Bennet used his skill on the floor to sweep them into a turn.

"Why must you say such things?" So much for focusing on the case. "Would you speak to Mrs Hendrie in this way?"

He laughed. "Thankfully, I did not take Mrs Hendrie to bed."

"You did not take me to bed. I issued the invitation." And it was becoming increasingly difficult not to do so again. "I know you like playing the dashing hero but—"

"I did charge across the lawn and save you from a fate worse than death. I have a faint bruise on my jaw as proof."

Drat! Yes, he had been magnificent in every regard. "You did, and I'm eternally grateful, but you mustn't say things you don't mean."

He firmed his grip and pulled her closer. "Did we not love each other as children? Are we not as attracted to each other now as we were then?" He grinned. "Well, perhaps it's not quite the same. You buried me in sand when we were young. Now I long to bury myself deep inside you."

She stumbled again. "If Monsieur Pernoir were here, he'd be cursing. All that money spent on dance lessons, all those hours wasted."

"You dance beautifully." He gripped her hand a little tighter. "And you look breathtaking in that gown. People aren't staring because of your lineage. They're staring because you're the most beautiful woman in the room."

Oh, merciful Mary!

"Are you trying to seduce me?"

"Trying implies one is likely to fail. *Determined* is the appropriate term."

Whatever she said, he would follow with something salacious. Best to stick to solving his problem, as she was being paid to do.

"Mr Ashwood was right to suggest coming tonight. Miss Ponsonby told me something you'll find interesting."

"Please tell me it has nothing to do with ghosts."

Julianna laughed. Miss Ponsonby was obsessed with the supernatural. "No. She said Isabella Winters had secret liaisons with Mr Branner. By all accounts, she visits him in his cottage whenever she comes to Witherdeen."

Bennet firmed his jaw and muttered a curse. "The man needs lessons in loyalty. How the hell can I trust him to keep my accounts when he schemes behind my back?" His face paled in anger. "How long has it be going on?"

Those gathered around the dance floor, watching their every move, would assume they were arguing about Miss Winters.

"She didn't say, but it would explain why Miss Winters came to Bramley. We'll know if Mr Branner visited her at the coaching inn when Mr Cole returns."

Was that why Mr Branner had been so attentive to Julianna when they visited the village? Like Bennet, did he have a penchant for red-haired women? Or was he simply trying to befriend her, to discover what she was really doing at Witherdeen?

Julianna looked up at Bennet, but he was glaring at Miss Winters. "Let's confront her with what we know. We'll tell her Branner confessed. See if we can drag the truth from her lying lips."

"I doubt she'll speak to us." And they could hardly bundle the woman into a room and hold her captive. Still, Rachel Gambit wouldn't dally and dither. She'd simply walk up to Bennet's ex-mistress and demand an audience.

You're Giselle de Lacy's daughter.

You know how to command a room.

Rachel's words of encouragement flitted into Julianna's mind.

She lifted her chin. "You're right. A courtesan's reputation is based on her allure. Miss Winters will want to speak to me."

"To compare notes," he teased.

"She will want to know how I managed to steal you from her bed."

CHAPTER 15

LORD NEWBERRY'S library didn't smell of musty old books or
tart ink, nor did it carry the woody aroma one expected from a
room lined with oak shelves. Stale cheroot smoke clawed at
Bennet's throat, along with the unmistakable tang of a sexual
encounter.

The couple who'd vacated the dark room mere moments ago
had done more than seek a quiet place away from the din of the
ballroom. They'd been rampantly celebrating their alliance.

Bennet crossed the room and took his position behind the
thick curtain, his thoughts turning to Julianna, as they always did
of late. He laughed to himself, recalling he'd been a boy of ten
the last time he'd taken to snooping in the darkness. Julianna had
asked what their parents did when they locked the study door
and made an awful racket.

"They're shouting and banging yet sound oddly happy."

Bennet chuckled aloud at the memory.

No boy wanted to see his naked father tied to a chair while
his mistress bounced on his lap. No girl wished to see her
mother sliding up and down a stiff cock. Julianna had squealed,
and all hell had broken loose.

They'd been kept apart for two weeks after that. Yet each
night, they crept from their beds at the witching hour and met
secretly within the shadowy walls of Witherdeen Abbey.

His mind turned to the night she'd been prised from his grasp and dragged into Denver's carriage. They could have ripped his heart from his chest and it would have been less painful. After falling into a permanent state of melancholy, his father sent him away to school, then Eton, then St John's College, Cambridge. He'd made friends, focused on his studies. Soon Julianna became nothing but a beautiful memory, one he visited nightly during those peaceful moments before sleep.

The creak of the library door jerked Bennet from his reverie. He parted the curtains a fraction and peered out into the gloom. Two people entered and quickly closed the door. The couple began conversing in breathless pants, then lunged and locked lips.

Hellfire!

A guttural groan rent the air. "God, Maria, you drive me wild."

"Be quick. My husband thinks I'm in the retiring room. Hurry!"

The devil's grunts accompanied the rustling of material and a pleasurable moan as he thrust home. Forced to listen to the woman's crude descriptions of his actions, Bennet winced.

"That's it! You're in! Yes! I feel you now, Lowbridge."

Lowbridge!

Good God! Did Miss Ponsonby know of her lover's indiscretion?

"How lovely. Good Lord! I'm taking all of you. How delightful."

"Hush."

"Yes! What a fine instrument!"

"Then be quiet and focus on the rhythm."

"Yes! What a pretty tune!"

"Madam, I cannot finish if you keep talking."

Poor Lowbridge attracted women with a penchant for rambling.

"But you're so hard, sir. I might be coming. Yes! Oh, yes!"

"For the love of God, be quiet!"

"There's no need to be rude."

Bennet pursed his lips, but a snort escaped.

"Did you hear that?" Maria panted.

"Damnation! You'll have to suck me to completion."

Even with her mouth stuffed full, Bennet could hear the woman's incoherent mumbles.

Lowbridge finished on a frustrated groan.

Bennet shoved his fingers into his ears, fearing Maria might describe the gift Lowbridge had deposited in her mouth. He took to musing while he waited for them to straighten their clothes and leave.

Daventry's plan had been a stroke of genius. Or so Bennet had thought when the man suggested Julianna reside in St James' Square. Now he wasn't so sure. Pretending to love Julianna was as easy as breathing. Having her in his home posed no great hardship, even if he did walk around in a constant state of arousal.

But the niggling voice of his conscience grew louder, more insistent with each passing hour. Now it had taken to prodding and poking to get his attention. Everything about the situation was wrong. Bennet would emerge from this fiasco unscathed. The rakes would pat him on the back and welcome him to the elite club of men who'd bedded a de Lacy. The gossips might accuse him of being as fixated as his father, but his conquest would be forgotten when another on dit tickled their fancy.

The same was not true for Julianna.

She was the last person he wanted to hurt. But she would be forever tainted for only pretending to be his mistress. He'd not understood her need to leave for Paris. Paris! What the devil would she find in Paris that she couldn't find in London. Now he knew.

Peace. Freedom.

With a heavy heart, he made a snap decision. One he should have made the second he discovered she worked for Lucius Daventry. He would hire another agent. Give Julianna the money Daventry promised, drive her to Dover, watch her board a ship, knowing he would never see her again.

His throat tightened.

He would miss her more now than ever.

Bennet peered through a gap in the curtain, relieved to find Lowbridge and Maria had vacated the library. Suspicion surfaced.

Lowbridge's sneaky antics marked him as a devious devil. Cole had described the man as a self-serving prig. It was true. But had Lowbridge and Isabella concocted a scheme to torment him?

After bearing witness to tonight's caper, Bennet might black-mail his friend to get to the truth. Yes! He would rather threaten Lowbridge than have Julianna confront Isabella.

Bennet was about to yank back the curtain when the library door opened, and Isabella's irate voice severed the silence.

"This is tantamount to blackmail, Mrs Eden."

"I'm giving you an opportunity to prove your innocence." Julianna locked the door and removed the key. "Your actions suggest you have devious motives. Lord Devereaux intends to inform the magistrate you were trespassing on his land. That you started a fire in the stables. There are witnesses."

Damnation! Julianna had made her first mistake. Still, Bennet admired her courage in opting for a direct attack and was some-what relieved he'd not had to listen to the women discussing his skill, or lack thereof, in bed.

"Lord Devereaux is the acting magistrate while Sir Henry's replacement is being decided." Isabella gave a mocking snort. "What will Devereaux do? Report me to himself?"

A brief silence ensued.

"Who told you that? Mr Branner?"

"Who?"

"Mr Branner. The steward at Witherdeen. The man whose cottage you were seen entering. Your accomplice in the plot to murder the Marquess Devereaux. Incidentally, a new magistrate has been appointed. Lord Hankin is notoriously harsh in his punishments."

Clever.

"Who are these witnesses? Let me guess. That fusspot house-keeper and her army of miserable maids." Isabella huffed. "If this is a ploy to hurt your lover's ex-mistress, save your breath. Lowbridge has just made me an offer, and I'm inclined to accept."

Lowbridge! The sneaky rat.

Julianna's sardonic laugh sounded fake to Bennet's ears, hope-fully not to Isabella's. "What a shame you didn't arrive minutes earlier. While waiting in the alcove along the corridor, I saw Mr Lowbridge leave this room with a woman. They were both dishevelled, and he was busy fastening the buttons on his satin breeches."

"You're lying."

"I shall find the woman, and you can ask her yourself. The person who should be affronted is dear Miss Ponsonby. The man is scheming behind her back. Where is your loyalty to your friend?"

"Friend! She's an annoying harpy who never stops jabbering. Lowbridge wants rid of her. A pretty face and lush figure can only sustain a man for so long. As no doubt you will discover when Devereaux casts you aside and takes a wife."

The last jibe affected Julianna. She looked away to gather her composure. Isabella seized the opportunity to flex her fangs and inject more venom.

"We look so similar, Mrs Eden. Surely you must wonder who Devereaux is thinking of when he's bedding you. You're nothing more than a fresh bit of skirt. Someone to warm the bed while he chooses his marchioness."

Bennet gripped the curtain, ready to dart out of his hiding place and put Isabella firmly in her place. He'd been waiting an eternity for Julianna to return. Now, he'd be the one left behind —the one to mourn the loss.

But Julianna raised her chin and mustered her mother's courage. "You confuse me with other courtesans, Miss Winters. I'm a de Lacy. I say who deserves a place in my bed. I decide if it's to be the Marquess Devereaux. A de Lacy does not wait for men to tire of her as you have done. She rips out men's hearts and leaves them wanting."

Isabella gawped.

"Know this," Julianna continued with steely determination. "Mr Branner may not be a titled gentleman, but like all the pathetic lords here tonight, he knows how to manipulate women. During my short visit to Witherdeen, he invited me to his cottage on numerous occasions."

Curse the devil to Hades!

Bennet prayed it was another ruse to gain a confession. Even so, the urge to punch his steward left his fists throbbing.

"Perhaps Branner pitied you because you lack my sophistication," Isabella countered.

"Or perhaps Mr Branner discovered I am not Lord Devereaux's mistress, and it's merely a ruse to catch a criminal."

Good Lord!

Julianna was to play the doting mistress, not confess to being an enquiry agent. Would Daventry want her to reveal intimate details of her work? Shouldn't she consult her client before revealing his secrets?

Isabella's laugh held no hint of amusement. "You certainly take after your mother, Mrs Eden. You're full of elaborate tales."

Julianna must have read Bennet's mind because she started answering his questions. "I'm not supposed to reveal the fact I work as an agent of the Order. Have you heard of the Order?"

"The group of men who help peasants?" Isabella spat.

"The group of men who help the innocent and pursue the guilty."

Isabella burst into fits of laughter. "Oh, you are funny, Mrs Eden. An agent of the Order, indeed. As if anyone would employ a woman to solve crimes."

To Bennet's surprise, Julianna chuckled. "Truth be told, I'm a useless agent, and have tendered my resignation."

Isabella fell silent.

"Still, I am a de Lacy, and I intend to solve my only case even if I have to lie and cheat to uncover the truth. So you see, Miss Winters, I shall make your life a living hell unless you tell me what I want to know."

Isabella stood rooted to the spot.

"Of course, Lord Devereaux is wondering why I've been honest with you and not continued with our facade." Hell! Julianna gestured to the curtain. "You may show yourself, my lord. Miss Winters needs to realise we intend to see her incarcerated for her crimes against you."

Feeling like a boy caught spying on the maids, Bennet slipped out from his secret hiding place. Staying any embarrassment, he leant on a peer's trusty crutch—arrogance.

"Isabella." Bennet inclined his head. "Mrs Eden has shown you our hand, and now you're forced to wager your freedom in the hope she's wrong."

Isabella glanced nervously between them. "If Mrs Eden is not your mistress, why put an end to our arrangement?"

Bennet couldn't expect honesty from Isabella and then blatantly lie. "Ours was a casual affair. But I cannot entertain thoughts of another woman now I've rekindled my friendship with Mrs Eden." He could feel the heat of Julianna's penetrating stare. "Mrs Eden is an enquiry agent working for the Order. The men are ruthless when it comes to catching criminals, and the female agents are equally unrelenting."

Isabella touched her hand to her throat. "I assure you, I had nothing to do with the fire in the stable yard."

"Did you come to Bramley with Mr Granger?" Julianna said.

"Yes, but the devil left me there. I had to take the mail coach back to London." She pursed her lips as if she'd tasted something sour. "Travelling with commoners is the worst kind of punishment."

"Did Mr Lowbridge tell you why his cousin left in such a hurry?"

Isabella scanned Julianna's gown with some contempt. "Lowbridge said you encouraged Granger's affections in a bid to get Devereaux's attention."

Bennet stared down his nose. "Granger's a disgusting lech who preys on innocent women. I doubt he'll make the same mistake again. Why did you come to Bramley?"

"To visit a friend."

"Who?"

Isabella failed to reply.

"Mr Branner said you arranged to meet him," Julianna interjected. "He said you've been using him to hurt Lord Devereaux, though wouldn't say why. You gave him the handbills to leave at Witherdeen. You had a penny boy deliver a handbill to Lord Devereaux's house in St James' Square. The penny boy gave a statement. The woman who hired him fits your description."

Isabella jumped. "What the devil are you talking about?

What handbills? The boy must be mistaken. I'm not the only red-haired woman in London. Perhaps you sent it."

Julianna caught Bennet's gaze. "My lord, we're wasting our time here. I think it's best if Sir Malcolm Langley takes Miss Winters to Bow Street for questioning. We have the evidence from the coaching inn, the record of her secret visits to Bramley, and Mr Branner's testimony. I'm sure if a constable searches her apartment, he will find my mother's gold gowns."

Isabella paled.

Bennet sought to play along. "I'll not have the *ton* knowing my damn business. Sir Malcolm is rather brutal when interrogating suspects."

"I must advise against a soft approach, my lord. We must pass the evidence to Bow Street. Mr Daventry wants this case solved quickly, and Miss Winters refuses to co-operate."

"Wait!" Miss Winters glanced at the locked library door. "If I tell you what I know, will you let me leave without alerting Bow Street?"

Julianna sighed. "That depends on whether we think you're telling the truth. Mr Branner believes you're a devious minx."

"Branner is a lying toad. At least Granger admits he's an immoral reprobate." Isabella started shaking. Clearly Branner had hurt her in some despicable way.

"What did Branner do?" Bennet wondered if beating profligates on his front lawn was to become a habit. That said, he'd not act solely on the word of this woman.

"You'd better tell us everything," Julianna added. "I'll not give you a second chance." She could be quite spirited when needed.

After a prolonged sigh, Isabella said, "I did pay a penny boy to deliver the letter, but Branner said it was a matter concerning the estate. I didn't know anything about handbills or why Branner would want to send one. But two nights ago, he asked me to deliver another."

Two nights ago?

She was consorting with Branner while Bennet dined with his friends?

"Another handbill?" Bennet gritted his teeth. He would murder Branner with his bare hands.

"A letter, but I broke the seal and saw what was inside. That's when I knew, knew he was trying to blame me for all the terrible things he's done."

Julianna's brow furrowed in suspicion. "Describe the letter."

"He had cut words from a newspaper and stuck them onto the page."

Isabella couldn't know the specific details unless she had seen the handbill or produced the letter herself.

"What did it say?" Bennet held his breath.

The way Isabella looked at Julianna chilled Bennet's blood. "It was a jumbled mess of words, terrible words about you, Mrs Eden. It said you died at the hands of your childhood friend. That it was a case of unrequited love. Consumed with sorrow, the Marquess Devereaux shot himself with a duelling pistol."

A heavy silence descended.

An unholy rage tore through Bennet. If he unleashed the violent tempest, he would throttle every man in sight. Perhaps that was Branner's intention. To have Bennet lose all sense and rationale. But why?

"Are you and Mr Branner lovers?" Julianna spoke in a voice thick with distrust. "Don't bother answering. Of course you are, else he wouldn't have asked for your assistance. How strange that you both blame each other."

"Are you partners in this bid to test my sanity?" Bennet growled.

"No!" Isabella reached for Bennet's hand but he stepped away. "What do you want me to say? That I was foolish enough to believe Branner's protestations? That because he's not a lord, I fell for his stories about love and marriage?"

"Did you?"

A tear trickled down Isabella's cheek. "He said we would move away. That he was to come into an inheritance and could support us both in the comfort to which I am accustomed."

Julianna sighed. "Believe actions, not words. That's what my mother always said though she rarely placed faith in either." She paused. "What else did Mr Branner ask you to do?"

"Nothing, other than I was to visit him at Witherdeen. We

arranged to meet at a coaching inn numerous times, but he came on one occasion."

Julianna gave a curious hum. "Were you to come to Witherdeen late at night and wait by the oak tree? Were you to wear my mother's gown? The one you stole from the attic?"

Isabella nodded. "He said he liked me in the gold dress. Told me to wait by the oak tree, and he would come when the coast was clear."

"You're lying!" Julianna snapped. "You couldn't have been at Witherdeen because Mr Granger brought you to Bramley two days later."

Bennet noticed the sudden flush rising to Isabella's cheeks. What excuse would she use to explain the cracks in her story? But then he realised it was a flush of anger, not embarrassment.

"Good God! You lied! You lied about having information from the innkeeper. Else you would know Granger brought me to Bramley two days early. You would know the devil made me share a room with him as payment for ferrying me from town."

Julianna's shoulders sagged. "I said I would lie to uncover the truth. Mr Granger took advantage of the situation, and my heart goes out to you, but you've deceived Lord Devereaux, and that's something I cannot condone."

Isabella thrust out her hand. "I'm leaving. Give me the key. I've told you everything I know and suggest you begin by questioning Branner. Ask Granger. He'll tell you that I called on him and asked him to ferry me to Bramley. He'll tell you that he agreed to leave right away and then proceeded to use me for his own end." Her hand started shaking. More tears fell, though she tried to fight the sudden sobs. "The k-key! Give me the damn key!"

Julianna gave her the key.

Isabella darted across the room. It took her three attempts to open the door, and then she was gone.

For a few seconds Bennet stared at the door. "Well, now we know who sent the handbills. Branner must have staged the scene with the gargoyle and lied about the gravestone."

"But Grimley saw the stone."

"Perhaps Branner caught him treasure hunting and threatened to tell me."

Julianna frowned. "You know about Grimley digging in the chapter house?"

"He's been doing it for years, hoping for a windfall. He's getting too old to work, and I thought to hide a pouch of sovereigns for him to find."

She shivered. "I get chills thinking about Mr Branner left to wreak havoc at Witherdeen. What if he should raze the house to the ground in your absence?"

"If that was his plan, he would have torched the house long ago."

"None of it makes sense. What motive could Mr Branner have for sending the letters, for lying and being so devious?"

Bennet shrugged. "I have no notion. We should speak to Daventry, have him accompany us to Witherdeen. After hearing about the handbill Isabella failed to deliver, I'll not take risks with your safety. Not until we've apprehended Branner."

The veiled threat had shaken her resolve, for she made no protest.

"Bennet, Mr Cole is at Witherdeen. Surely he should have been back by now. What if something terrible has happened to him? What if he's found evidence of Mr Branner's duplicity and your steward has attacked him with the sledgehammer?"

"There's not a man alive with the courage to threaten Finlay Cole." And yet a wave of dread washed over him. Branner knew the ruins better than anyone. Cole would be defenceless against a man pouncing in the dark. "Even so, we must leave for Witherdeen tonight."

Julianna looked up at him, her eyes swimming with unshed tears. "Bennet, I'm frightened. Frightened, Mr Branner has something terrible in store for you."

Bennet drew her into an embrace. He'd meant to hold her close, that's all, but he couldn't help but brush his mouth over her soft lips. She responded instantly, opening to him, letting him taste her fears, letting him explore every delicious aspect of her mouth.

The door burst open.

Julianna shot back and gasped in shock.

Lucius Daventry stormed into the library, dressed entirely in black and looking like a fallen angel. A haggard Finlay Cole followed behind and closed the door.

"Sloane said we'd find you here." Daventry scanned the room with his hawk-like gaze. "You're certain we're alone?"

"Indeed." Bennet's heart thudded.

From the grim look on Daventry's face, he was the bearer of bad news. Why else would the man attend a ball when he despised social events? And from Cole's dusty coat and windswept hair, he had recently returned from Witherdeen.

Had a fire ravaged Bennet's ancestral home? "Has something happened at Witherdeen?" Instinctively, he reached for Julianna's hand and gripped it tightly.

Daventry's dark gaze fell to their clasped hands. "There's no easy way to say this. The news will come as a shock." He paused, those silent seconds carrying the weight of his burden. "Branner is dead."

CHAPTER 16

"Dead? Mr Branner? How?" A host of gruesome scenarios formed in Julianna's mind. A blood-soaked body sprawled amid the ruins. The steward's charred remains unidentifiable amongst the rubble. She clutched a shaky hand to her chest. "Tell me there wasn't a fire. Tell me Witherdeen still stands."

A man had lost his life. Regardless of Mr Branner's deception, she should focus on how he met his untimely end. But Witherdeen was like a living, breathing thing. A custodian of the heart she'd left behind all those years ago.

Mr Cole cleared his throat. "Witherdeen stands. But Branner—"

"Wait!" Mr Daventry gripped Mr Cole's arm to silence him. "We'll discuss it in Hart Street. Find Sloane, and Devereaux's coachman, and tell them to meet us there. Say nothing to Devereaux's friends." His gaze shifted to Julianna's bare shoulders. "Have Vivienne collect Mrs Eden's cloak."

"May I ask when Mr Branner died?" Julianna recalled Miss Winters' statement. Was she the last person to see Mr Branner alive? Or had Mr Cole uncovered evidence that led to a fatal altercation?

"I'll not talk of it here," Mr Daventry reiterated in the stern voice only a fool would contest. "My carriage is waiting in the mews. We'll leave through the servants' quarters."

Without further discussion, Mr Daventry opened the door and beckoned them to follow. Mr Cole strode towards the ball-room while Julianna and Bennet took the back stairs, squeezed past harried servants in the corridors, and headed outside into Cavendish Square.

Bennet brought her to a halt on the pavement. "Wait. It's bitterly cold tonight. Wear this." He shrugged out of his coat and draped the garment around her shoulders. His fingers brushed the sensitive skin at her collarbone. More a lover's caress than an accident.

The last time she'd worn his coat, they'd made love in the cottage. Based on how he touched her, how her needy body responded, it was inevitable they'd make love again.

"Are you all right?" She noted his furrowed brow, the grim line of his lips. Since learning of Mr Branner's death, he'd hardly spoken, hadn't fired questions or demanded answers.

"There's nothing a man hates more than being taken for a fool. Still, I liked Branner and am at a loss to know why he'd want to hurt me."

Julianna quickly cupped his cheek, aware Mr Daventry stood staring at them from the cobbled alley leading to the mews. "We'll talk about it later. When we have all the facts." She forced a smile when Mr Daventry cleared his throat to hurry them along. "Perhaps it's a good thing I've tendered my resignation. Mr Daventry would never condone an agent fraternising with a client."

"Is that what we'll be doing later, Julianna, fraternising?" He captured her hand and pressed a lingering kiss to her palm. "Will we seek solace in each other's arms the way we did when we were children?"

Desire coiled in her belly. "We've both passed the point where a simple embrace will suffice."

She shouldn't say such things, but with Mr Branner dead, her work with Bennet Devereaux was almost at an end. Paris was but a heartbeat away. Soon they'd be hundreds of miles apart. The days would stretch to months, years, decades. The potent smell of his cologne, the rich cadence of his voice, the taste of his mouth, they'd be but distant memories.

Mr Daventry called their names and proceeded along the alley.

Suffering the disparaging glares from the ladies in the ballroom proved less intimidating than Mr Daventry's stare. He sat opposite them in his plush carriage, his unreadable gaze moving slowly from Julianna to Bennet to their hands resting less than an inch apart on the seat.

"How did Branner die?" Bennet gripped the overhead strap as the carriage lurched forward and clattered out of the mews. "Who found him?"

"He was beaten over the head numerous times with a poker. The coroner said he bled to death slowly, over a period of hours. Yesterday, when he failed to make an appearance to check the fire-damaged stable block, Mrs Hendrie went to his cottage."

Poor Mrs Hendrie. She must have had a dreadful fright.

"I need to return to Witherdeen tonight. I must put my staff at ease."

"A murder complicates matters. Once we've caught the culprit, the case will be heard at Crown Court. Sir Malcolm Langley spoke with Peel an hour ago. Based on your position and the seriousness of the crime, Peel instructed Sir Malcolm to conduct a thorough investigation. I had to tell him about the threatening notes, amongst other things."

Bennet muttered a curse. "A man is dead. Tell Sir Malcolm whatever he wants to know. We must alert Branner's family. I believe his mother lives in Bath or Bristol. No doubt he kept her letters. It shouldn't be difficult to find an address. I shall visit her myself."

Mr Daventry sighed.

Mr Daventry never sighed.

A strong sense of foreboding settled in the air.

"The coroner places the time of death almost forty-eight hours ago." Mr Daventry paused. He waited for them to realise they were at Witherdeen when Mr Branner was murdered. Had the poor man met his demise while they were fighting with Mr Granger, or while making love in the cottage?

Bennet sat forward. "But that's impossible."

"Did you visit your steward to tell him you planned to leave for London? Did you enter his cottage at any point on the night your friends came to Witherdeen?"

"Enter his cottage? No! I left in a hurry. I gave my valet notes for Branner and Mrs Hendrie, informing them I'd be back in a few days."

Julianna realised she had cause for alarm. "Sir, surely you don't think Lord Devereaux bludgeoned his steward. I can vouch for his whereabouts on the night in question."

"I'm sure you can, Mrs Eden. No doubt he can vouch for yours."

The comment caught her unawares. "Are you suggesting I had something to do with Mr Branner's death? What possible motive could I have for killing the steward?"

"You're in love with Devereaux and sought to punish the person who sent the threatening letters. Protecting a loved one is a motive for murder."

In love with Devereaux? Did he have to say that aloud?

"Sir, I'm forced to bite my tongue lest I say something wholly disrespectful. I'm grateful to you for giving me this position, for having faith in my abilities, but your reasoning is flawed."

"Flawed?" Mr Daventry's expression darkened. Then he laughed. Granted, it was only a mild chuckle, but his eyes crinkled all the same. "If only you could see what I see, Mrs Eden."

"Damn it, Daventry! Are you saying we're both suspects in Branner's murder?" Bennet answered his own question. "Of course we are. Everyone in attendance is considered a suspect."

"Mrs Hendrie saw the gruesome scene through the cottage window. She sent a groom to Basingstoke with a note for the coroner. By the time Cole arrived, the coroner had found the incriminating evidence."

Incriminating evidence!

Thank heavens! Surely that proved their innocence.

"The killer left a clue?" she said, though the rush of relief died when she met Mr Daventry's stare.

"Two clues. When the coroner prised open Branner's palm, he found strands of red hair. Next to the body was a sapphire stickpin. The same stickpin Devereaux is wearing in the portrait hanging in Witherdeen's drawing room."

Silence filled the cramped space.

It took a moment to absorb the gravity of their situation. The evidence placed them both at the scene. People were hanged for less. That said, a marquess wouldn't face the noose. The blame would rest squarely at Julianna's door.

"I lost that pin months ago."

Julianna studied Lucius Daventry. He seemed remarkably unconcerned that his agent and client might be guilty of murder. Yes, he wore an unreadable expression most of the time, but there was something reassuring about his cool demeanour.

"We secured a confession from Miss Winters tonight. Alas, Bennet and I are the only two witnesses to the fact she visited Mr Branner's cottage the night he was murdered."

Julianna explained all they had learnt from Miss Winters. "Had we known of Mr Branner's death, we would have brought her to Bow Street for questioning."

"No doubt she's on the first boat to anywhere," Bennet scoffed.

"Why would Miss Winters admit to being in Mr Branner's cottage if she murdered him with a poker?" Julianna doubted the killer would confess to visiting the scene. "Why confirm she had a room at the coaching inn in Bramley?"

"Now you're thinking like an enquiry agent, Mrs Eden. There are only two reasons why she would incriminate herself."

Julianna thought for a moment. "The first being that Miss Winters didn't attack or murder Mr Branner. The second being she hit him with the poker but doesn't know he's dead."

"Correct." Mr Daventry relaxed back in the seat. "Let's consider all the evidence so far. Cole has more to say on the matter, but I want to have a clear picture when we arrive in Hart Street."

Bennet exhaled deeply. "Allow me to relate the events. Branner sent the handbills. We assume he staged the scenes with the gargoyle and gravestone. I also believe he is responsible for the faulty pulley in the stable block."

"Yes," was all Mr Daventry said.

"Though his motive is unclear," Julianna added. "He used Miss Winters to assist him in his endeavour though she says she is ignorant of any wrongdoing. Maybe Mr Branner meant to implicate Miss Winters. After discovering he used her, she murdered him in a fit of rage."

"Interesting."

"Whoever killed Branner planted my stickpin and a lock of Mrs Eden's hair at the scene to incriminate us both."

Mr Daventry rubbed his firm jaw. "Or the hair belongs to Miss Winters, and she stole the stickpin. It all comes back to motive. Why would anyone seek to hurt you, Devereaux? That's the question we must answer."

●

The carriage rattled to a halt in Hart Street.

Mrs Gunning was expecting them. She had made tea, lit the lamps and stoked the fire in the drawing room. While they waited for the agents, Mr Daventry probed Bennet about his father's relationship with the staff.

The Sloanes arrived first. Vivienne handed Julianna her cloak, forcing her to shrug out of Bennet's warm coat. Mr Cole came five minutes later. The dark circles beneath his eyes said he'd barely slept.

They all sat around the low table, waiting for Mr Cole to discuss the terrible incident at Witherdeen. He began by relaying what they'd already learnt during the carriage ride across town. Then described the gruesome scene in graphic detail.

"The coroner can't decide if Branner died because of a blow to the head or fell after being hit with the poker and cracked his skull on the grate. Either way, Branner never regained consciousness and bled to death."

Bennet asked about Mrs Hendrie and his staff.

"Mrs Hendrie took to her bed for a few hours. She suspected Branner had lied about seeing the gravestone but had no proof."

"But Grimley swears he saw the gravestone," Julianna said. Mr Bower had confirmed the fact on numerous occasions.

Mr Cole looked at Bennet. "Branner caught Grimley digging inside the chapter house. Branner threatened to inform you unless Grimley told a small lie. I had to scare the gardener out of his wits to get to the truth."

So, Bennet's theory proved correct. Smashing the gravestone had seemed like an odd thing to do. "Mr Bower searched the pit for hours, looking for the broken remnants. He found no evidence to support Mr Branner's claim."

"Evidence suggests Branner played the part of the ghostly monk, too." Mr Cole struggled to suppress a yawn. "Hidden under the boards in his cottage were robes and an incense burner."

Bennet threw his hands in the air. "But why?"

A tense silence ensued. Mr Cole looked at Mr Daventry and arched a brow. A covert message of sorts.

The master of the Order turned to Julianna, his eyes holding the hint of compassion she'd seen twice before. "Mrs Eden, I'm afraid I must ask you some uncomfortable questions. Should Sir Malcolm seek to inspect the journals and the letter found in Branner's cottage, he will draw the obvious conclusions. No doubt you would prefer to direct your answers to someone who believes you're innocent."

Innocent?

Julianna frowned. "Sir, I'm at a loss to know what you mean." And yet her stomach sank. Mr Daventry did not play games with people's emotions. He must have some justification for speaking out.

"If you prefer, we can speak privately," Mr Daventry said.

"I have nothing to hide, sir, and have no idea why I'm suddenly a person of interest in this case."

"I believe it has something to do with what my father wrote in his journals," Bennet said, his voice thick with regret. "He resented your mother for leaving and sought to make her life difficult."

"More than difficult," Mr Cole scoffed. "So difficult, Mrs Eden has every reason to seek vengeance. The letter suggests she knew Branner before agreeing to take your case. One might commend her for spinning quite a clever deception."

Letter? What letter? She scoured her mind, but drew a blank.

"Sir, I sit here ignorant of my crime, yet I assure you I have known Mr Branner for only a few short days."

"And I've known Mrs Eden for a few short hours," Vivienne interjected, "but I'm willing to vouch for her character. Whatever it is you're suggesting, Cole, there must be another explanation."

"I agree." It was Bennet's turn to argue a case for the defence. "Regardless of what evidence you have to implicate Mrs Eden, I'm confident she has nothing to do with any of this. I introduced her to Branner and would have sensed if something were amiss."

Mr Sloane snorted. "With all due respect, Branner has been deceiving you for months, if not years, and you do not know why."

Bennet firmed his jaw and looked ready to retaliate, but Lucius Daventry said, "Enough! No one here doubts Mrs Eden's word, but she must account for the letter found in Branner's cottage."

"I have never written a letter to Mr Branner." For the love of God, how could she write to a man she didn't know? "Perhaps he has a friend or relative with the same name."

Mr Daventry reached inside his coat pocket and withdrew a folded note. He stood and gave the tatty paper to Julianna.

"The coroner found it in Branner's coat pocket."

The second she gripped the letter, she knew exactly what it was. Relief rippled through her in waves. Thank the Lord. She thought she'd lost it at Witherdeen, feared Bennet had found it and said nothing.

Forced to peel back the folds and examine her own penmanship, Julianna read the words she had written to Bennet Devereaux. During those lonely nights when Edward and Justin expressed their love, she left the house, lay under the stars with her letter and her memories.

When you look to the heavens, do you think of me?

Tears welled, but she gathered her composure. "I wrote this letter, but nowhere on the page does it state the name of the recipient."

"But you agree it's a love letter."

"It is a love letter, sir. One that is never far from my heart. Mr Branner must have entered the cottage without my knowledge and rummaged through my belongings."

Bennet looked aghast. "You wrote a love letter to Branner?"

"Of course not. Mr Branner is a stranger to me, a man I met mere days ago. I wrote a letter meant for my eyes only. A private outpouring." The thought that Mr Cole and Mr Daventry had read her innermost thoughts left her mortified.

Bennet held out his hand. "May I read the letter?"

Good God, no!

"It's a personal keepsake. It pains me to think others have been privilege to my dreams and aspirations."

Mr Cole had the decency to incline his head by way of an apology. "Mrs Eden, the letter was found at the scene. I would not have read it otherwise."

Bennet sat forward. "The fact the letter might incriminate you in Branner's murder suggests it must be written to someone."

Julianna did not reply. She looked at Lucius Daventry. "Can I keep the letter, or is it considered evidence?"

"The coroner found it on a murdered man's body." Mr Daventry spoke with a degree of empathy. "It's listed in his report. I shall speak to Sir Malcolm, explain my thoughts on the matter, but ultimately he must rule on its significance."

"Because I am still a suspect in the steward's murder?" she asked.

"The letter, it was meant for me," Bennet interrupted, looking more than intrigued. "There are only two reasons why it might be considered as evidence. If you were conspiring with Branner, which I know you were not, or if it proved you were defending me. Therefore, you wrote the letter with me in mind."

Her chest tightened.

She swallowed many times, still her mouth felt dry.

"The person I wrote about doesn't exist. How could I write about you? We've not seen each other for seventeen years."

She'd promised never to lie.

Some lies were necessary.

"Then let me read the letter," he challenged.

"No."

"Why not?"

Mr Daventry coughed into his fist to get their attention. "The letter is unimportant. Mrs Eden's explanation supports my belief that Branner suspected she was at Witherdeen to spy, and so he entered the cottage while she dined with your friends and stole the letter. We can only assume he planned to use it to frame Mrs Eden for the crimes, should he fail to blame Miss Winters."

Bennet's expression darkened. "You mean he might have killed me and told the authorities it was a case of unrequited love."

"That's assuming Mrs Eden had you in mind when she wrote about the only time in her life she's been truly happy."

Curse the devil! Why didn't he just snatch the letter and read it aloud? It was unlike Mr Daventry to be so obtuse.

A quick change of subject was needed to calm her nerves. "You said Lord Devereaux's father mentioned my mother in his journals. I understand he was unkind. I remember her saying he made life unbearable and even attacked Lord Denver in the street. But why would I blame the marquess for his father's poor judgement?"

Mr Daventry stood abruptly. "Would you care to accompany me to the study, Mrs Eden? We won't be long. What I have to say requires privacy." He asked politely, yet something about his tone said she shouldn't refuse.

She caught Bennet's anxious gaze, saw the same fear she'd witnessed the night she'd be abducted from Witherdeen. Did he know of this secret Mr Daventry was compelled to disclose? Did Bennet know why she would have a reason to hate him now?

Mr Daventry led her into the lit study across the hall. He closed the door, gestured for her to sit while he perched on the edge of the imposing desk.

"The job of an enquiry agent is a dangerous business." Mr Daventry folded his arms across his chest. "A man cannot take risks with people's lives."

Julianna wasn't sure where the conversation would lead. "You take your responsibility seriously. I've never known anyone be so thorough."

He inclined his head at her compliment. "I never hire an agent without checking their background. I knew of your connection to Lord Devereaux before I decided you would work his case."

It wasn't a complete surprise. Still, she was forced to ask, "Do you know why Edward Eden married me?"

"No. Your mother's history is of more interest to me. Giselle amassed enemies, and I cannot afford for those with a hidden agenda to disrupt our work here."

"My mother had many lovers. Most of them grew to hate her."

"None more so than the Marquess Devereaux."

"He told terrible lies, blackened her name." Giselle had cursed him to hell many times. "His aggression stemmed from the loss of a woman he claimed to love. There's a reason it's called a broken heart. Some cling to the hopeful half, the half that appreciates things change, that life has more to offer. Some grab the bitter half and hold it until it withers away, and they're nought but an empty shell."

"Leaving Witherdeen broke your heart."

"Leaving Bennet broke my heart."

"Your letter implies you clung to hope."

"After the life I've had, I have every reason to be bitter. But I've seen how it ravages the mind and body, and I would never choose a life like that."

Mr Daventry pursed his lips as if reluctant to speak. "I pray you always choose hope. I pray you break the destructive cycle adopted by your mother."

Julianna sat there, uncertainty coursing through her veins. Unlike Giselle, Mr Daventry gave no warning he was about to turn her life upside down. The only sign to suggest she would be packing her valise again was the slight downturn of his lips.

"Delaying will not spare my feelings, sir."

"No," he said softly.

"I'm hardened to anything concerning my mother."

He remained silent for long, drawn-out seconds. "While you

were at Witherdeen, I spoke to the lords Denver, Carstairs and Montgomery."

Strange how she could barely remember the nights Giselle dragged her away from those gentlemen's homes.

"I wasn't sure whether to believe their claims, but having read the journal Cole brought back from Witherdeen, it seems their suspicions were founded."

Oh, the wait proved torturous. "Forgive my bluntness, sir, but would you get to the point."

Mr Daventry smiled sympathetically. "The marquess blackmailed every lover your mother had, beginning with Denver. He bought their vowels, bribed friends and relatives to gain the men's secrets, used every means necessary to make them banish your mother from their lives."

Julianna had known Lord Denver was the first man to give Giselle her marching orders. Consequently, her mother's confidence had taken a knock, later a thump, then a battering.

"My mother despised the marquess, though she never said why. No doubt his aim was to force her back to Witherdeen."

Love and hate were sides of the same coin.

"Did she say why she fled to France?"

Julianna raised a brow. "Sir, you ask a question yet know the answer."

"Yes. Because it was the only way she could escape the marquess. But an incident that occurred after Montgomery threw your mother out made life difficult."

With a heavy heart, Julianna recalled the event. "We took a room at the Dog and Pheasant. Someone entered while we slept and stole my mother's jewels."

Thankfully, Giselle kept her diamond ring and ruby earrings in a secret pocket sewn into her corset. And she met a gentleman in Calais who kept them in reasonable lodgings for the next year.

"In the journal, the marquess mentions buying vowels, spreading gossip, making sure no one extended Giselle an invitation."

"As I said, he clung to the bitter half of his broken heart."

When Mr Daventry paused, Julianna held her breath.

"Montgomery said the marquess paid someone to steal the jewels. In the journal, the marquess wrote that his man had a successful night at the Dog and Pheasant. You fled to France to escape the marquess. He's the reason your mother lost everything, the reason she sold you to Edward Eden."

For a moment, Julianna felt nothing.

The first flicker of anger caught her by surprise. Each painful memory fed the beast. The insults hurled at them in the street. The cruel way men discarded them without a thought for their welfare.

Then the tears came, along with a knot of doubts and insecurities. Why hadn't her mother loved her as much as she loved men? Why was she not enough for the woman who constantly chased happiness? Why had Giselle sold her to Edward Eden? She had known the truth and committed the worst kind of betrayal.

I'm not selling you, silly girl.

He's paying for the privilege of being your husband.

Edward loves you.

"Mrs Eden." Mr Daventry's words sliced through the chaos.

"Please don't call me that."

She was not Miss de Lacy or Mrs Eden. Both names seemed abhorrent now. The lies. The deceit. The evilness. It was like a swirling vortex, threatening to drag her down, hold her under.

The urge to run took command of her senses. She pushed out of the chair. "I must go. I must leave London." Tears slipped down her cheeks. "I beg you, sir, release me from my contract. Mr Cole can help Lord Devereaux prove his innocence."

In a shocking gesture of solidarity, Mr Daventry stood and touched her gently on the upper arm. "I cannot let you leave, Julianna. Sir Malcolm insists you remain in St James' Square while he attempts to prevent a scandal."

"A scandal?"

"There'll be riots if a respected peer is accused of murder. Though I'm confident it won't come to that. You *were* with Devereaux all night?"

She had no choice but to answer the embarrassing question. "Yes, until I roused Mr Bower and asked him to bring me home."

"When Devereaux followed you from Witherdeen, I knew you were more than friends. I suspect he will follow you to Paris."

Her hands started shaking. Not because she believed Bennet was a controlling fiend like his father. But because she was not strong enough to resist him.

"Lord Devereaux must marry and sire an heir, sir. There is no place for him in Paris. As his friend, I pray you will make him see sense." Her mind scrambled to think how she might make their separation easier. "Perhaps I could stay with the Sloanes in Little Chelsea. Would that not satisfy Sir Malcolm?"

"I've confirmed you're staying with Devereaux. If you remove to Little Chelsea, people will assume he killed his steward."

She glanced at the closed study door, feeling much like a caged bird with clipped wings. She couldn't abandon Bennet in his hour of need. No, she had no choice but to deal with her dilemma.

"Then might you grant me one request? Might your coachman take me to St James' Square? I'd like some time alone before Lord Devereaux returns home."

Time alone wouldn't solve her problem.

Time alone wouldn't stop her loving Bennet Devereaux.

CHAPTER 17

ACROSS THE HALL, a door creaked open. The patter of footsteps echoed on the tiled floor, accompanied by a mumbled conversation. Another door opened and closed. Bennet listened intently to every sound, wondering why the hell Lucius Daventry needed a private audience.

The matter concerned Bennet's father.

Bennet had read the journals, had told Julianna of the bitter remarks, of his father's need to force Giselle de Lacy back to Witherdeen. It wasn't a secret. So why squirrel her away to another room and fill her head with nonsense.

"Branner went to a great deal of trouble to torment you, Devereaux." Finlay Cole was known for being blunt. "I assume you checked his references before hiring him as your steward."

Bennet tried to keep his temper. "My father employed Branner six months before he died. He never hired a man without a recommendation."

"May I ask how he died?" The question carried Cole's apparent suspicions. "He must have been no older than sixty."

"Sixty-two. His heart failed. Branner didn't kill him."

"Perhaps the timing is a coincidence," Cole mocked. "Branner never gave you a reason to doubt his loyalty?"

"Never." Bennet was tired of the probing questions. He didn't give a damn about the case, cared only about the wicked words Lucius Daventry was busy spouting.

As if conjured by thought alone, Daventry returned and closed the door.

Bennet shot to his feet. "Where is Mrs Eden?" Panic left his heart pounding. Was she drying her tears? Were those her footsteps he'd heard in the hall? Had she made a hasty escape?

"Sit down, Devereaux." Daventry raised his hand, a plea for patience, and waited for Bennet to sit. "Cole, go home and get some sleep. Before you go, I need to know where Branner's mother lives. Did you find anything in the cottage with her direction? Devereaux thinks it could be Bath or Bristol."

"I found no personal effects. Nothing to suggest he has any living relatives. Though there was a book borrowed from the Bristol Library Society and never returned." Cole removed a small notebook from his coat pocket and flicked through the pages. "A library in King Street, Bristol."

"Excellent. Sloane, tell Sir Malcolm that Devereaux and I are journeying to Bristol tomorrow to see what we can discover about Branner's background. We'll be gone for two days—"

"Two days!" Bennet stood again. "I'm not leaving Julianna alone when there's a murderer on the loose. The handbill Isabella Winters refused to deliver said Julianna died by my hands. Someone plans to hurt her and blame me." Bennet glanced at the door. "Where is she? For the love of God, tell me you've not let her leave."

"We'll discuss it in a moment."

"We'll discuss it now!"

Daventry's grey eyes darkened like a gathering storm. "Solving the case and saving your life is of paramount importance. You will wait while I lay a trap for the blackguard. I trust you told Roxburgh the truth."

Bennet huffed. "Yes, and he was at a loss to know why one of our friends would go to such extreme lengths. What can any of them hope to gain by my death?"

"Do you suspect him?"

"Roxburgh? No! We shoot and fence together. He could have

killed me many times and made it look like an accident. Besides, he can barely raise the enthusiasm to dress each morning."

Daventry gave a curt nod. "Sloane, we'll leave at first light. Visit Roxburgh at nine—"

"Nine?" Bennet snorted. "Roxburgh never rises before noon."

"Drag Roxburgh from his bed. Tell him Devereaux and Mrs Eden are leaving for Bristol to locate Branner's family. As a matter of urgency, he's to visit all those who were at Witherdeen the night Branner died and inform them the man is dead, casually mention the trip to Bristol."

Mrs Sloane spoke up. "The villain must believe it's possible to find them before they reach Bristol, before they find Mr Branner's mother."

Daventry pursed his lips while in thought. "Do you recall the case where Sir Frederick Marley blamed his captain for stealing a tobacco shipment? We caught Sir Frederick paying the real thief at a coaching inn just outside Bristol."

"The Golden Eagle?" Cole said.

"Sloane, tell Roxburgh that Devereaux is staying at the Golden Eagle. Make sure Devereaux's friends and Miss Winters know they'll find him there."

Sloane nodded.

Through the means of silent communication, Daventry informed his agents it was time to leave. They made their excuses, said good night and headed for the door, though Mrs Sloane asked Bennet to convey a message, a desire for Julianna to visit her in Little Chelsea once they'd solved the case.

Daventry waited until his agents had left the house before speaking. "Now we're alone, we'll get back to the matter of Mrs Eden."

"Where is she?"

"Gone home."

"Home? To Howland Street? To bloody Paris?"

"To St James' Square, but you'll allow her time alone before giving chase." Daventry crossed the room to the drinks cabinet. "Care for a brandy?"

Bennet's temper flared. He imagined grabbing the man by

the scruff of his coat and shaking the truth from his arrogant mouth. But Daventry raised a glass as an enticement to stay.

"If I lose her, I'll blame you. Sod your agents. I'll make your life a living hell. Do you hear?"

Daventry smiled. "Despite every effort to the contrary, you sound like your father. He persecuted Giselle, made *her* life hell, all in the name of love."

Bennet firmed his jaw. "I'm nothing like my father."

"No, you're not." Daventry closed the gap between them, thrust a glass of brandy at Bennet and raised his in salute. "You're so in love with Mrs Eden, you would turn your back on your responsibilities and move to Paris."

Bennet relaxed, all thoughts of fighting abandoning him. "I'm so in love with her, I would do whatever she asked. But I'm a man at war with my conscience." It was a gruesome battle between happiness and duty.

Daventry knocked back his brandy and panted to cool the burn. "God, I'm glad I was born a bastard. Do you know what I find so amusing about the nobility?"

"No doubt you plan to enlighten me."

"You have immense power yet are slaves to your position. You're the Marquess Devereaux. You can do what the hell you please. No one will dare stand in your way. If you were a gambler, a whoremonger, you'd still be invited to fancy balls and routs. But woe betide you marry someone outside the select little club."

Bennet swallowed a mouthful of brandy. "Breeding is everything. That's what we have thrust down our throats from an early age."

"Surely you can see how illogical it sounds." Daventry snorted. "You would choose a debutante who whimpers because of muddy slippers over a woman like Mrs Eden?"

"Mrs Eden is superior in every regard."

"Then marry her. You need a wife, and she has everything you could want in a marchioness." Daventry winced. "Though after what she's learnt tonight, she may not have you. To marry you, she must betray her mother's memory."

"What the devil did you say to her?" Fear fuelled Bennet's temper now.

Daventry relayed the stories told by numerous lords, tales of blackmail and revenge, of jewels stolen from the Dog and Pheasant, of Giselle's mistreatment at the hands of his father.

Shame left Bennet gripping the nearest chair and dropping into the seat. He'd known a milder version of events, knew his father was prone to bouts of cruelty, but what he'd done beggared belief.

"He died a lonely man." Bennet recalled the deathbed conversations. The deep regrets that skulked out of the shadows when one's life ebbed away. "But he was a master of his own destiny."

Daventry refilled his brandy glass and then sat on the sofa. "Now it's time to decide what sort of man you are, Devereaux. Are you a man who bows and nods and does what is expected? Or a man who challenges the rules and paves the way for the next generation? A man capable of choosing his own bride?"

Bennet's heart swelled at the thought of marrying Julianna. If she refused him, he was destined to spend his life alone. He could not stand in church and exchange vows with any other woman.

"Life will be difficult for our children."

"Difficult? Living from hand to mouth is difficult," Daventry mocked. "Cowards choose the easy path. You're not a coward, Devereaux. Raise children with the strength to do what is right. Perhaps your daughter will marry my son, and they'll turn society completely on its head."

Everything Daventry said made sense. But Julianna would refuse his suit. A courtesan's daughter did not become a marchioness. And having resigned from the Order, all she wanted was peace.

"Your work for the Order is really a plot to take over the world, Daventry. You're playing matchmaker. Marrying peers to sensible women so their children have the backbone to challenge convention."

Daventry raised his glass and then downed the contents. "My father-in-law died trying to change the world. His death cannot be in vain. Our country needs rebels. Sons and daughters with the courage to confront their peers."

They sat for a while, discussing how a forward-thinking man might rock the foundations of the House of Lords. The topic moved to the case, and Daventry warned Bennet that his steward might well have been his bastard brother.

The thought had crossed Bennet's mind. He'd have welcomed Branner with open arms, treated him like kin. Perhaps it would have filled the void left by his estranged family. But without a confession, what proof was there?

Bennet made to leave, but Daventry spent the next ten minutes discussing arrangements for their trip to Bristol.

Keen to drag himself away, Bennet bid the master of the Order good night. "There's nothing left to talk about unless you know of a secret mantra that might persuade Julianna to marry me."

"The desire to have you spouting nonsense all the way home is tempting. Just remember, she's in love with you. She'll put your needs before her own. You must convince her your needs are the same."

"The Augustinian monks were of one mind and one heart. I'll keep their motto in mind when deciding what to say to Julianna."

Daventry smiled. "What words could convey centuries of wisdom?"

"It's a motto you could use—nothing conquers except the truth."

●

Julianna shuffled down beneath the bedsheets and hugged the pillow to her ears so she wouldn't hear Bennet pacing the floor in the adjoining room.

He'd come home ten minutes ago, entered his chamber but not said a word, not called to her through the locked door, not whispered good night. He'd dismissed his valet, insisting he would manage, asking to be left alone.

Alone.

Her soul ached at the thought. Every instinct urged her to open the door, to race into his arms and live for the moment. A hardened heart could cope with anything. That was another one of Giselle's platitudes. But Julianna knew she would never recover from this.

Desperate to distract her mind, her thoughts turned to Mr Daventry's revelation. Had Giselle not lost her precious jewels, would she have sold them to purchase a cottage in an idyllic location, away from the glittering lights of the ballroom? Would she have become a doting mother, loved Julianna more than she did a lover's attention?

No. Never.

Giselle was as addicted to men as she was to laudanum. Fifty fawning lords could not satisfy her craving. Julianna needed only one man to feel completely content.

She let go of her pillow and sat up in bed.

All was quiet.

Did Bennet's reticence stem from guilt? Did he believe his father's misdeed had led to Julianna being sold to Edward Eden?

It wasn't true.

The blame lay with Giselle, the manipulating devil who'd never been a mother. The blame lay with Julianna for being a fool to believe the lies, for not being strong enough to escape a loveless marriage.

"Julianna." Spoken in a voice tinged with uncertainty, her name echoed from the room beyond. "Julianna. Are you awake?"

Her heart thumped hard in her chest.

"Julianna. I need to talk to you."

She should ignore him, feign sleep, but his magnetic pull had her slipping out of bed and padding over to the connecting door. "Bennet, it's late. Can we talk tomorrow?" If she faced him tonight, she would be a slave to her wants and desires.

He responded by sliding a folded note beneath the door.

With trembling hands, Julianna took the note and peeled back the folds. A smile formed. It was a privilege pass written in Bennet's elegant penmanship, declaring himself the winner of the race from the ruins to the quaint cottage.

"We made a pact," he reminded her. "Whoever won the pass can make demands. And I wish to use mine to make you open this door."

She pressed her palm to the wood as if it were Bennet's chest. "This isn't a game, Bennet. We're not those children anymore."

"Still, you don't want to break another vow. Let me in, Julianna."

She hadn't broken the first vow. She had returned to him every night in her dreams. A part of her would always live with him at Witherdeen.

Rousing what little strength she had, she folded the note and pushed it back through the gap beneath the door. "I can't talk to you tonight. Perhaps tomorrow we—"

"We're leaving for Bristol before dawn."

"Bristol?"

"I can't talk to you through the door. And we'll be stuck in a carriage with Daventry for the best part of fourteen hours. No doubt we'll speak of nothing but catching a killer."

Julianna rested her forehead gently against the door. The man had the power of an ancient god, for his essence managed to penetrate the wood and seduce her senses. She closed her eyes and breathed deeply. "Then we should sleep, else we'll be good for nothing tomorrow."

"Let me in, Julianna. Don't make me ask again."

"Why? Have you inherited your father's need for control?"

Her stupid question was met with silence.

For lengthy seconds she stood there, knowing she had hurt him, wanting to make things right. "Bennet. I'm sorry. You could never be like him."

Silence.

If this was their last night together, she didn't want it marred by one foolish comment. Giselle used spiteful words to hurt men. Julianna would never be her mother's daughter.

She quickly took the key from the nightstand, unlocked the door, and yanked it open. Bennet stood there in nothing but his breeches, his muscular arms braced against the door frame, his mischievous grin reaching his eyes.

The sight hardened her nipples.

His heated gaze skimmed her loose red curls, her plain night-gown, dipped to her bare feet. "Even in white cotton, you steal my breath."

Her breath hitched as he prowled towards her, this merciless hunger for him refusing to abate. "You're a dangerous man, Bennet Devereaux. One look from those tawny eyes, and I'm entirely at your mercy."

"Then I intend to put my powers to good use." He came closer, captured her chin, and stroked her bottom lip with his thumb. "I know what my father did, and I shall spend my life making amends. I need you. I'll never have the strength to let you go."

"You must."

"Don't you want me, Julianna?"

She'd spent forever wanting him.

The time for honesty was nigh. "I could never share you with another woman. Even if I had your heart, it wouldn't be enough. I want all of you, Bennet, and I cannot accept anything less."

He bent his head and kissed her, those captivating lips moving so slowly, so softly, the coil of desire tightened in her belly. "I meant what I said earlier. I have loved you from the day you stole an apple from the kitchen and came to sit with me beneath the stairs. I will love you, and only you, my whole life."

Unshed tears blurred her vision. She would never forgive herself if she left without letting him know how much she cared.

"I've tried to suppress my feelings, Bennet, but it becomes harder each day. I will always love you. Indeed, my love for you is so great I know I must let you go."

A tear slipped down her cheek, and he dashed it away.

He gestured to the sumptuous pale blue bed hangings. "You see this splendid room. No one but you will ever cross the threshold. No one but you will ever sleep in that bed. No one but you will carry my name or bear my children. It's you or no one, Julianna."

Emotion caught in her throat. "C-carry your name?"

Surely he didn't mean—

"Marry me. Be my marchioness, my wife, my lover, my friend. And if Edward Eden has poisoned your mind to marriage, then we'll move to Paris and live in sin."

Marry him? For a few seconds, she let his words infuse her

mind, body and soul. She bathed in the possibility of all her wildest dreams coming true.

Reality reared its head. "You cannot marry a courtesan's daughter."

He tapped her playfully on the nose. "I'm the Marquess Devereaux. I can marry who the devil I please. Besides, I have Lucius Daventry's permission to court you, and there's not a man in England who'd dare challenge him."

"But you'll be cast out. Our children will—"

"Be so strong of heart and mind society will crave their approval. The world is changing, Julianna. Our children will have to please no one but themselves. Do you know how liberating that will be?" He chuckled. "I've already agreed our daughter will marry Daventry's son, so you can't refuse me now."

This was a dream, a beautiful dream full of endless possibilities. Would she wake to find herself alone in a cold bed?

"Our daughter will be free to choose her own husband."

Bennet's eyes widened. "Does that mean you accept?"

"It will be difficult."

"Living from hand to mouth is difficult."

She recalled the day she'd sat on the Registry's steps, alone and without hope. She owed Mr Daventry a debt far greater than she could ever repay.

"We'll discuss marriage when we've caught the devil who wants to kill you." A man was dead, murdered by his accomplice, though Julianna felt certain Miss Winters lacked the heart for such a grisly deed. "We should focus all our efforts on solving the case."

"All our efforts?" He slipped his arm around her waist and glanced at the bed. His gaze was so hot she could warm her cold hands. "Surely we're allowed a little self-indulgence before we leave at dawn."

Heat pooled between her thighs at the prospect of joining him in bed. "By all accounts, Mr Daventry gave you permission to fraternise with his agent. And who would dare challenge such a formidable gentleman?"

"Who indeed?" He stripped her bare with his smouldering gaze. "Invite me into your bed, Julianna."

Need surpassed embarrassment. Although her heart fluttered wildly, bit by bit, she drew her nightgown up over her thighs like a wicked wanton.

"Come to bed, Bennet." She pulled the gown over her head, let it slip from her fingers to pool on the floor.

Bennet hissed a breath. He rubbed his chest as if starved of her touch. "Love, I plan to devour every inch of you."

Entranced by the noticeable bulge in his breeches, by his lean hips and solid thighs, she dared to tease him. "What are you waiting for?"

With a self-assured grin, he stripped out of the garment, freeing his impressive erection. "Well? Do you like what you see?"

"Indeed." Julianna stared at his manhood, so thick and gloriously hard. "I pray you won't break your last vow."

"The one where I promised to love you forever?"

"No. When you promised to pleasure me before a roaring fire, vowed to use your mouth to taste every inch of my flesh."

Bennet glanced at the flames flickering in the grate. "I'm glad you reminded me. That's one of many vows I intend to keep." He closed the gap between them. "Before we take to the floor, there's something I would like to do first. Something I imagined doing when I trapped you against the bedpost yesterday."

She wanted nothing more than to be caged in his masculine prison.

With her body thrumming in eager expectation, she took his hand and drew him towards the bed. "Tell me what you want, Bennet. There must be no secrets between us."

Hunger flared in those amber pools. "Turn around, love, and grip the bedpost."

She did as he asked.

He came behind her, the heat of his body caressing her bare skin, his hot breath breezing down her spine, whispering over her buttocks. She breathed his musky scent, inhaled the potent smell of his arousal. He was achingly close. Soon he would touch her, slide those large hands around her waist and drive her dizzy with desire.

Every muscle was strung as tight as a bow. Lust left her panting.

"Touch me." Sweet heaven. She was mindless with need.

"Close your eyes, love."

She squeezed them shut, silently urging him to hurry.

And then she felt him. The soft brush of his lips across her right shoulder. The gentle suck on her neck. A moan burst from her when his hand skimmed her hip and cupped her breast. Then he was everywhere at once—kissing her neck, grazing her nipples with his thumbs, his erection pushing against her buttocks in an intoxicating rhythm.

"It's always been you," he whispered in her ear as he massaged her sex in tantalising strokes. "You're the reason I spend most of my time at Witherdeen. The memories are like magic."

His fingers were like magic.

"I'm going to spend my life finding ways to pleasure you," he drawled.

She pushed back against him, needing to open herself, needing to feel his solid shaft sliding into her sex. "Take me like this, Bennet. We can move to the floor later. Take me. Take me now."

Oh, did he oblige!

He gripped her hips and pushed slowly into her body. The sensation of him stretching her, filling her, there wasn't a pleasure like it in the world.

"You're so wet, love, so tight, so damn warm."

She clutched the bedpost, a little bereft when he almost withdrew completely. "I need you inside me, Bennet."

He drove into her sex again and again, in and out of her in long strokes. The audible slapping mingled with his guttural groans and her high-pitched pants.

"Can you feel me, Julianna? Is this how you imagined our reunion? Did you touch yourself when you slept under the stars, thinking about me?" He thrust to the hilt and stilled, slipped his fingers between her thighs, and teased her sex. "When we're married, I'll flood you with my seed. You'll get all of me, Julianna, every last drop."

Pleasure pulsed through her. Heat coursed through her veins. The quickening in her core left her shaking and convulsing around his solid length.

But he didn't wait for the powerful waves to ebb. He slammed into her, quick and hard, telling her he loved her, assuring her they would never be parted again.

CHAPTER 18

TRAVELLING in a coach for a few hours resulted in stiff knees and an aching back. Travelling in a coach for twelve hours, having had little sleep, had exhaustion tugging at Bennet's eyelids, at every muscle, every limb. He needed to stretch and release a lengthy groan, but Julianna's head rested on his shoulder, and he'd not disturb her slumber.

Bennet closed his eyes briefly, his thoughts turning to their lovemaking, to Julianna's soft thighs hugging his hips as she rode him to completion. The memory hardened his cock. As did the thought of them spending the night together in a coaching inn— until another vision dampened his ardour. One where his bed partner snored like a hog and had stubble. Curse the devil. What if he were forced to share a bedchamber with Lucius bloody Daventry?

From the seat opposite, Daventry withdrew his pocket watch and checked the time beneath the light of the carriage lamp.

"We'll not reach Bristol before nightfall." Bennet spoke quietly so as not to wake Julianna. "Even if Branner's murderer follows us here, he won't reach the coaching inn tonight."

"He? You presume the villain is a man?"

"It was merely a turn of phrase." Lowbridge and Granger were the only men who could have killed the steward. Bennet would wager everything he owned on Roxburgh's innocence.

"Surely the ladies lack the strength to overthrow a man as strong as Branner."

"Sir Malcolm disagrees. He's convinced Miss Winters reached the end of her tether and hit Branner while in an uncontrollable rage. It's one possibility."

Sir Malcolm had insisted Bower keep watch over Isabella's apartment and had instructed him to apprehend her should she decide to flee. The magistrate thought luring the villain to Bristol was a pointless exercise. But Branner's motivation for hurting Bennet had to stem from something in his past.

"It's late." Bennet yawned. "Too late to visit the library."

"Then we'll find the man with the key." Daventry could navigate his way around any problem.

"Branner could have had that book for years. He worked for Lord Morton before coming to Witherdeen. Should our sojourn to Bristol fail to reap results, I shall visit the lord and make enquiries."

"There's no need. Tomorrow, we'll be heading back to London having solved the case." Daventry's confident gaze shifted to the woman sleeping beside Bennet. "When this is over, I hope I'm not ferrying my agent to Dover."

Bennet glanced at Julianna and drew the wool blanket over her lap. "Let's just say that St James' Square will soon be her permanent residence."

Daventry didn't hide his victorious grin. "You wanted her the moment your eyes met and you had to pick your chin off the floor."

"I've loved her for as long as I can remember and cannot let her go. You helped me come to a decision quickly, but I would never have let her leave for Paris." Bennet suspected Daventry had been manipulating events from the beginning. At this rate, all his female agents would be married by the summer. "You've been so instrumental in our affairs, one wonders what you have in store for Miss Gambit."

The glint in Daventry's eye said his mind was a nest of intrigue. The man was plotting something. "Miss Gambit is to meet her potential client soon."

"To see if she will take the case?" Bennet got the impression it was more complicated than a conversation in the Hart Street drawing room.

"To see if he will allow Miss Gambit to work alongside him. She must go through a series of tests. If she passes, which I'm sure she will, Hunter will hire her to help solve his problem."

"Hunter?" The man sounded like a blood-thirsty beast who took no prisoners. "I cannot recall a lord of that name."

"Hunter isn't a lord."

"From what I hear, Miss Gambit is a formidable woman who goes straight for the jugular." Was Daventry hoping his agent would form an attachment to Hunter while solving his case?

"Yes. It will make for an interesting pairing."

They fell silent for a time.

Bennet closed his eyes and drifted off to sleep, woke as the carriage rumbled into the Golden Eagle coaching inn. Daventry booked rooms, gave false names. He demanded to see the layout upstairs before persuading the innkeeper to give them chambers close to the taproom.

It was eight o'clock that evening when Daventry's carriage drew up alongside the library in King Street. The Palladian-inspired building of limestone ashlar stood shrouded in darkness.

Daventry opened the carriage door and vaulted to the pavement. "Wait here while I check the premises." He unlatched the iron gate and entered a flagged courtyard, knocked on the door numerous times before disappearing around the side of the building.

Julianna peered into the gloom. "There's no one here at this late hour."

"Daventry's confident he'll get the information we need."

"Someone peered through the curtains in the cottage next door. Perhaps the librarian lives there." Regardless of Daventry's instruction to wait in the carriage, Julianna lowered the steps and climbed down. "It's worth taking a look."

Bennet followed her to an L-shaped row of stone cottages, accessed through another wrought-iron gate. Daventry caught up with them outside the first cottage.

Julianna knocked.

A man of middling years appeared at the window.

"Good evening." Julianna spoke to him through the glass. "Do you work at the library?"

The fellow squinted and cupped his ear.

"The library?" she repeated. "Do you work there?"

He waved for them to wait and appeared at the door moments later.

"Sorry for disturbing you so late at night, sir, but we have pressing business with the keeper of the library."

After straightening his crooked spectacles and combing straggly brown hair over his bald pate, the man cast a wary eye over Lucius Daventry. "There's nothing in the library but books." Clearly he feared they'd come to steal the coin box.

Daventry stepped forward. "I believe introductions are necessary. Mrs Eden is an enquiry agent from London. My name is Lucius Daventry." He gestured to Bennet. "Allow me to present the Marquess Devereaux."

Daventry omitted to mention he was the son of a duke. Bennet suspected he would rather say he was the son of a cobbler.

Bennet removed an engraved silver case from his pocket and handed the fellow a calling card.

The poor man's eyes bulged as he studied the elegant script. "My lord, what an honour. I'm Mr Davies, keeper of the library. Please, please, come in out of the cold."

Bennet had to duck to clear the lintel. His stomach rumbled when he caught a delicious waft of beef stew. Mr Davies lived alone but for a lazy tabby cat. Despite numerous efforts to shoo the devil from its seat, the creature refused to vacate the fireside chair.

"We're investigating a murder in Hampshire." Julianna perched on the edge of another chair while everyone else stood. "We found a book at the scene, borrowed from your library some time ago, and we're looking for the address of the person who failed to return the volume."

Mr Davies scratched his head. "We keep a record of non-returns and issued fines. Do you know the title or author of this book?"

Julianna looked at Bennet, and he gave an inconspicuous shrug.

Daventry knew the answer, of course. Finlay Cole was extremely thorough. "William Enfield's *The History of Philosophy*."

Julianna turned to the librarian. "Perhaps a generous donation to the library might convince you to examine your records. We seek information regarding the gentleman who borrowed the book."

Mr Davies nodded. "I cannot let you into the library after hours, but I shall fetch the ledger. Might you have the gentleman's name? It will help to locate the records."

"Branner. Jonathon Branner." Plagued by a sudden pang of remorse, Bennet was compelled to add, "Had he spoken about his problems, his death might have been avoided."

Mr Davies offered his condolences and promptly left the cottage.

With its master gone, the cat leapt from the chair to investigate the newcomers. They spent the next fifteen minutes stroking the affectionate thing.

Bennet breathed a sigh of relief when Mr Davies returned carrying a heavy brown ledger.

"I found no record of a Jonathan Branner." He placed the musty tome on the small dining table and flicked to the relevant page. "Jonathan Blanchard borrowed Enfield's book four years ago and failed to return it. That's the only fine ever issued. Mrs Blanchard paid for the book and cancelled his subscription. I have her direction here."

Blanchard, not Branner?

The name meant nothing to Bennet. A point he reiterated when Daventry asked him to cast his mind back to his father's journals. Still, it could not be a coincidence.

"Either way, Mrs Blanchard's son is dead. We must inform her at once." Daventry reached into his pocket and withdrew a folded note. "I believe I'm to make this payable to the Bristol Library Society."

Behind his crooked spectacles, Mr Davies' eyes brightened. "Goodness. That's very generous, sir. Very generous."

"Do you have pen and ink?"

Mr Davies hurried to a cupboard in an old oak cabinet and brought the wooden inkstand to the table. "We appreciate any amount you can spare."

"I'll need Mrs Blanchard's address." Daventry dipped the nib in ink and scrawled his signature on the note. He handed the pen to Mr Davies, who scribbled Mrs Blanchard's address onto a scraggy bit of paper.

The men exchanged notes.

They·thanked Mr Davies and left the cottage, spent a minute brushing cat hair from their clothes before climbing into the carriage.

Before settling into his seat, Daventry instructed the coachman to take them to Great George Street. "Think, Devereaux. Can you not recall seeing the name Blanchard amongst your father's papers? Has your father ever had a mistress of that name?"

"No." It was an unusual name, and he would have remembered.

Julianna touched Bennet's hand. "Mr Branner must have had cause to give a false name. He must have used the alias when he worked for Lord Morton. Else you would have noticed the discrepancy on his reference."

Daventry glanced at the scrap of paper in his hand. "Instinct says we're about to find out why."

●

Great George Street consisted of a row of elegant townhouses on a steep incline facing an extensive park. Daventry's carriage followed the trail of lit street lamps to the top of the hill and stopped outside a house of the same architectural design as the library.

Bennet peered out of the window at the impressive facade. "You're sure Branner lived here?"

Daventry glanced at the note. "This is the address recorded in the ledger."

Doubts surfaced.

Mr Davies must have made a mistake. Why work as a

steward when one's family were wealthy? The answer was obvious. Branner worked at Witherdeen to be close to Bennet. And he wished to be close because he held a grudge. Still, it tested all logic and reason.

"Bennet, knock on the door and present your calling card." Did Julianna realise she had spoken his given name? "It's late. We shall all look rather intimidating gathered on the front steps."

Daventry nodded. "Sometimes it pays to have a title."

Aware of the resplendent coach parked outside, the butler opened the front door as soon as Bennet stepped onto the pavement. Daventry's equipage had an air of grandeur, despite the scruffy coachman hired from the Golden Eagle.

Bennet introduced himself. He offered his card and asked if he might speak to Mrs Blanchard. The butler invited him into the hall and went to fetch his master, not his mistress.

"My lord." An elderly gentleman with thinning white hair appeared wearing a green silk banyan. His bow reflected the depth of his esteem. "Welcome. Welcome. What a pleasure it is to receive such a prestigious guest."

Would the man be as welcoming if he knew Bennet was to marry a courtesan's daughter? "Mr Blanchard?" In his excitement, the gentleman hadn't offered his name.

"Blanchard? No. No. Good heavens, no."

"I've come seeking Mrs Blanchard."

The gentleman beamed. "I knew your uncle. John Devereaux."

John Devereaux?

Bennet froze. Pieces of the puzzle slotted into place. "I'm sad to say I never met him." It wasn't a lie. Loneliness had plagued him since his father's death. Perhaps long before that.

The gentleman seemed surprised. "That is sad. He was a remarkable fellow. I lived at number seven when he owned this house."

Bennet observed the elaborate gilt furnishings and grand staircase. "This was once John Devereaux's house?"

"Indeed. Indeed."

But Bennet's uncle had lived on an estate in Kent. "Forgive me. I was told Mrs Blanchard lived here."

Compassion coloured the man's pale cheeks. "Yes, yes. She used to live here, many years ago."

Keen to save the fellow any embarrassment, Bennet came straight to the point. "She lived here when my uncle owned the house?"

"Indeed. Now she lives in the cottage at the bottom of Bigwood Lane. Take the first right, and it's but a minute's walk." He sighed. "It's not been easy for her. I helped her when your uncle died, helped put the boy through school."

The boy? He surely spoke of Branner.

Bennet might have asked a host of questions but knew not to trust second-hand information. He thanked the man, declined the offer of supper and port and an opportunity to warm himself by the fire, then returned to the carriage and told Julianna and Daventry what he'd learnt.

"Mrs Blanchard must have been your uncle's mistress. Mr Branner might be John Devereaux's son. It would explain why the handbills bore the title *The Reckoning*." Water welled in Julianna's eyes. She reached for Bennet's hand. "In all likelihood, Mr Branner was your cousin."

"Or Mrs Blanchard was related to John Devereaux by some other means." Daventry did not race to conclusions.

But Bennet felt the loss too keenly for there to be another explanation. If only Branner had told him of their connection. Bennet would have acknowledged him publicly. Yet some murdering devil had robbed them both of the opportunity to heal old wounds.

"We'll all visit Mrs Blanchard." Daventry opened the carriage door and vaulted to the pavement. "Her son is dead. Based on your father's mistreatment of John Devereaux, you may receive a frosty reception."

A frosty reception was an understatement.

The frail, grey-haired woman gripping the door stumbled back upon hearing the name Devereaux. The painful silence lasted seconds before she charged at Bennet, cursing him to the devil, shouting and screaming for him to leave and never darken her door again.

Bennet took her abuse.

He took the blame for his father's cruel deeds.

Julianna intervened. She wrapped her arms around Mrs Blanchard and whispered soothing words to calm her spirit. "Bennet Devereaux is a good man. He's nothing like his father, but we must come inside and speak to you. We have news of your son."

Mrs Blanchard jerked to attention. "My son? You've seen him?"

"Let's go inside."

Hearing Julianna's grave tone, Mrs Blanchard burst into tears. "He's dead, isn't he? He's dead. I've known it for years." She turned on Bennet. "You devil. Hell will freeze over before you set foot in my house."

"Lord Devereaux wishes to help you. You may have every faith in his character." Julianna hugged the woman and led her into the cottage. "He knew nothing about you until a few minutes ago."

For an hour, Bennet sat in a threadbare chair in the small parlour, listening to Mrs Blanchard's wails and racking sobs. Julianna spoke of Branner's vendetta, explained how the terrible deeds had led to his death, paused periodically to hug the distraught woman and to make tea.

Eager to confirm Branner was indeed Jonathan Blanchard, Daventry asked, "Were you aware he was working as a steward at Lord Devereaux's estate?"

"No. He left four years ago. I've not seen him since."

"But Jonathan was John Devereaux's son?"

The woman nodded then launched a scathing attack on Bennet's father. She cursed his black soul, blamed him for killing her lover, killing her son, spat vile words.

"Why would he choose the name Branner?" Daventry was persistent in his need to prove the men were one and the same.

"Branner was my mother's name."

Daventry's shoulders relaxed a little.

Mrs Blanchard stared at Bennet as if he were the devil reincarnate. He was innocent of any crime, yet guilt flowed through his veins. In the end, he could not remain silent.

"If I had known we were related, I would have spoken to your son. I would have tried to help him, but he went to great lengths to hurt me. We believe his accomplice is responsible for his death. Despite all he's done, we won't rest until we've apprehended the villain."

The woman turned ashen. She put her hand to her mouth as if she might retch. "Oh, Lord! It's all my fault. I let bitterness fill my heart. We should have moved back to Somerset, closer to my family. But when you lose someone you love, all you have are the memories."

Bennet met Julianna's gaze. They exchanged a silent message—a promise to grasp happiness with both hands. A promise they would both keep.

"My father deserved your contempt. John lost a substantial sum in the mining scheme. People say the stress of it killed him."

"It broke him, broke his spirit." Mrs Blanchard—who used the title merely to hide the fact she'd had children out of wedlock with her married lover—dabbed her eyes with her handkerchief. "I hated your father, hated him for what he did, and I made sure my children inherited that hatred. It's their only legacy."

Mrs Blanchard continued to express the depth of her loathing, complained that John had been forced to sell their house, that she'd hated his wife as much as she hated the old marquess.

But one word uttered in passing hit Bennet like a lightning bolt.

Daventry was as sharp as ever and waited for Mrs Blanchard to take a breath before saying, "Children? You had more than one child with John Devereaux?"

Tears tumbled down the woman's cheeks. "Oh, poor Portia. Does she know about her brother? They left for London together and will have surely kept in contact. You must find her. Explain—" Mrs Blanchard stopped abruptly. She gripped the arms of the chair and froze in horror.

Bennet didn't want to suggest her daughter was Branner's accomplice and was rather thankful Julianna spoke up.

"Mrs Blanchard, you must give us a description of your daughter. She may have assisted her brother in his campaign against Lord Devereaux. We must find her, reason with her, save her if we can."

Bennet feared it was too late.

During an argument, Portia had probably killed him.

Mrs Blanchard looked up at Julianna, perched on the arm of the woman's chair. "You say you're an enquiry agent, Mrs Eden, yet Lord Devereaux looks at you as if you're lovers. Take my advice. The life of a mistress is a life of loneliness and heartache."

Perhaps Mrs Blanchard should have some compassion for John Devereaux's wife. Was her life not blighted by loneliness and heartbreak, too?

Julianna opened her mouth to correct Mrs Blanchard's assumption, but Bennet said, "Mrs Eden is not my mistress. She is soon to be my wife."

The woman almost slipped off the chair in shock. "You'd marry a widow who works for a living?"

"I would marry a widow who works and whose mother was a courtesan." And be blissfully happy for the rest of his days.

Julianna's eyes widened in silent reproof. "I haven't accepted his proposal, but everything his lordship says is true."

Mrs Blanchard stared at Bennet for the longest time. "Is it too late to save Portia?"

Bennet couldn't lie. "If she intentionally killed her brother, then yes. But we won't know until we find her. If she kills me, she will most definitely hang."

"We have a list of possible suspects," Daventry said. "We need you to confirm her identity."

After an evident tussle with her conscience, Mrs Blanchard nodded. "People always commented on her hair. Mine was the same when I was young. It's one of the things John loved about me. You've hair like spun gold, he used to say. Portia is the same."

Julianna gasped. "Is your daughter fond of talking?"

"Heavens, no. She's always been the quiet sort. You often find that with pretty girls. Portia would be a diamond of the first water if she'd not been born on the wrong side of the blanket."

CHAPTER 19

"COME TO BED, BENNET." Julianna came up on her elbows, her gaze finding his muscular silhouette in the darkness. Dressed in nothing but a pair of breeches hanging low on his hips, he stood at the window of their chamber in the Golden Eagle, staring out into the night. "Even if Miss Ponsonby hired a carriage, she won't reach Bristol tonight. And Mr Daventry said the next mail coach from London doesn't leave until first light."

Bennet ran his hand through his hair and cast her a sidelong glance. "Get some sleep, love. We must have our wits tomorrow, and you hardly slept a wink last night."

Was it only last night that he proposed marriage and made love to her twice? When Mr Daventry said they were to share a bedchamber, Bennet had grinned like a schoolboy and clearly hoped they'd be intimate again.

"I'll not leave Mrs Eden alone in a chamber when there's a murderer on the loose," Mr Daventry had said when they arrived. "And I'll not sleep in a room with anyone but my wife. I told the innkeeper you're married. Gave your names as Mr and Mrs Drummond."

But Bennet had been plagued by a crippling sense of guilt since learning of his cousin's identity. And Julianna couldn't give herself to him knowing Mr Daventry occupied the room across the hall.

Despite the frosty nip in the air, Julianna slipped out of bed and padded to the window. She ran her hand over Bennet's shoulder and massaged the tense muscles. "Nothing about this situation is simple."

He sighed. "My mind is in turmoil."

"Because you don't want to believe Miss Ponsonby killed her brother?"

"Because when I think of her situation, I think of you." He glanced over his shoulder and covered her hand with his. "Was your father married? Did he love Giselle more than his wife?"

Talk of her father tugged at the wound she thought had healed. "My mother refused to tell me his name. She said men like to own things, and I was not for sale. Later she proved she was just as calculating and callous."

"It wouldn't be hard to find him."

"He knew my mother had a child." All a child wanted was love and recognition. "If I was important to him, he would have moved heaven and earth to find me."

"Nothing would keep me from seeing my child."

No, he was extremely determined with those he loved.

"I stopped blaming myself for my parents' failures. No one is perfect. You must stop blaming yourself, too, Bennet."

He fell silent and stared out over the deserted stable yard.

Julianna wrapped her arms around his waist and hugged him. There was something about the warmth of his skin, the natural masculine scent that made her feel safe, content, protected.

Her thoughts turned to Miss Ponsonby, or Miss Blanchard, as she should call her now. The friendly chatter had been an act—a means to get close to Bennet. Surely the ultimate aim wasn't to kill him?

Bennet stepped out of her embrace and drew the curtains. "You're right. I can't stand here all night watching the shadows." He took hold of her hand. "Let's go to bed. Lying next to you will ease my mind for a time."

They climbed into bed. Bennet drew her close to his chest, and she twined her legs with his. The conversation turned to Miss Ponsonby.

"If she killed her brother, there is nothing I can do to save her. If she harms you, Julianna, I will see her hang." Bennet stroked her hair, pushed an errant lock behind her ear. "When this is over, I must visit Mary Devereaux, see what I can do to mend the feud my father started."

"I'm sure she'll welcome you, for her children's sakes."

They fell into companionable silence and closed their eyes.

Julianna was almost asleep when Bennet said, "Miss Gambit is to meet her client soon. Daventry spoke about it on the journey. Perhaps you should warn her the man is a hard taskmaster."

Rachel had an assignment?

Julianna shot up. "Who's a hard taskmaster? Mr Daventry or the new client?" Either way, Rachel would finally get an opportunity to prove her worth.

Bennet smiled. "The client. Miss Gambit must pass a series of tests before he'll agree to hire her."

"Tests? What sort of tests?"

"Who can say?"

"Do you know who wishes to hire her?" Rachel would be beside herself with excitement. She'd breeze through the tests and show her client she was just as formidable as the men. "It might help her prepare."

"No, but with the name Hunter, he's more than a match for Miss Gambit."

"Hunter! He sounds like a savage." Still, Rachel was equally skilled with weaponry. "Oh, there's no chance of me sleeping now."

His sensual hum said he sought to take advantage of the fact. "As I'm to blame for the disturbance, let me massage your shoulders as you did mine. Help you relax."

Julianna arched a brow. "Are you sure you mean to massage my shoulders? Why do I suspect you failed to pay attention in anatomy class?"

His husky laugh turned her blood molten. "Turn over, love, and face the wall."

"Shouldn't I lie face down?"

Bennet chuckled softly. "I plan to start at your thigh and slowly work my way up to your shoulder. Concentrating on those areas that throb and ache most."

Unable to suppress the flutter of excitement, she turned over and let him have his way. She had no complaints. Those magical fingers soothed all her woes. When he fondled her breasts and entered her from behind, when he drove slow and deep to limit the noise, she had to muffle her moans with a pillow.

"I've spent many nights imagining holding you like this," he whispered against her neck as they came down from the dizzying heights of their pleasure. "Now I've found you, I'll never let you go."

"I've spent many nights thinking of you, too." She caressed his arm in soothing strokes, lulling him to sleep. Julianna knew he'd succumbed when his breathing slowed and his limbs relaxed. And yet she lay awake, the old fears and doubts surfacing.

She had been ripped from his embrace once before.

Was their love destined to end in tragedy again?

●

Julianna woke to a faint tapping noise. She glanced around the dark room. The embers in the grate had died, and the air carried a bitter chill. Below stairs, she heard mumbled voices and the clip of footsteps on the flagstones. The clatter of horses' hooves on the cobbles outside said a coach had entered the stable yard.

"Devereaux?" Bennet's name whispered through the room, followed by more tapping on the bedchamber door. "Devereaux?"

Julianna shook Bennet awake. "Bennet. There's someone at the door. I think it's Mr Daventry." It was definitely a man's voice.

"Devereaux!" came the urgent plea.

Bennet dragged himself out of bed and padded to the door.

Julianna's gaze followed his firm buttocks and solid thighs. She would never tire of ogling his naked physique. She would never tire of sleeping next to the man she loved.

"Give me a moment." Bennet's voice was still thick from sleep. To protect his modesty, he opened the door a fraction. "Daventry? What time is it?"

"Three o'clock. Get dressed. Roxburgh's carriage has just

pulled into the inn. I'm right in saying his crest carries a flaming torch?"

Roxburgh? Julianna's breath caught in her throat.

Why would the lord make the fourteen-hour journey to Bristol when he complained about the drive to Hampshire? She'd wager all she owned he was not involved in the threats made against Bennet, but it looked mighty suspicious.

"It can't be Roxburgh." Bennet echoed Julianna's sentiment, but she'd never known Mr Daventry make a mistake. "He wouldn't come all this way unless—" Bennet paused and exhaled deeply. "Wait there. I'll be two minutes at most."

Bennet closed the door and quickly reached for his breeches.

A hundred questions filled Julianna's mind. "Lord Roxburgh must have left at noon to arrive so promptly."

Bennet seemed agitated. "What if Miss Ponsonby—or whatever the hell her name is—has exacted her revenge by torching Witherdeen?" He dragged his shirt over his head and thrust his arms into the sleeves. "She knew she couldn't catch us before we found her mother and so avenged her father's death by sticking to their original plan."

"That's physically impossible. It would take a minimum of five hours for news of Witherdeen to reach London. And it's a fourteen-hour journey to Bristol."

"Then what the devil is Roxburgh doing here?" Bennet dropped onto the bed while tugging on his boots. "What possessed him to journey a hundred miles? The man hates the drive to Witherdeen."

"I'm sure there's a reasonable explanation."

Like a thief in the night, doubt slipped into her mind. Trust no one—that was the lesson she'd learnt long ago. Mr Branner had been kind and affable and had proven false. Miss Ponsonby brightened a room like a ray of sunshine, and she was a deceiving devil, too. Was Lord Roxburgh hiding hatred in his heart?

"I shall dress and come downstairs with you." Julianna pulled back the bedsheets and climbed out of bed. "We don't know who to trust anymore."

Bennet thrust his arms into his coat. "No. Stay here and lock the door. Don't let anyone into the chamber. Roxburgh must have some justification for being here. If I'm wrong, you'll hear us fighting in the taproom."

"What if he means to shoot you?"

Bennet gave an incredulous snort. "In front of Daventry and the innkeeper?" He crossed the room, kissed her forehead, and reiterated, "Lock the door. I'll return and put your mind at ease as soon as I've spoken to Roxburgh."

He slipped from the room, leaving Julianna alone with her thoughts and a crippling sense of dread. She couldn't settle, took to pacing the floor, her mind a whirl of questions.

Was Lord Roxburgh playing the dutiful friend?

Had he come all this way merely to offer his support?

It seemed unlikely.

The icy nip in the air saw her throw her pelisse over her nightgown and fasten the buttons. Then she continued pacing while determining why the hairs on her nape prickled to attention, why she felt a sudden frisson of alarm.

So, the carriage clattering into the stable yard belonged to Lord Roxburgh. She walked over to the window and parted the curtains, expecting to see the young grooms removing the harnesses and brushing down the horses.

No one attended the carriage with the unusual crest.

But wait! Movement inside Lord Roxburgh's vehicle caught Julianna's eye. How odd. Mr Daventry said the lord was waiting downstairs in the taproom.

Hiding behind the curtain, she took a tentative peek at the conveyance. The outline of a woman's bonnet caught her eye, but it was impossible to note any identifying features in the dark. It could be Mrs Thorne. The widow clung to the lord like knotweed. Could it be Miss Ponsonby? If so, why had she not followed Lord Roxburgh into the inn?

Was the plan to lure Bennet to the carriage and shoot him dead? Would Lord Roxburgh really risk his life and reputation to assist Miss Ponsonby in her devilish plan?

There was only one way to find out.

Julianna pushed her feet into her boots, tied the laces and ferreted around in her valise for the pretty bottle of pepper and small blade given to her by Rachel Gambit. She slipped the weapons into her pocket and unlocked the bedchamber door.

Mr Daventry had spent five minutes explaining every route out of the building in case they found themselves pursued by Mr Branner's killer. And so, Julianna left the room and took the rear stairs leading to the stable yard.

She paused on the bottom step and took a deep breath.

Every instinct said Miss Ponsonby had come to Bristol.

Every instinct said Julianna was about to confront a cold-blooded killer.

●

Bennet strode into the dimly lit taproom to find Roxburgh leaning against the crude oak counter. "What the devil are you doing here?" Bennet came to a crashing halt. "God's teeth! You look like you've crawled from the pits of hell."

Roxburgh never looked anything but immaculate. Now his ruffled clothes, bloodshot eyes and pale face spoke of severe fatigue.

"Fourteen hours of torture does that to a man." Roxburgh dragged his hand down his face and rubbed his bristly jaw. "It hurts to stand, hurts to sit. Every bone in my body creaks. I crave a hot bath and a woman's pliant fingers to massage the knots."

Daventry closed in on the lord. "You were given a simple task. Inform Devereaux's friends of our plan so the villain might follow us to Bristol. The fact you're here leads me to question your innocence."

Roxburgh jerked back. "If I was going to kill a man, I'd shoot him between the brows, not hit him with a fireside implement."

"Who told you Branner was killed with a poker?"

The innkeeper slammed a large glass of whisky on the counter.

Roxburgh knocked it back in two gulps.

"Sloane woke me at an ungodly hour and described every gory detail." Roxburgh panted as the liquor scorched his throat. "He said I was to make the tale sound gruesome, judge our friends' reactions. Said the villain would do something to rouse my suspicion."

Daventry gestured to a round table. "Sit down. Explain why you saw fit to ignore simple instructions."

Roxburgh dragged out a chair. "Can a man not use his initiative?"

They sat around the table. Roxburgh summoned the innkeeper and ordered another drink. Bennet declined the offer of refreshment, as did Daventry. Men hunting a brutal fiend had to keep their wits.

Daventry fixed the lord with a stare. "Well?"

"Miss Winters was detained while attempting to book passage on the Edinburgh stage at nine o'clock yesterday morning. Cole, and that burly fellow who lifts rocks like they're pebbles, caught up with me outside the townhouse Lowbridge keeps for his mistress."

Relief settled over Bennet's shoulders like a warm blanket. So they were not hiding in a coaching inn waiting for a killer. Isabella had murdered Branner in a fit of rage. Yet the pang deep in his gut said not.

"Where is Isabella now?" Bennet snapped.

"Being questioned by the magistrate at Bow Street. Cole said I was to tell our friends that Miss Winters killed the steward."

Daventry leant forward. "Did you?"

Roxburgh nodded. "Sloane was right. Miss Ponsonby's reaction gave me cause for concern. She suddenly recalled seeing Miss Winters running across the lawn in a blood-stained gown. Said Miss Winters told her she had stolen Devereaux's stickpin as a keepsake. Lowbridge suggested she go to Bow Street and give a statement."

"How did she react when you told her Branner was dead?"

"The Miss Ponsonby I know would have swooned before asking a myriad of questions. Would have wanted to know every gruesome detail. I found her stone-cold silence unnerving. Not as unnerving as what happened when I left the house."

"What did Miss Ponsonby ask you to do?" Daventry spoke as if he knew the answer. He waited for Roxburgh to inhale a pinch of snuff. "I guarantee she had more important matters on her mind than visiting Bow Street."

"She followed me, had a sudden fit of hysterics. Insisted we come to Bristol. She ranted about Miss Winters' wickedness, about needing to put your mind at ease, Devereaux. She whined and made a host of excuses for needing to reassure Mrs Eden. Pleaded with me to act at once."

A shiver ran the length of Bennet's spine. "Tell me you left her in London and are here purely to pass on the information." Had Miss Ponsonby made such a nuisance of herself, Roxburgh had agreed to her demands? "For the love of God, tell me you didn't bring her to Bristol."

Roxburgh glanced at the taproom door and lowered his voice. "Sloane said the person who murdered Branner will likely follow you here. Is it not better to keep the devil in one's sights?"

In one's sights?

"Cursed saints!" Bennet jumped to his feet and sent the chair crashing to the floor. "Where is she?"

"Asleep in the carriage. I left—"

"Damnation!" Sick with fear, Bennet darted across the taproom and mounted the stairs. He hammered on the bedchamber door. "Julianna. It's me. Quickly, open the door." A frantic scan of the dark corridor said a murderer wasn't lingering in the shadows. "Julianna!" He knocked louder this time, loud enough to wake the dead. He tried the doorknob to put his mind at ease.

The door opened without any resistance.

Nausea rolled through Bennet. He entered and searched the darkness.

But Julianna was gone.

CHAPTER 20

THE NIGHT WAS COLD. A bitter breeze wound its way under the hem of Julianna's clothes, raising goose pimples to her skin. The air smelled crisp, sterile, but for the stench of manure and the faint odour of fear.

She hid in the shadows, gathering her wits, before creeping towards the vehicle. There was no way to surprise the lady, and so Julianna had no option but to yank open the door and climb into Lord Roxburgh's carriage.

She slammed the door and dropped into the seat, caught a whiff of Miss Ponsonby's perfume before meeting the woman's shocked gaze.

"Mrs Eden!" Miss Ponsonby's throat worked tirelessly while she scrambled to compose herself. "Oh, thank heavens it's you. Have you seen Roxburgh? Damn the man for making me wait in the stable yard in the dead of night. Who leaves a woman alone to defend herself against ruffians?"

Julianna decided to play along for a while. "Roxburgh has no shame. He said coaching inns are eerie places, that during the witching hour you're bound to see a ghost."

The lady kept her hands nestled inside her white muff. "I'd like to meet the ghost of a headless horseman. Men are much more tolerable when they cannot speak or think." She laughed. "Perhaps you should write a book about haunted hostelries."

Julianna laughed, too, though shuddered inside at the depth of this woman's deception. "Please tell me you've not travelled fourteen hours in a carriage with Lord Roxburgh just to see a ghost. I don't imagine he's much of a conversationalist."

Miss Ponsonby huffed. "It was the worst fourteen hours of my life. The man mumbles erotic fantasies in his sleep. Oh, the air was blue with his crude descriptions. But never mind that. We came to bring news of Miss Winters, to tell you she's been taken to Bow Street on suspicion of murdering the steward. Indeed, you must come home at once."

Miss Winters arrested for murder! It was a surprising development. In all likelihood, the woman was innocent.

"Miss Winters killed Mr Branner? Good heavens!" Julianna wanted to bombard her with questions, but it could wait. No doubt Lord Roxburgh had come to Bristol to relay the shocking news. Miss Ponsonby had come for devious reasons.

"You ventured all this way just to tell us about Miss Winters? You should have waited. We're returning to London later today."

"Today?" Panic flickered in the woman's eyes. Fear coated every word when she said, "Why? Have you concluded your business already?"

Miss Ponsonby's prying questions hadn't bothered Julianna before. She'd found them quite endearing. Now it was evident she had an ulterior motive for everything she asked.

"We planned to go into town tomorrow. Poor Mr Branner had a library book in his cottage, from King Street, Bristol. We hoped to gain his address from the library's records, hoped to visit his family and pay our respects."

"But I'm sure someone said the steward's mother lives in Bath." Miss Ponsonby clung to her story like a spider did a web.

"They were mistaken. Mr Branner's mother lives near Great George Street in Bristol. Lord Devereaux wished to visit and express his condolences."

Miss Ponsonby fell silent.

Miss Ponsonby never fell silent.

"Luckily, we arrived early enough to travel into Bristol last night. We spoke to Mrs Blanchard. It seems Mr Branner used a false name when he worked at Witherdeen, to disguise the fact he was the marquess' cousin."

Miss Ponsonby's bright blue eyes darkened. "How odd."

That was all? Where were the gasps of shock, the excited titters? Where were the rambling questions that usually followed every statement?

"Mr Branner was John Devereaux's illegitimate son." Julianna observed the woman, waiting for the mask to fall. "What shall we discuss first, Portia? The fact you've been lying to everyone? Or that during a heated argument, you killed your brother?"

The air turned oppressive.

Julianna held her breath for a few suffocating seconds.

"No one likes a snoop, Mrs Eden," came Miss Ponsonby's bitter reply. Her charming smile vanished as quick as a spectre. The playful innocence shrank into the shadows, replaced with a demonic-like contempt. "You think you're so clever, so smart, so bloody perfect. The ingenious mistress saves the day. Hurrah for Mrs Eden! Hurrah!"

"And you've made a stupid mistake. I'm not Lord Devereaux's mistress. I'm an enquiry agent for the Order, hired by the marquess to discover who sent the obituaries." She felt quite proud of the fact, truth be told. Yes, she would never make a good agent, but she had helped to solve this case.

The news came as a shock, but Miss Ponsonby soon recovered.

"It seems we've been deceiving each other, Mrs Eden." Her hateful gaze could bore through one's soul. "So, you're the hired help. Perhaps all is not lost. Perhaps we might strike a bargain. I shall give you a share of the inheritance once we've killed Lord Devereaux."

An icy chill penetrated Julianna's bones. Mrs Blanchard had raised devils. Devils who didn't know that bitter people always perished. Devils who didn't know that forgiveness was about saving the victim's soul, not the perpetrator's.

"Why would you think there's an inheritance?"

The woman grinned. "John Devereaux wrote to Jonathan and said he was aware we were his half-siblings. If he inherits the marquessate, I shall prosper, too."

"But at what cost?" Wickedness came at a price. "Your brother is dead. Killed by your own hand." Julianna took a wild stab in the dark. "He didn't want to kill Lord Devereaux. People will believe he was the architect of this harebrained scheme, but you're the master manipulator."

Portia's nostrils flared. "The fool wanted to tell Devereaux everything. He'd taken a fancy to Miss Winters and changed his mind about blaming her. It would have been so easy to frame that conceited bitch for murder. But no! Jonathan said the marquess would welcome us as family. There'd be no need for John Devereaux to inherit."

When this was over, and assuming Julianna survived, she would let Miss Winters know that Mr Branner had spoken in earnest. Such a simple thing as the truth might determine how she conducted herself in future.

"But your brother had missed the point." The only way Miss Ponsonby could honour her father and get vengeance was by ensuring she stole everything from Bennet. "It was all about *The Reckoning*, about getting even."

"And it still is, Mrs Eden. My father died because of the Marquess Devereaux, and I intend to make sure his son dies because of me. An eye for an eye. Isn't that justice?"

"You've misunderstood the principle." Resentment had left the woman somewhat deranged. "But why the elaborate notes? Why smash gargoyles and lie about the gravestone? Why go to the trouble of causing a fire in the stable block?"

Portia grumbled incoherently. "Because I want Bennet Devereaux to suffer the same mental cruelty inflicted on my father. My mother told me all about the marquess' systematic torture. It's only right his son experiences the same injustice."

Julianna considered her next move. There was no hope of saving Miss Ponsonby. Her heart and soul had withered and died.

There but for the grace of God, Julianna thought. She had every reason to seek vengeance, too. She might have grown to hate Bennet Devereaux were it not for that wonderful year spent at Witherdeen.

"I must be honest with you, Miss Blanchard." Julianna stressed the woman's real name. She drew all the strength she could muster. "I'm to marry Bennet Devereaux, and so I cannot help you in your scheme. Indeed, I cannot let you leave this carriage. So it appears we've reached a stalemate."

The woman's sinister smile said otherwise. "Not a stalemate, Mrs Eden." Miss Blanchard pulled her hand from her muff, cocked and aimed her pocket pistol. "I believe it's checkmate."

●

Bennet ignored the sick feeling in his gut. He tried to ignore the cruel words assembled on the last handbill, a portent to the evil he feared was about to unfold. Holding on to the last threads of composure, he focused on the only important thing—finding Julianna.

Daventry and Roxburgh entered the bedchamber.

Daventry scanned the empty room. "Mrs Eden left of her own accord. There's no sign of a struggle. We would have heard a commotion had Miss Ponsonby taken her under duress."

He spoke so matter-of-factly, Bennet had to curb his temper.

"Why would she leave?" But Bennet knew the answer. Julianna sought to protect him. Her inquisitive mind had her hunting for all the reasons Roxburgh had journeyed to Bristol. Logic said she'd overheard the conversation in the taproom or glimpsed Miss Ponsonby exiting the carriage.

"Why the devil would Miss Ponsonby kidnap Mrs Eden?" Roxburgh said.

"Her name isn't Miss Ponsonby. She's my cousin seeking vengeance for her father. It's a long story. I'll explain later."

Bennet noticed a gap in the curtains though he recalled closing them before climbing into bed. He strode to the window and peered into the yard. Roxburgh's vehicle sat in darkness.

"Julianna must have seen Miss Ponsonby in your carriage."

Daventry nudged Bennet aside and observed the stables with hawk-like intensity. "Roxburgh, what's Miss Ponsonby wearing?"

Roxburgh gave a nonchalant shrug. "When a man has no interest in bedding a woman, he pays little attention. But if I had to hazard a guess, then a blue bonnet and pelisse, a muff the size of a small dog. She cradled the thing as if it were a beloved pet. I had to resist the urge to strangle the blighter and bury it in a roadside grave."

Daventry swung around. "Miss Ponsonby doesn't know me. I shall enter the stable yard and check the carriage. Devereaux will wait at the window for my signal. Roxburgh, return to the taproom and wait outside. Miss Ponsonby has no means of travel and so plans to remain in the area."

Without further comment, Daventry marched out of the bedchamber.

Roxburgh looked at the crumpled bedsheets. "One suspects there was a little tussle in here tonight."

"Do be quiet. You're the fool who brought the devil here. If anything happens to Julianna, I shall castrate you and send you to live in a monastery in France."

"It's good to see you've not lost your sense of humour." Roxburgh attempted to brush the creases from his coat. "And I spoke with Daventry's agent before leaving London. Finlay Cole waited outside Lowbridge's house. He witnessed Miss Ponsonby playing the hysterical maiden and suggested I bring her to Bristol. He said he would follow, though I've not seen hide nor hair of him since."

The information failed to calm the panic pounding in Bennet's chest. He sent Roxburgh back to the taproom, turned to the window, and watched the yard through a gap in the curtains.

Daventry appeared, moving like a panther on the prowl. His sleek steps spoke of a man who'd stalked many crooks and criminals. He came up alongside the carriage and glanced inside before moving to the stables. Daventry spoke to a young groom who pointed to the woods.

Everything happened quickly then.

Daventry beckoned Bennet downstairs.

Bennet took to his heels and was in the yard in seconds.

"Two women left the coach. They walked arm in arm and entered the woods. Took the track leading to the old church." Daventry gestured to the bank of shadows swaying in the breeze. "Miss Ponsonby told the groom to wait for ten minutes before alerting you."

"Then why the hell are we standing here?" Bennet's blood pumped through his veins at too rapid a rate. "They can't be far ahead." He caught himself. "You believe Miss Ponsonby has a weapon. Julianna would have overpowered her otherwise."

"Precisely. Follow the path but proceed with caution. The groom said I can access the church by another means. He'll show Roxburgh a third route. Together we'll corner her inside the ruin." Daventry gripped Bennet's shoulder. "The aim is to capture Miss Ponsonby without bloodshed."

Bennet wasted no time. He darted across the cobbled yard, stopped to hone his senses, and then disappeared into the woods.

A man would think he'd entered Satan's underworld. Darkness swamped everything. Trees were but tall, black shadows surging up from the earth like Lucifer's army. The air smelled deathly cold, smelled of earth and rotting vegetation. Twigs cracked like bones beneath his feet.

In the distance, streaks of moonlight caught the mossy green walls of a ruined church. Ivy, rich and verdant amid the bleak landscape, clung to the walls like God's supporting hands.

Bennet headed to the vast stone archway, a gawping mouth of an entrance, and paused. Angry voices sliced through the stillness—a harsh contrast to the wind's gentle whispers.

"Portia!" he cried. "It's me you want. Let me take Mrs Eden's place."

"Bennet! Don't come any closer!" Hearing Julianna's voice proved reassuring and terrifying. "She has a pistol and means to use it."

If she killed Julianna, she'd be ripping out Bennet's heart and soul, too. But he drew comfort from the fact Miss Ponsonby was unlikely to have a good aim, and he was her intended victim.

"Portia! Why didn't you tell me who you were?"

Silence.

He slipped into the church, kept his back pressed to the damp walls. "Portia! We're family. Put the pistol away and let's talk."

"It's too late!" came Portia's irate reply.

Bennet followed the sound of her disgruntled mumbling,

moved stealthily through a hole in the wall and entered what must have been the nave. All four walls stood intact. All four walls had a doorway or opening of some sort. Even if Roxburgh and Daventry approached, Portia could use the remaining exit.

"Stay back, Bennet." Julianna stood in the middle of the roofless nave, near an oak tree that towered twenty feet high. Terror kept her eyes wide, her body rigid. "Please, don't come any closer."

Portia thrust Julianna forward, using her as a shield. A sliver of moonlight caught the barrel of a small pistol she held against Julianna's temple.

Merciful Mary!

Fear lanced through him.

Bennet raised his hands in surrender and took a few tentative steps closer. "If you'd told me who you were, this could have been avoided."

Portia snorted. "Your father murdered mine. Nothing but your death will suffice. Had that fool Granger not attacked Mrs Eden, I would have crept into your bedchamber and slit your throat while you slept. Of course, I would have left a lock of red hair to incriminate Miss Winters."

"Just like you did when you murdered your brother?" Bennet rubbed his neck, though was unwilling to accept a reprobate like Granger had unwittingly saved his life. "You were an infant when your father died. By all accounts, he was a kind and loving man."

"He was generous and giving, and your father killed him."

John Devereaux was hardly a saint. "A man might wear an affable smile and make benevolent gestures, but it's his actions to those he loves that tells the most about him."

"Yes!" she cried. "He loved us more than anything."

"Did he? A man who loves his family does not leave them destitute, does not leave them to accept the charity of their neighbours."

Portia's hand shook. She struggled to hold the pistol to Julianna's temple and was forced to push the muzzle to her back instead.

"We lost everything because of the marquess."

"No. You lost everything because your father sought to

betray his vow to his wife, to betray the child he had in wedlock, and take another family who were destined to suffer for his self-ishness."

Portia shook her head. "What? No! That's not what happened."

"It's exactly what happened." Hopefully, if Bennet kept pressing her, she would take aim and fire at him. "John Devereaux let lust cloud his judgement. He was a slave to his appetites."

"No! No! Your father ruined everything."

Bennet's father was guilty of driving the man to the edge of insanity. He was not responsible for his brother's moral conduct.

"John Devereaux was weak, and his children inherited the same trait. Weak people destroy themselves in the name of vengeance. Happiness is the best revenge. It takes courage, one single act of forgiveness, to mend a feud. Had you come to me, I would have welcomed you as family, and we might have salvaged something worthwhile from our fathers' misdeeds."

Daventry stepped into the nave through the doorway to the west. Seconds later, Roxburgh entered from the east. Both men blocked Portia's escape.

Like a frightened doe, her gaze darted left and right. Her only route out was through the crumbling hole in the north wall.

Tension thrummed in the air.

"Lower your weapon, Miss Blanchard." Daventry's menacing tone echoed through the ruins. "Don't make matters worse by shooting an innocent woman. Devereaux does not deserve to die for his father's failures."

Portia was panting as she struggled with her dilemma. Then, like the calm before the storm, she shoved Julianna aside and confronted Bennet.

"My brother was a coward, a traitor to his family. One of us must make our mother proud. One of us must make the Marquess Devereaux pay." Portia aimed her pistol at Bennet. "I'll hang for my brother's murder. I may as well hang for yours."

Bennet might have darted for cover had Julianna not thrown the contents of a glass bottle in Portia's face.

"Argh!" Portia coughed and sneezed. She dropped the pistol

and rubbed her eyes. "No! No!" She stumbled, bent forward and cupped her face. "I can't see!"

But it was another example of her superb acting ability. Indeed, she kept her head buried in her hands while plotting her escape. Without warning, she grabbed her skirts and bolted through the only exit.

Bennet took to his heels and shouted for Daventry to give chase.

"Wait!" The master of the Order charged after Bennet and grabbed his arm just as he reached the north wall. "Don't move!"

"What? We can't let her leave!" Portia Blanchard would make her way to Witherdeen and seek another opportunity to murder Bennet. He'd be forever looking over his shoulder, forever worried about losing Julianna.

"The groom said the terrain to the north is unsafe. An old underground tunnel connects this church to one a mile away. That's why—"

A high-pitched scream rent the night air.

Bennet strained to listen, but heard no pained groans, no cries for help, heard nothing but deathly silence.

"Damnation!" Daventry swung around. "Roxburgh, fetch the innkeeper. We need someone to guide us through these woods. Bring lanterns. Hurry."

Roxburgh didn't offer a witty quip about being the errand boy, but sprinted through the east door with surprising agility.

Bennet's thoughts turned to Julianna.

She stood motionless, dazed, hugging her chest as she stared into the gloom. Bennet quickly closed the gap between them and wrapped his arms around her trembling body.

"It's all right, love. She can't hurt you now." He kissed her temple, told her they were safe, that fate had better plans for them. "You don't need to be afraid."

She held on to him as if she might never let go. "I wasn't scared for myself, Bennet. I was scared for you. Fate has been unkind to me in the past. It's hard to believe we'll ever be happy."

"When it comes to happiness, there are no guarantees. But we have each other. We have honesty and trust and a desire to let love be our focus." It seemed like the perfect recipe for happiness.

She looked up, her eyes glistening with unshed tears. "With your strength of heart, we're bound to succeed. I could kiss Mr Daventry for pairing us together on this case."

"Daventry is busy scouting around the nave for sticks, so you'll have to kiss me instead." Bennet stole the opportunity to press a chaste kiss to her lips.

The pounding of footsteps on the hard ground caught their attention.

Finlay Cole darted through the east doorway. "Roxburgh's following behind with the innkeeper in tow."

Lucius Daventry did not seem surprised to see his agent so far from home. The man was rooting through debris and merely glanced up. "We need sticks to test for unstable ground. Help me find some."

The men spoke in hushed whispers and continued searching the dead vegetation until Roxburgh arrived with the innkeeper and lanterns.

"It's madness to trek through the woods at night," came the innkeeper's warning. "A woman's missin' ye say?"

"She left through the north door and screamed less than a minute later." Daventry twirled his four-foot stick as if preparing for combat. "Stand in the doorway and direct me. Everyone bar Cole will wait here."

"I should be the one to go." Bennet would not have two men risk their lives while he waited like a milksop. "It's a family matter. I must insist."

Julianna tugged his arm. "No."

The innkeeper's beady eyes widened. "Yer a few eggs short of a dozen if you venture out there at night." That was the extent of his helpful comments.

Daventry considered Bennet for a moment, though Lord knows what he was thinking. "You'll follow me, Devereaux. Watch where I place my feet. We'll walk slowly, three paces apart. Do you understand?"

"Yes."

"Cole, hand Devereaux your stick." Cole threw the baton to

Bennet, and he was somewhat relieved he caught it with ease. When dealing with the men of the Order, anyone would feel inadequate.

Bennet kissed Julianna on the forehead. "There's nothing to fear. I'm with Lucius Daventry. The man has nine lives."

She grabbed his arm. "Hurry back. I'll be waiting."

Taking slow, tentative steps, Bennet followed Daventry through the hole in the north wall. Each carried a lantern in one hand, a sturdy stick in the other. They moved hesitantly along the narrow walkway leading through dead bracken. Bennet grew accustomed to the rhythmical beating of Daventry's stick hitting the hard ground. But when they passed a danger sign and entered a clearing, the repetitive thuds became eerie echoes.

Daventry came to a crashing halt. "Stop! The tunnel runs beneath us." He used his stick to prod and poke the earth.

Bennet held his lantern and searched the clearing. "There's a dark mass ahead. She could have fallen into the tunnel."

"Wait here while—"

"No. As head of the family, it's my responsibility." Despite everything she'd done, Miss Blanchard was still his cousin. "It looks like the tunnel runs in a straight line from the church. I'll approach from the right. The ground should be stable enough there."

They agreed it should be safe for both of them to approach.

The dark mass was a hole with a twelve-foot drop.

Bennet raised his lantern aloft but almost dropped the damn thing when he met Portia's lifeless stare. Blood left a glistening trail down her cheek. Blood pooled thick and red around her head.

"Portia?" Bennet called her name repeatedly but received no response.

Daventry gripped Bennet's shoulder and said the words he'd been expecting to hear. "I'm sorry, Devereaux. Miss Blanchard is dead."

CHAPTER 21

BENNET PLUNGED his hands into the washbowl and splashed water over his face. He stood, elbows resting on the oak table, rivulets running down his cheeks, dripping off his chin.

Julianna watched from the bed, knowing guilt and remorse filled his heart. The case was solved; the culprits punished. Mr Branner's fate—to be murdered by his kin—seemed crueller than if he'd swung from the gallows. In some ways, Miss Ponsonby's death reflected the horror of her crimes. She had died alone and unloved. Died in a hole in the ground crawling with insects and vermin.

Things could have been so different.

Again, Bennet drenched his face with cold water and exhaled a sigh that reflected the depth of his despair.

"We should go down to the taproom and sit with Lord Roxburgh. He professes to be a man without feeling, but the news of Miss Ponsonby's death disturbed him."

Bennet dried his hands and face on a towel. "I need time alone before Daventry returns with the magistrate and coroner. They'll need to access the tunnel to retrieve her body. Be prepared to stay at the inn tonight."

She didn't care where she slept as long as they were together. "Then if you wish to be alone, I shall venture downstairs and keep Lord Roxburgh company." Julianna pushed off the bed and made for the door.

Bennet reached the door before her and blocked the exit. "Love, I meant I want to be alone with you. I need to feel your comforting touch, hear the sweet timbre of your voice."

Julianna cupped his bristled cheek. "I'm sorry, Bennet. I wish things could have ended differently. I wish I'd been a good enough agent to confront Mr Branner, wish I could have stopped Miss Ponsonby before she committed a crime."

"You did everything you could. They deceived us all."

"Still, I wish I could have spared you the loss."

At the mention of loss, he squeezed his eyes shut. "You might have died tonight. Don't do that to me again. Don't leave me fearing I've lost you."

She hugged his waist, lay her head against his shoulder. "I thought I could reason with her, but she was beyond help. Years of hatred had corrupted her heart. Mr Branner thought to torment you, but never intended to go through with the threats. In her frustration, she killed her only sibling."

He captured her chin and looked deep into her eyes. "We'll work to banish the hatred. Love will be the focus of everything we do."

He bent his head and kissed her, kissed her in the slow, sensual way that curled her toes, that had her pressing her body to his. Her insides melted when he slipped his warm tongue over hers and made love to her mouth.

"You were right. Your uncle was far from a saint. We must make sure Mary Devereaux and her children become part of our family. Your cousin John, too, when he returns from India. We must heal the rift, Bennet."

"We?" He looked hopeful. "Does that mean you accept my proposal?"

No matter what hardships lay ahead, they would navigate them together. "It's selfish of me, I know, but I would like to hear you ask again. And pinch me, so I know I'm not dreaming."

He didn't pinch her. He settled his hot hands on her buttocks, drew her to his hard body, and let her feel the evidence of his growing erection. "Does it feel real now, love? Marry me, Julianna. Come home to Witherdeen."

Home to Witherdeen.

She loved the house, but Bennet made Witherdeen special. Bennet made life worth living. "Nothing would make me happier than being your wife. If we can cope with this, we can cope with anything."

"Can you cope with a wedding in St George's, Hanover Square? I want the world to know I'm in love with you. I'll show everyone why I want you to be my marchioness."

Julianna nibbled her bottom lip. She wanted to make him happy, but parading in front of those who willed their marriage to fail was not how she wished to celebrate their union.

"Julianna?" Bennet prompted. "Shall we marry in St George's?"

"If that's what you want." She would walk down the aisle to the whispers of her mother's name while the organist played Handel or Haydn. When prompted by the minister, no one would step forward to present her hand to Bennet.

"What do *you* want, Julianna?" He paused. "I want to marry you. I don't care where or when."

"It will take weeks to have the banns read. I thought we might marry by licence."

A slow smile formed on his lips. After the horrors they'd witnessed tonight, it was a beautiful sight to behold. "Perhaps I could apply for a special licence, and we could marry at Witherdeen. Do you recall the time I gave you flowers, and we paraded arm in arm through the nave, pretending we had wed?"

"With remarkable clarity." She'd felt as if she belonged with Bennet even then. "I pretended to toss the bouquet, and Mrs Hendrie caught it."

He laughed. "We were always good at stretching the limits of our imagination, though I do know Milford holds my house-keeper in high regard."

It seemed wrong to marry anywhere but the house they loved.

"Let's marry at Witherdeen." Joy filled her heart. "We cannot deprive Mrs Hendrie of a chance to catch a posy. And a celebration is just what's needed to banish the ghosts."

"Agreed." Bennet cupped her face. "I promise you Witherdeen will be a happy home." He kissed her nose, kissed her chin. When his mouth captured hers, when she felt the power of their love deep in her soul, it occurred to her they had kept their pledge.

Promise you'll find me when you're old enough.
Promise you'll return if you can.

●

Witherdeen Hall, Hampshire
Two weeks later

"I'm sorry I can't stay tonight, Julianna." Rachel Gambit glanced over her shoulder, saw Mr Daventry conversing with Bennet, and turned back to the group of ladies who worked for the Order. "I hate to miss the wedding celebrations, but I'm to meet my client tomorrow night at Vauxhall. He's given specific instructions. One mistake, and he will choose another agent."

"You were here for the ceremony, and that's what matters." Julianna's stomach performed a somersault. She was the Marchioness Devereaux. More importantly, she was Bennet's wife. "Besides, you've been eagerly awaiting an assignment, and I'm confident you'll impress the gentleman."

Eliza Dutton's eyes widened. "I'm sure he will choose you, Rachel. But it's a shame you can't stay. Julianna is to give us a tour of the ruins tomorrow."

Rachel laughed. "There's every chance he'll reject me. In which case, I shall hop on the first stage back to Hampshire."

Julianna took one look at Rachel's vibrant countenance. Any man would be a fool to cast her aside. "Mr Daventry said you're to undergo tests."

Rachel shrugged. "It's all a bit dramatic if you ask me. The first test involves identifying him amid the crush at Vauxhall's masquerade. Mr Hunter wishes to test my intuitive powers, to make sure I can think on my feet. He's quite precise in his requirements. I'm to wear a red gown. Red slippers. A red mask."

Honora Wild touched her hand to her throat. "Vauxhall? In February? Surely you're not venturing there alone."

"It's a special event, open for one night. Mr and Mrs D'Angelo are to accompany me until Mr Hunter appears."

"You won't be the only woman in red." Julianna wondered why he insisted Rachel wear such a vibrant colour. "It's a rather odd request."

"Indeed. Mr D'Angelo said the man favours black."

Eliza suddenly gasped and skirted behind Honora. "Don't look now, but the lord is staring again."

Julianna turned to see Roxburgh leaning languidly against the wall, watching them. "Ignore him, Eliza. He's a rake and a rogue and loves nothing more than to appear intimidating." Still, Julianna was rather fond of the man, and Bennet needed a friend he could trust.

Bennet must have sensed Roxburgh was up to no good, for he joined the lord and thrust a glass of brandy into his hand. They conversed while glancing in Eliza's direction. Miss Trimble must have noticed the lord's lecherous gaze, too, because she hurried across the room to join their group.

"If that man asks any of you to stroll in the gardens, tell him you've twisted your ankle." Miss Trimble was an attractive woman of thirty who was rather guarded when it came to her personal affairs. Still, protecting her ladies was her life's mission.

Julianna laughed. "Knowing Lord Roxburgh, he'll have two footmen fetch a sedan." She caught Bennet's eye, and he beckoned her over. "I believe my husband needs me, but please, make yourselves at home. And avoid the stairs leading to the west wing. Lord Roxburgh often prowls there after dark."

"Perhaps I could use the lord to practise my verbal sparring," Rachel replied. "No doubt he's tamer than a man named Hunter."

Julianna left Miss Trimble chastising Rachel for mentioning a client's name aloud. She joined Bennet and Roxburgh, whose wandering eye had caused such a stir.

"You're making my friends nervous, my lord." Julianna tapped Roxburgh playfully on the arm. "Now you've parted ways with Mrs Prickle, don't think to choose a mistress from this group."

"Who's the lady with hair as black as my heart?"

"I'm not telling you. Forget you've seen her."

Bennet tsked. "I've told him she's an enquiry agent for the Order, that Lucius Daventry will kill him if he even looks at his agent in the wrong way."

"Perhaps I shall find a reason to hire her services," Roxburgh drawled.

"She doesn't provide the sort of services you require."

"I might need help finding my conscience."

"I doubt a man with Daventry's skill could locate that," Bennet said. "Now, drink your brandy and behave. I wish to walk to the ruins with my wife." There was a sensual tone to his voice that said they'd be doing more than walking.

Roxburgh merely grinned. "Don't concern yourself with me. I shall engage the ladies in conversation and be my usual charming self."

"I'm not concerned." Julianna took hold of her husband's arm. "Miss Trimble will flay you alive at the merest hint of disrespect."

Bennet slapped his friend affectionately on the back, then led Julianna into the hall where Mrs Hendrie stood holding a green velvet pelisse. The housekeeper had cried with happiness upon learning Julianna was to marry Bennet, and had worn a permanent grin all day.

"Thank you, Mrs Hendrie." Bennet accepted the proffered pelisse.

Bless her! Mrs Hendrie walked away with a skip in her step.

"It's rather cold out, and it's my duty to protect you." Bennet helped her into the garment and set about fastening the buttons. "Though you won't need gloves as I intend to stop every few minutes and warm your hands."

She gazed into his captivating eyes. "Do you think I should

have told Roxburgh that Eliza's father was a reckless gambler who left his daughter destitute?"

"No, he's bound to make a flippant comment, and he needs a strong woman to put him in his place. Perhaps you should have told him Miss Gambit always carries a weapon. We'll likely return to find a blade pinning his coattails to the console table."

Julianna laughed. "That's a sight I wouldn't want to miss."

Bennet glanced at the cubbyhole under the stairs. He clasped her hands. "When you left on that stormy night, I thought my world had ended. I never thought I'd see you again. Now you're the love of my life, my darling wife."

Julianna brought his hands to her lips and pressed a lingering kiss to his knuckles. "I've come home to you, Bennet."

"Let's make a promise never to let our problems consume us. Let's promise to be as playful with each other as we were when we were children."

She arched a brow. "I think we're far more playful than we were then. The games you like to play would have seemed shocking."

Those sensual amber eyes raked her body. "Who will decide what game we play tonight? Might I suggest the first one to the cottage earns a privilege pass?"

"In long skirts, I'm at a disadvantage. Might I suggest we walk to the cottage?" Once there, she would have him out of those clothes in a flash. "Let's conserve our energy. I think we're going to need it for a far more intimate pursuit. Don't you?"